Praise for

SOMETIMES I DREAM IN ITALIAN

"Wry, charming . . . Ciresi [is] a resonant voice chronicling the lives of Italian-Americans." —*Publishers Weekly*

"The genius of Rita Ciresi is her gift for mixing humor with heartbreak. Anyone who ever had a family, Italian or otherwise, will find themselves at home with the Lupos—the love, the exasperation, the earnest hopes, the broken dreams. *Sometimes I Dream in Italian* is charming, warm, and universally true. I love this book." —David Haynes, author of *All American Dream Dolls*

"A heartwarming, hilarious tale." —*Abilene Reporter-News* (Texas)

"With her customary wit and pathos, Ciresi . . . again mines the psyches of women: 13 interrelated stories about two sisters growing up in the working-class Italian-American section of New Haven. . . . Classic Italian-American fiction: characters and situations rendered with such skill and honesty, of such understanding and feeling, that they are instantly and universally recognizable." —*Kirkus Reviews*

"Rita Ciresi turns her unerring radar on that intersection between old-world parents and their new-world daughters; her exquisitely rendered Italian-American domestic interiors illuminate the joys and sorrows of all families. *Sometimes I Dream in Italian* will haunt your dreams."
—Mameve Medved, author of *Mail* and *Host Family*

"Rita Ciresi has distilled the essence of an Italian female childhood in this funny, moving, and lively collection about two sisters coming to grips with their Old Country upbringing. . . . A perceptive, completely involving portrait . . . You don't have to be Italian to get caught up in this book, or to root like crazy for the stubborn, fiery Lina or the self-questioning, observant Angel. These stories are rich, full of hilarious and authentic detail and dialogue, and dead-center accurate about the burdens and treasures that 'good Italian Catholic girls' carry into adulthood."
—Christina Bartolomeo, author of *Cupid & Diana*

Also by Rita Ciresi:

Pink Slip
Blue Italian
Mother Rocket

Sometimes I Dream in Italian

Rita Ciresi

DELTA TRADE PAPERBACKS

A DELTA BOOK
Published by
Dell Publishing
a division of
Random House, Inc.
1540 Broadway
New York, New York 10036

Library of Congress catalog card number: 00-029451

ISBN: 0-385-33494-X

Reprinted by arrangement with Delacorte Press

Manufactured in the United States of America
Published simultaneously in Canada

November 2001
10   9   8   7   6   5   4   3   2
BVG

For my mother and father
and my sisters
with love

THE STORIES IN this collection appeared in slightly different form in the following journals: "Soda Man" in *Hawaii Pacific Review*, "Big Heart" in *Italian Americana*, "Orphan Train" in *Southern Humanities Review*, "Miss Liberty" in *Natural Bridge*, "La Stella d'Oro" in *Voices in Italian Americana*, "Why Girl" in *Short Story*, "The Little Ice Age" in *Pleiades*, "Sometimes I Dream in Italian" in *Voices West* and *Sunscripts*, "I Am Happy, Are You Happy?" (under the title "A View of Venice") in *Dominion Review*, and "God Moves the Furniture" in *So to Speak*. Thanks to the Pennsylvania Council on the Arts and the Ragdale Foundation for their generous support.

CONTENTS

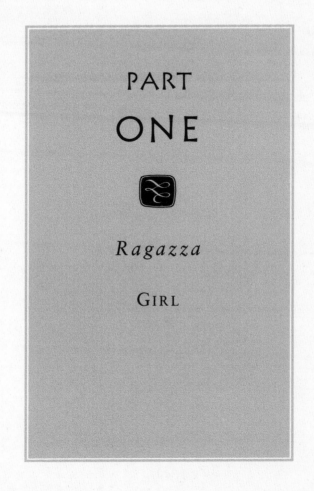

PART
ONE

Ragazza

GIRL

BIG HEART

HE CAME OUT OF the back, his apron bloody. The butcher Mr. Ribalta had the biggest belly I had ever seen. When he leaned into the case to grab a handful of hamburger or lop off a rope of sausage, his stomach grazed the meat. I wanted to poke his fat, to see if my finger would sink into it like pizza dough, or press my ear against him, to hear his insides sloshing and grumbling. But I hung back from the meat counter until he crooked a plump finger and beckoned me forward.

"Oh, Swiss Girl," he called. "Yo-do-lo-do-lo-do-lay."

I always eyed his Swiss cheese. I wanted to take a chunk of it home and slip it between a wedge of sharp pepperoni and a slice of salty prosciutto on a seeded roll. But Mama refused to buy it. "I don't pay good money for holes," she said. She frowned when Ribalta reached into the case to cut me a sliver.

People said Ribalta had a big heart, but Mama was convinced his heart longed for only one thing: to turn her into a big spender. Every Saturday morning before we left the house for the market, she armed herself with a black plastic wallet stamped with a picture of the Leaning Tower of Pisa, a shopping list, and a green pencil stub she had pocketed after playing miniature golf at

Palisades Park. Since my sister, Lina, thought she was too old for such outings, Mama took me—a mere nine-year-old who didn't yet know how to protest—as a witness. I was supposed to make sure Ribalta didn't try any monkey business, like doubling the wax paper or pressing his thumb down on the scale. Although Mama had patronized Ribalta for years, she still didn't trust him. "It's not like he's family," she said.

The market stood on a corner, the front windows lined with white paper, lettered in blue, that announced the weekly specials. Above the shop, behind windows hung with yellowed lace curtains, Ribalta lived with his mother. Mama called her Signora. For years I thought that was her first name.

In cold weather or warm, Mama and I found Signora out front, sweeping the dirt and litter off the sidewalk with a ragged broom that had lost half its dirty bristles. Signora reminded me of La Befana, the skinny old Italian witch who rode her broom over the rooftops on the Feast of the Three Kings, leaving toys for good children and coal and ash for the bad. She wore a black cotton coat over a flowered shift and scuffed gray mules with no stockings. Her brittle ankles and calves were mapped with thin blue veins. Signora was practically bald, but what little tufts of gray hair she had left on her pink scalp she clamped around wire curlers fastened with big silver clips. She held her broom still just long enough to peer at us through her cat glasses. When she was satisfied she had recognized us, she resumed sweeping.

Ribalta's shop officially opened at nine, but we always walked in a little after eight-thirty. Brass bells clattered as the door swung behind us. Mama headed down the first narrow aisle, stopping once or twice to inspect some canned goods that sat on the high wooden shelves. "Cheaper at the A&P," she announced loudly.

At the back of the store stood the gleaming white meat case, lit with fluorescent tubes that made the unit hum and vibrate. Behind the case was a swinging door and, behind that, the mysterious room where Ribalta butchered his meat while Radio Italia played. Mama went up to the counter and hit the silver bell on top with the flat of her hand. The radio went dead. We heard water running. Then Ribalta came out of the back, his breath heavy as he wiped his hands on a clean white cloth. He pushed his gold wire-rimmed glasses up on his nose. He was the only shop-keeper in our neighborhood who ever smiled at Mama.

Mama nodded back, her eyes on the case. Ribalta stocked it so the contents ranged from the reddest and rawest meat to the cleanest, tidiest rolls of processed food. First came the organs—bloody bulbs of liver, tough-looking necks, and limp hearts—packaged in clear plastic containers. Then came ground beef pressed in an aluminum tray, rump roast and flank steaks, coils of sausage, and a quilt of overlapping bacon strips. Cuts of pale pork and veal were followed by moist chicken breasts and piles of stippled yellow legs and scrawny wings. In a separate section of the case, Ribalta kept logs of prosciutto, mortadella, Genoa salami, and blocks of cheese.

Mama checked each item on her list against Ribalta's prices. Then she placed the list on top of her wallet and firmly crossed off some items with the pencil stub. "Here's what's left," she said. It always took Ribalta a long time to fill the order. Mama made him display each cut of meat, back and front, before she allowed him to put it on the scale. And when she said she wanted half a pound of something, she meant eight ounces, no more and no less. Ribalta knew better than to ask Mama if *a little bit over* was okay. He patiently lifted chop after chop onto the scale, while Mama watched the gauge waggle back and forth until it settled as close to the weight she had asked for as it would ever get.

After Ribalta had wrapped the meats in stiff white paper, tied each bundle with red and white string, and marked the price with a black wax pencil, he crossed his arms and rested them on his big belly. He knew exactly what Mama was going to ask for next.

"Any scraps today?" she said.

"For the dog, eh?" Ribalta held up one finger, meaning Mama should wait. He disappeared into the back.

I never understood why Mama kept up this charade. We didn't have a dog and never would. "Good for nothing except to bite and bark," Mama said, whenever I pleaded for one.

"If you hate dogs so much, why do you tell Ribalta we have one?" I asked.

"I tell him no such thing."

"But you let him think we do."

"I can't help the ideas he gets in his head," Mama said.

She waited impatiently for Ribalta to return with the scraps. He came back balancing a pile of metal pans. He displayed the contents to Mama and the haggling began.

"Veal bones," he said. "With plenty of meat. Chicken necks, close to ten of them."

Mama rejected the necks and offered fifteen cents for a bag of bones.

"Make it a quarter," Ribalta said.

"For those sticks?"

"These are beautiful bones. Juicy. Tender. Flavorful."

"Twenty cents," Mama firmly said.

Ribalta never said *done, fine,* or *okay.* He simply moved on to his next offering. "Giblets. Fresh this morning. And these hearts, I saved them just for you."

They went back and forth like that, until Ribalta ran out of scraps and Mama was satisfied she had bled him for whatever she could get. Ribalta stacked the white packages in a box. Then he winked at Mama and peered over the case at me.

"Oh, Swiss Girl," he said. "Yo-do-lo-do-lo-do-lay!"

He turned, wiped off a cleaver, and reached into the case to whack off a hunk of the cheese. He handed it to Mama. She frowned when she gave me the cheese. "Say thank you," she told me, before I could even open my mouth. To Ribalta she said, "You're too generous."

"Why not?" he replied as he wiped the cleaver. "Life is short."
Then he came around the side of the case, carrying Mama's box.
We followed him up the aisle. The strings of his apron stretched
tightly across his broad backside. They were tied in a simple knot
because there wasn't enough give for a bow.

Up in front, behind the squat glass counter, Signora now sat on
a wooden stool. Ribalta lowered the box onto the counter and
left Signora to figure the bill with a pencil and paper. Signora
lifted out the bundles one at a time and wrote down each price,
totaling as she went along. Mama kept her eyes on that rising
sum. Signora counted out aloud: *"Due più cinque? Otto. Mi
scusi, sette. Otto più tre? Dodici. Mi scusi, undici."* Nothing
would have made Mama happier than nailing Signora in a mathe-
matical error. But Signora always caught her mistakes and confi-
dently bellowed the sum the way a railroad conductor announced
the next station: *"Sei dollari e sesanta due centi, per favore!"*

Mama opened her wallet and counted out the bills. Signora
took them, recounted them, then reached below the counter for a
rusty Maxwell House coffee can full of coins. With her gnarled
fingers, she dug through the coins to make Mama change.

Mama left the market with a satisfied look on her face. But
after a block or two, when the box grew heavy and she switched
the weight from one hand to the other, she bit her lip and wrinkled her brow, convinced that Ribalta had gotten fat off her business and hers alone. *"Grassone!"* she said. "Thinks I don't notice
that diamond ring."

On his right pinky, Ribalta wore a thin gold band studded with
a diamond. Mama often remarked on it. "Who else do you know
owns such a swanky thing?" she asked me. I shrugged. No other
man I knew wore jewelry—not even a wedding ring—except the
archbishop, who came to our church once a year to give Confir-
mation. He wore a huge gold ring on his right hand that was supposed to hold a sliver of Christ's cross. On our way out of church,
we all knelt down and pressed our lips against the cold, pale blue

jewel. The archbishop wiped his ring with a little red cloth after each person had kissed it, the same way Ribalta wiped his cleaver before and after he cut me a piece of cheese.

Ribalta didn't go to church. Sundays, my mother and my aunts gathered together on the sidewalk after mass and stared after Signora, who hobbled home alone. Then they turned back into a circle and began their attack against the butcher.

"What does the man eat, *pasta e fagioli* six times a day?"

"How can he breathe with a belly like that?"

"How does he move his bowels?"

"The size!"

"The smell!"

"They say he sings in a band."

"Fat as an opera singer."

"If he sings so well, why isn't he in the choir?"

"Have you ever seen him at mass?"

"He should be there."

"He's a bachelor."

"That's his problem."

"He'll have a heart attack."

"He's unhealthy."

They blamed Signora. They said she spoiled him, babied him, cooked him whatever he wanted. They said that after she died, he would lose a little weight. Find himself a girl. Get married and have children. Why not? He was still young enough. He had a kind face. Most important, he owned a family business. In our neighborhood, that was the ultimate sign of having done well for yourself. The only thing better was getting in with the post office or phone company.

※

Every afternoon when I fetched the newspaper off the front porch, Mama paused a few moments from her housework to scan the obituary page. One day she snapped the newspaper open and pointed to a picture with triumph.

"Ribalta's mother," she said.

I looked for the helmet of hair clips and wire curlers, the scraggly neck crisscrossed with lines, the silver cat glasses and pinched cheeks. But the hair was full as a wig and the face smooth, as if air had been pumped into it.

"That's not her," I said.

"Stupid," said Mama. "It's an old photograph."

"The name's wrong too."

"What? Gelsomina Ribalta, that's right."

"But you called her Signora."

Mama laughed. She spent the rest of the afternoon on the phone, repeating the story to my aunts. "Imagine, I had to tell the *bimba* it meant *Mrs.* How much more American can these kids get? I wonder who'll sit behind the counter now. He'll have to find some girl, and quick too. Yes, tonight, at the Torino Funeral Home. Burial on Tuesday, the paper said."

For three days after the funeral, the shop was closed. A black ribbon hung from the door, and upstairs all the shades were drawn. The weekly specials remained the same. I made a sign of the cross as I passed on my way to school. I was frightened that Signora's spirit still lingered in the world, that I'd hear the swish of her broom on the sidewalk and the clatter of her bony fingers, sorting through the Maxwell House coffee can to make change.

On Saturday morning I stuck close to Mama on the walk to the store. When we arrived, the front door was locked. Mama pulled at the handle to test it again. Then she peered through the door. The glass grew foggy with her breath. A boy stood in the front aisle, stacking loaves of bread on the shelf. He turned. Mama rapped at the glass. The boy held up his wrist, pointed to his watch, and then went back to stacking the bread. Mama was astounded.

"The sign says open at nine," I pointed out.

"That sign has hung there for years. Signora always opened." Mama bit her lip, then rapped at the glass even harder.

"Aspettino," the boy called out.

Mama turned away. "Figures," she said. "A real *paesano*. Speaks no English. Lazy."

I could tell she wanted to knock even harder at the door, pull at the handle, and yell at him. But Mama held herself back out of respect for Ribalta. We waited two or three minutes in the cold before the boy came to the door. He was older than he seemed at first, about twenty, and short and erect, with muscled arms and a firm chest that swelled beneath the bib of his clean white apron. He had close-trimmed black hair and dark, liquidy eyes with long black lashes, high cheekbones, and a moist, pouty lower lip. A gold medal hung on a chain around his short, solid neck. I fell in love with him instantly.

"It's about time!" Mama huffed when he let us in.

He looked at us as if he didn't understand. Mama strode past him without even a nod. "Off the boat," she muttered, as I followed her down the first aisle. I turned back to look at him. Maybe he didn't understand English, but I was sure he caught the drift of Mama's loud *Cheaper at the A&P*. He stood with one hand on the counter and watched as Mama hit the bell on the meat case. Ribalta came out slowly, wiping his plump, squat hands. Radio Italia continued to play.

Two new things in one morning were more than Mama could handle. "You forgot to turn off your radio," she said.

"My cousin likes the music," Ribalta answered.

Mama looked back down the aisle at the boy. "That one there is your cousin? Funny, I don't remember him at the funeral."

Ribalta hung his head to show his sorrow. Then Mama got ahold of herself and rolled out her standard sympathy speech. "Torino did a wonderful job with your mother," she said. "She looked so peaceful. And Father said a beautiful mass, don't you think? The flowers were lovely. I've never seen so many in my life. Sent by relatives?"

"I ordered most."

I could tell Mama was racking up the price of that in her head, adding it to the cost of the fancy coffin Signora had been buried in and the white headstone that had an angel with outstretched wings. "A real tribute to your mother," she said. "I pray my children do the same for me."

"Not too soon, I hope."

"You never know, do you. God has His plan." She scanned the meat case. If she was hoping Ribalta would be running some specials to lure his customers back into the store, she was disappointed. She crossed about half the items off her list. "Start with the hamburger," she said. "That's fresh, I hope."

"I always sell fresh."

"Three-quarters of a pound, then."

I stood with my back to the front of the store. I felt the cousin's eyes on us. I was embarrassed by my childish red earmuffs and red wool mittens, by Mama's flat black boots and shabby wool coat. The haggling was long and intense that morning. I stood there awkwardly. I blushed when Ribalta called me the Swiss Girl and yodeled at me. I quickly ate the piece of cheese as we followed Ribalta to the front of the store. Mama's undisguised astonishment at what she found on the counter mortified me. Ribalta's cousin stood behind a cash register, a green metal box with smart red buttons.

"What's this fancy machine doing here?" Mama said.

"We're joining the modern age," Ribalta said.

Mama looked dubious. "Pencil and paper was good enough for Signora," she said. She watched the cousin carefully as he sorted through the box and rang up the paltry sums scribbled on the packages. When the insubstantial total popped up on little silver tabs in the window of the cash register, I wanted to die of shame.

Mama regarded the numbers suspiciously. "Is that it?" she said to the boy.

He pointed to the total. I turned my back as Mama drew the bills out of her Leaning Tower of Pisa wallet. The impatient way she held out her hand for the change annoyed me.

"Slow as molasses," Mama said after we left the store. "And sloppy too. Packed the bones on top of the meat."

Just as Gelsomina Ribalta became known simply as *The Mrs.*, the boy became known as *The Cousin.* "So what do you think of Cugino?" my aunts polled one another, with little smiles on their faces. Too many muscles, they decided. Too long nails. He took forever to figure out the total and too long to pack the box back up. He was too handsome for a man. Good looks spelled trouble, you better believe it!

"Heartbreaker," my Aunt Fiorella pronounced him, nudging me. "Look out!" Then all my aunts cackled. I turned red, both from the shame of knowing that Cugino would never be interested in a silly girl like me and from fear that Mama and my aunts would guess my secret. I had never been in love before, and I was sure it was written all over my face. But if Mama caught on to it, she said nothing. She was distracted by other things at the market. She made it her business to find out more about Cugino. The more Ribalta refused to be pinned down, the harder she hammered him.

"So where is this cousin of yours from?" she asked.

"Calabria."

"I thought your family was *napoletana.*"

"My mother's side, God rest them, yes."

"Oh, so this *cugino* is from your father's side? But his last name isn't Ribalta? He's your father's sister's son, then?"

"Second cousin, actually."

Mama hesitated, then probed again. "I hear you sing in a band," she said.

"That's right."

"Your *cugino*, he's in show business too?"

"He plays horn, yes."

"What sort of music—Sinatra, that kind of stuff?"

"We'll be giving a concert downtown—"

"Downtown!" Mama said, as if traveling five miles to the center of New Haven took Ribalta to a distant (and depraved) country. "You go downtown?"

"Just to Wooster Square. For *Carnevale*. Come hear us play."

Mama was taken aback. No one ever invited her anywhere. She looked down at her list, and for a moment I thought she truly was considering it. I imagined us standing in the square, bundled in our winter coats. Up on stage, Ribalta snapped his chubby fingers and crooned into the microphone. Then Cugino stood up from his folding chair, lifted his gleaming trumpet to his lips, and staring me soulfully in the eyes, played a lilting solo that sent the audience into a frenzy of applause. People hooted and roared, knowing that the next day they would have to don black, go to church, and fast for Ash Wednesday. . . .

"I don't go to *la festa*," Mama said. "Too many people. The whole world is there." She paused. "Your *cugino*'s parents, they'll be there?"

"They're dead."

"Orphaned so young. How old is he anyway?"

"Nineteen."

"He'll be married soon," said Mama. "He has a girlfriend, I guess?"

"Not at the moment."

"You should fix him up. There are plenty of nice girls in the parish."

"We don't go to church."

"You should."

"What for?"

"To find God."

"God is in our hearts," Ribalta said.

"He's at Sunday mass," said Mama. "And you should be there too, with your *cugino*. Who knows? You both might meet a nice girl."

"We already have our favorite," Ribalta said, and smiled at me. "She's called the Swiss Girl. Yo-do-lo-do-lo-do-lay!"

I prayed I would be Cugino's favorite. My mind was always on him. In the middle of a spelling bee at school, or during the Eucharistic prayer at church, I would feel warmth envelop me and suddenly Cugino would be by my side, his thick fingers clasping my upper arms. We were rolling over and over again in a bed of grass, lying together on the beach as the waves lapped in on the sand. We kissed and embraced . . .

Then I misspelled *sacrifice* and Sister Thomas made me sit down. I forgot to say *amen* after Father said *Body of Christ,* and he had to repeat it. I didn't care. I loved Cugino so much I hated everybody else: Sister and Father and all nuns and priests, my aunts, my mother and her wallet, even Ribalta. I was sure my heart beat louder and stronger than any of theirs. Only love was real, and mine was all for Cugino.

I desperately wanted to impress him. On the way to the store I tried to convince Mama to spend more money.

"Let's get some Swiss cheese today," I said.

"You'll get your piece for free."

"All my friends bring baloney sandwiches to school."

"Peanut butter isn't good enough for you anymore?"

"It sticks to my mouth," I said.

"So put on some jelly."

"We're almost out of jelly, I noticed this morning. We'd better get some at Ribalta's."

"It's cheaper at the—"

"Stop talking about the A&P!" I said. "Especially in the store."

"Who can hear me?" Mama asked. "Ribalta's blasting the radio in the back and Cugino *non capisce*."

"He understands from the way you say it."

Mama sniffed. "I've got nothing to hide from his type."

"Why don't you put your wallet in a purse?"

"Because I've got two hands."

"Don't you want a new wallet for your birthday?"

"This one works just fine."

"Aren't you tired of the Leaning Tower of Pisa?"

"When it falls over, you can buy me a new one."

I tried to wean Mama from haggling over the scraps. But the bargaining grew even more intense as the weeks went by. Mama was convinced Ribalta was offering her less of a choice. One minute she wondered if he was holding back on her; the next she was worried some other housewife was beating her to the best of the pickings. She insisted on leaving even earlier for the store to make sure Cugino didn't let anyone in before us. She stood outside the shop door, talking about him loudly as he stacked the bread. "It's that cousin," she said. "He probably steals the scraps and gives them to his friends."

"Ssh," I said. "He does not."

"He's taking Ribalta for a ride, believe you me."

"He is not."

"One of these days he's going to clean out that fancy cash register and be long gone."

"He won't leave."

Mama snorted. "That would break somebody's heart."

"It would *not*."

She looked at me. Then she laughed. "Oh, so you're wild about him too?"

My face felt warm. "Am *not*," I said. I looked down at the dirty sidewalk. The word *too* resounded disagreeably in my ears. "Who else likes him?"

Mama snorted again. "Are you thick in the head?" She gestured with a limp wrist toward the store. "*Tutti frutti* in there," she said.

I bit my lip. *Tutti frutti* was a phrase my father used to describe that strange, grinning man in the sparkling cape who played the white grand piano on Sunday-night TV. I couldn't believe that Ribalta—and Cugino—were of the same ilk as Liberace. But when Cugino came to the door and Mama pushed past him, I noticed he wore something gold and sparkling on his finger—Ribalta's ring.

I kept my eyes on Mama as she marched down the first aisle, her fingers tightly clasped around her wallet. I hated her. She had killed my dream of being with Cugino as neatly and cleanly as Ribalta chopped the head off a chicken. I'd get her back. My heart pounding, I waited while she made her selections. When she was through, Ribalta folded his arms over his belly.

"Any scraps today?" Mama asked.

"For the dog, eh?" Ribalta answered.

My blood raced. "We don't have a dog," I announced.

Mama gave me a murderous look. Ribalta opened his mouth and nothing came out. He swallowed. In a sad voice that showed his disappointment in me, he said, "I know that," before he disappeared through the swinging door.

The moment he was gone, Mama smacked me soundly on the back of the head with her wallet. "That'll teach you," she said. "I'll never take you here again."

I turned and walked halfway down the soup aisle. The black letters on the Campbell's cans blurred. I was crying. Mama had put me to shame. I heard Ribalta come back and I walked down the rest of the aisle. Cugino, fortunately, was nowhere in sight. I went out the front door and around to the side of the store. The yard behind the market was blocked off with a high wooden fence. I peered over the gate.

Through the back window of the shop, I could see into the room where Ribalta did the butchering. It was illuminated with long fluorescent tubes that gave off a bluish hue. A huge refrigerator—five doors long—lined one whole wall. Above the triple sink hung knives as long as swords, cleavers that looked like they would fell a tree, and an assortment of scissors to trim and snip the meat after it had been sliced and gutted. From metal hooks on the ceiling, slabs of meat hung like punching bags waiting for someone to pummel them. On a wire stretched across the room, plucked chickens dangled—long, skinny, and naked as Mama's bras hanging on the clothesline. Radio Italia was playing opera. Cugino moved around the room, then came out the back door carrying a bucket. He held it above his head as he descended the stairs. Then from the back of the yard trotted three lambs, their coats gray and covered with bits of grass. Their hooves sounded sharp on the frozen ground. They nuzzled up against Cugino's white apron, licking him and looking up at him with glassy, expectant eyes. Cugino waited until he had gotten to the center of the yard before he dumped the bucket. There, on the ground, lay beet stalks, shredded turnips, carrot and potato peels—and what little of Mama's coveted scraps Cugino hadn't seen fit to put into a soup or stew. The lambs crowded in to feast on the mess.

Cugino looked up and saw me. He said something in Italian, broke it off, then beckoned. He came over and unlocked the gate to let me in. Cugino gestured that I should pet one of the lambs. I stroked the matted fur of the smallest, which had a black face and knobby knees.

Cugino gestured toward the lambs, then smacked his lips and rubbed his stomach. I screwed up my face to show I didn't understand him.

"*Per la Pasqua,*" he said.

"Yes," I said. "Easter pets."

He smacked his lips and rubbed his stomach again, smiling. He kept grinning and gesturing, pointing first to the lambs, then to his belly. I noticed his teeth were crooked and his stomach was a little bit flabby. He looked like an actor in a silent movie trying to get a laugh. I wondered how I ever could have loved such an idiot.

"*Capisci, capisci?*" he asked. When I kept on staring at him, obviously not understanding what he was driving at, he grabbed one lamb by the wool on top of its head, held out one finger, brought it up to the lamb's neck, and dragged it across, in the gesture of an executioner.

I took my hand away from the lamb I was petting. I couldn't decide who was more evil—Ribalta for butchering the lambs, or Cugino for telling me he was going to do it. Tears welled up in my eyes. Cugino looked confused. Then he reached out and took my hand. After all those weeks of dreaming he would touch me, his grasp felt tight and cold. I was about to pull away when Mama appeared at the gate, against the broad white backdrop of Ribalta's figure.

Mama tried to open the gate, then rattled it. She began to sputter incoherently. *What was this? Crazy nut! Drop her hand! Disgraceful! My daughter! He'd go to hell for this! Sick turkey!*

Ribalta's fat seemed to quiver as he gestured at Mama. "Calm down," he said, reaching over her to fumble with the lock. "Please be calm, Signora."

Mama made a fist and shouted something evil-sounding in Italian. Cugino dropped both the bucket and my hand and raised his fists at Mama. The lambs scattered. Mama gazed at the beets and turnips and the last of her scraps on the grass. That was the final straw. When Ribalta finally popped open the gate, she marched in and dragged me out of the yard. "Family business!" she said to Ribalta as she pulled me down the sidewalk. "More like *funny* business you've got going on here. And you'll pay for it, just you wait and see."

On Easter, I refused to come down to dinner. I lay on my bed, trying to recapture the feeling of being in love. I tried to melt into a dreamy state, to smell the meadow and hear the waves. But it was useless. I couldn't get it back, no matter how hard I tried. I had lost Cugino, the same as Ribalta.

For Cugino was gone. They said Ribalta stuffed his pockets full of money and sent him packing. The butcher had his business to think of. Mama talked loud and word spread fast that something just a little bit fishy was going on over at that meat market, and never you mind what, although you could take a guess.

Knowing she wouldn't meet up with Cugino at the market ever again, Mama returned to Ribalta's on Holy Saturday and acted as if nothing had happened. She came back with a boxful of packages and reported, with satisfaction, that a very nice older woman—perhaps a relative of Signora's—sat behind the counter. She was quite pleasant and spoke good English too.

As I lay on my bed, trying to block out the squeak of knives scraping against the plates, I heard Mama telling my aunts, for the umpteenth time, how she had bargained Ribalta rock-bottom low on the lamb. It was such a good deal she even bought some mint jelly. Why not? Life was short. "Try it," she urged them. "I got it on special. Delicious."

SODA MAN

BEFORE FIRST GRADE, I never gave much thought to Babbo. He simply was who he was: our father, who was quick to remind us that his hard work was the only thing that kept food on the table, a roof over our heads, and clothes on our backs. The first day of school taught me to look at Babbo differently. Sister Sebastian—a stern black presence in the front of the room, whose tight voice could make even the call to recess seem like a threat—made us stand up one by one and recite our name and address. Then she grilled us about our families. How many brothers and sisters did we have? Did our grandparents live at home? I had no trouble answering until she came to *What does your father do for a living?*

I stared straight ahead at the wall, where an illustrated chart of the alphabet reduced the world to twenty-six simple statements: A is for apple, B is for bee, C is for cat. Sister stared at me impatiently. "Don't you know what your father does all day?" she asked. "Or maybe he's out of work, is that it?"

I shook my head.

"Has he passed away, then?"

At that moment I gladly would have sunk Babbo to the bottom

of the sea in order to truthfully reply yes, he was dead. I shook my head again. My answer burst forth from my mouth like a cork from a bottle.

"Soda man!" I said loudly.

"What?" Sister asked.

"Delivers soda!" I said, and sat down, defying one of Sister's strictest rules, which was never to resume your seat without her permission. My cheeks and ears blazed as she made me stand up and sit down all over again. Behind me, I heard a girl's nasty little twitter.

It turned out everyone else in class had a father just like mine. Giuliana Selmone's father wore a powdery white apron and bagged Danish pastries and kaiser rolls for customers at the bakery. Mario Cusini's father worked at the Welling Box Factory, where at 11:55 you could see him clutching his tin lunch box and thermos behind the chain-link fence, waiting for the noon whistle to blow and the gates to open that would release him for exactly half an hour from his hot, stuffy imprisonment. Anna Maria Milletti's father pushed a broom at Saint Raphael's Hospital, and later in the school year the rumor—never substantiated—would surface that on Saturdays he wore a white pointed hat to sell popcorn and peanuts at the Yale football games. Didi Dellavone's father was a plumber, yet she could brag that her family had living-room furniture so nice it was kept under plastic wraps. I thought that was the height of elegance. At the A&P I used to pester Mama to buy Saran Wrap so we, too, could cover our shabby three-cushion couch and stuffed armchair.

"What are you, nuts?" Mama asked. "Covering perfectly good furniture meant to sit on? That's the limit. How much more *pazza* can you get?"

I sulked. I was dissatisfied. I longed to be elegant, but I felt branded for life as a girl whose father was only A Man—an anonymous male who went from store to store and house to house, knocking on doors and sending girls upstairs shrieking with exaggerated fright—silly little girls like my older sister, Lina, and me. "What are you acting so nuts for?" Mama hollered at us when we ran from the sound of the back doorbell. "It's only the oil man." Or it was the gas man. The furnace man. The milkman. The mailman. Any male who appeared at our door—be he the Fuller Brush man or the paperboy—sent Lina and me flying up to our room, where we pounced on our beds, kicked our legs in the air, and giggled madly until the deep-voiced, loud-mouthed intruder left our house.

Even though he lived in our home—and paid for it—Babbo, too, seemed like an invader. When the Dixon Park Soda truck rumbled up our driveway, Lina and I used to run to the kitchen and peek out the sheer yellow curtains, then bolt for the living room as he got out of the truck. We pretended to be grossly absorbed in our books or dolls or crayons when Babbo came in. We dreaded the moment he sat down on the couch with the newspaper. He always examined the sports page first. He let out a hefty sigh. Then came the fatal words, uttered to no one in particular: *Think I'll rest my tootsies awhile.*

Lina and I looked at each other with dismay. Babbo leaned over and untied his shoelaces, then grasped each heel and pulled his black shoes off one at a time. We stared, fascinated, at Babbo's white socks, gray on the bottom and stained with dark brown spots at the toes where his nails, rarely clipped, had squished too close together and cut the skin. Babbo peeled the top of his sock down over his ankle and gave a sharp yank at the end. We sucked in our breath. His feet—cracked white at the ankles and undersides, calloused at the toes, and blistered on the heels—stunk royally. But he seemed unaware of it. He dropped his socks to the carpet and propped his legs on the orange vinyl hassock in front of the couch. "Aaah," he said. "That feels better. Yes."

I bit my lip. Lina began to hum a loud, ominous-sounding tune, until she reached an unsurpassable crescendo and had to exhale and pull in more air. My face felt as if it were turning blue.

I looked at her beseechingly. She nodded. Grabbing a fistful of crayons or a doll by the leg or the hair, we bolted the room, pinching our noses so hard our nostrils ached. Upstairs we collapsed on our twin beds, panting and gasping.

Downstairs we heard Babbo shake open the newspaper. "What's the matter with those girls now?" he sometimes called out to Mama in the kitchen.

"They're half your kids," Mama said.

Babbo sighed. "One of youze half-mine girls," he called out, "remember to bring down my slippers!"

Even though we swooned at the overpowering smell of his feet, Lina and I loved Babbo enough to fight over him. We tussled to win the favor of fetching his slippers and squabbled over who would get to wear the thick red and gold band that came on the Rey Corona cigar Babbo smoked in the backyard while we played after dinner. Babbo gave the cigar ring as a consolation prize to whoever lost the game of four squares, Seven-Up, or hopscotch. Since Lina was much more athletic and terrifically competitive, I often got to sport the ring on my finger. Lina used this as rationale for claiming the privilege of getting Babbo's slippers on Mondays, Wednesdays, and Fridays.

I had to be content with entering the otherwise forbidden territory of Mama and Babbo's room on Tuesdays and Thursdays. The floorboards creaked as I tiptoed past the dark wooden bed covered with a nubby white spread Mama had pulled tight with hospital-like precision. I peeked under the pillows just to see if Mama and Babbo had anything hidden there. Just Mama's old nightgown, the lace torn at the collar. Then I opened the heavy door to Babbo's closet. Tied on a hook to the right, one of Mama's old stockings held a cluster of waxy white mothballs. The odor made me sneeze. On the rack, white and blue dress shirts hung to the left, black dress trousers and jackets hung to the right, and two somber ties hung over the rack in the middle. Babbo wore those clothes only to Sunday mass and weddings and funerals. On weekdays during the summer he wore thick brown cotton pants and white T-shirts that got soaked with sweat. In winter he wore the same gray V-neck sweater five days a week, which he discarded every night on one of the living-room chairs. When Mama wasn't looking, I liked to pull the pills off the sleeves.

I lingered as long as I could in front of the closet. Then I pulled the slippers—black leather with fur lining worn almost completely away at the heels—out of the shoe bag that hung on the back of the door. I ran downstairs, plopped the slippers on the floor beside Babbo, and ran back upstairs, where I reported on this nonevent in whispered, conspiratorial tones to Lina.

"He didn't look at me," I said. "But he said thank you."

"I saw wax in his ears yesterday," Lina bragged.

"So what?" I countered. "I saw hairs in his nose."

"I saw a piece of hot-dog relish between his teeth," Lina said. "When he kissed me."

Babbo always favored Lina because she was prettier. "Who wants a kiss from him, anyway?" I asked, in a sourpuss voice. "His face feels like an S.O.S. pad—all rough and stubbly."

"Some women like that," Lina said.

"You're not *some women*," I said. "You're half his daughter."

Lina curled a lock of hair around her finger. "I've been thinking," she said. "Maybe he's not our father. You know, like in books, where the kids get switched in the hospital, or they're left on the doorstep in a laundry basket."

"Maybe we're orphans," I said.

"I bet we have a long-lost father," said Lina. "Someday we'll be reunited. He'll own diamond mines. He'll have a treasure chest full of gold and silver coins."

"He'll come home to us someday," I said, "with his pockets stuffed with sapphires and emeralds, pearls and rubies." I sighed. Babbo came home every night with one pocket full of loose change and the other stuffed with a crumpled yellow handkerchief. Yet I couldn't forget that occasionally he gave us some of that change—the pennies and the nickels, if not the coveted quarters. He did other nice, fatherlike things, like telling us we looked pretty in our pastel Easter coats and hats. He carefully peeled two oranges and crafted the rinds into matching sunglasses, which we wore until they rotted. He put a bell on Lina's used green bike; he painted my wooden scooter a glossy red. Sundays he went out early and brought home soft, seeded rolls, hard cookies that snapped between our teeth, and gooey lemon pastries from the bakery. On my birthday he planted an awkward kiss on my right cheek and whispered, "Angelina, my angel," before he kissed the other cheek and said my name again, as if to confirm I was some winged creature just descended from the heavens.

"If he isn't our father," I told Lina, "that means we can marry him."

"Let's spy on him," she said. "To find out who he really is."

So a silly, secretive game began, with a record of Babbo's sadly predictable comings and goings.

He goes to work in the morning, Lina wrote down in her notebook, *and comes home around four in the afternoon. He eats dinner. He smokes a Rey Corona cigar. Then he falls asleep on the couch.* She bit her pencil. "There's got to be more to his life than that."

"Maybe he goes out later, after we're asleep," I said.

"Yes," Lina said. "He probably *carouses.* Goes out with other men to bars." She carefully wrote that down in her notebook.

"Friday nights he goes bowling," I offered.

Lina added that to her list. Under the heading of Saturday, she wrote, *Tells Mama he's going to the Knights of Columbus, an obvious lie.* She leaned back in her chair and surveyed the evidence. "I smell something fishy about Fridays," she said. "They're definitely suspicious. Keep your eyes open. Remember— first one to find out gets to wear the Rey Corona ring forever."

We sneaked about the house. When Babbo went out into the

yard, we ran upstairs, knelt on the floor in front of the window, and raised our eyes above the sill. When he went to the bathroom, not bothering to completely close the door, one of us stood outside. Lina claimed she actually saw the arc of his piss once, but all I ever could glimpse was the white toilet tank and the pink plastic shower curtain, frosted with faded silver. When Babbo was on the phone—a rare event—we stood at the top of the stairwell and listened. We didn't have to strain our ears. As if he were speaking on a public phone in a bowling alley (the balls smacking the pins and rumbling down the gutter), Babbo shouted into the receiver in a strange language we could not decipher.

"What's an exacta?" I whispered to Lina.

"I think it's a kind of cigar," Lina whispered back.

"Then what's a trifecta?"

"Three cigars."

"And a perfecta?"

"A perfect cigar!"

We giggled.

When Mama went out for groceries, we plundered Babbo's drawers. Mama's drawers we didn't care about—we knew her all too well, and our imaginations could conjure up only dreary, baggy white underwear, thriftily preserved until the elastic around the waist and legs had totally lost its snap, and heavy, seamed bras with wide straps and three sets of double hooks in the back. There also would be plain, flesh-colored stockings and white garter belts, worn only on Sundays.

But Babbo's drawers—his T-shirts and socks bleached white by Mama, the polo shirts he wore for bowling, and the green plastic container full of Clubman talcum powder that he sprinkled on the back of his neck before he put on a dress shirt—fascinated us. He had a black leather box into which he emptied his change every night. Lina and I were tempted to steal a coin or two but didn't, somehow convinced that Babbo knew the exact amount of his savings to the penny. We fingered the passbook issued to Babbo from the Greater Hartford Savings Bank and were tempted to take it out of its plastic case to see exactly how rich Babbo was. "How much do you think is in there?" I asked, and Lina told me at least one hundred dollars.

One hundred dollars! If only I had that kind of money, I thought, I could have a fur coat and high heels, a diamond ring, and a toy poodle. I could have a house shaped like a Swiss chalet, and an oval-shaped swimming pool with a bright blue slide that dropped into the deep end. Lina scoffed at the very idea. "You dunce," she said. "You need at least a thousand to be as rich as that."

Sometimes in the leather box we found tickets with either one number or three numbers printed on them. Other times we found no tickets but only the brown-tinted pictures of Babbo's mother and father standing stiffly in front of a curtained backdrop in a photographer's studio. Nonno wore a white suit and held a dashing wide-brimmed hat in his hands. Nonna had on a black lace dress and shoes that buttoned. Stacked below these were pictures of Lina and me sitting on the lap of the Santa Claus who appeared yearly at Macy's Christmas Wonderland (Lina squirmed in Santa's arms; I cried), posing in our Communion dresses on the front steps of the church, and leaping in our too-tight bathing suits beneath the sprinkler on a hot summer day better spent at the beach.

But the most fascinating photo was a black-and-white shot of a thin woman in a sharp double-breasted suit and nonchalant little hat. She stood on a boardwalk overlooking the shore, and the wind coming off the water fluttered the veil on her hat over the top half of her face. She had a happy, carefree smile. Who was she? On the bottom white border of the photograph, Babbo's faded handwriting boldly proclaimed: *mine*.

"Wow," Lina said, clutching the photograph tightly in her

hand and holding it up close to her eyes, as if she were Nancy Drew inspecting the fatal evidence. "Look at this. Babbo's got a girlfriend."

"He does not," I said, although the picture told me otherwise. "He can't. He's married to Mama."

"So what?" Lina said. "Lots of married people do bad things."

"Like what?"

Lina smiled. She didn't take her eyes off the picture. "She's his girlfriend," she whispered. "She's all his, I bet."

"So when does he see her?" I asked.

"On Fridays. When he's supposed to go bowling."

"But he takes his bowling bag," I said.

"He's got to do something to throw Mama off track."

"So when does he call her?"

"On his way home from work. From a public phone."

"Why doesn't she call here?"

Lina looked at me as if I were a colossal dope. "Because one of us might answer," she said.

I stood perfectly still, listening to the silence of the house and praying that the phone would ring that very instant. I longed to hear her sultry, passionate voice on the other end of the line. I desperately wanted the chance to speak to the kind of woman that Mama, scorn oozing from her voice, would refer to as *a brazen bombshell* or *a shameless hussy.*

"Do you think she's married too?" I asked Lina.

"She's definitely a working woman," Lina said. "Maybe she's a hairdresser."

"Maybe she sells perfume at Macy's."

"Maybe she sells cigars," Lina said. "Yes—perfectas! Let's look for her next time we go out."

"Okay," I said. And for a while our mutual goal was to find this slutty young heartbreaker. Everywhere we went, we tried to sniff her out. In the backseat of the car, we kept our eyes glued to the windows as we scoured both sides of the street. We looked for her at church, on our way to school, at the beach, and even in the crowds at Palisades Park and Yankee Stadium. "That's her, that's her!" I nudged Lina from time to time.

"That's who?" Mama turned to ask once. Lina practically toppled me to the floor of the car with a shove. "A movie star," she told Mama at the same time I said, "Nobody."

"Couple of kooks," Mama muttered. "Living in a dream world. Just remember, crazy girls turn into crazy women."

I saw Lina looking at Mama funny after that. She squinted at Mama, as if she were trying to examine her in a blaze of glaring sunlight, or as if she was searching for something she was afraid to find in Mama's face. She must have found it, because she grew sulky—as only Lina could—after that. She didn't want to play with me or talk to me, except to tell me I was childish. She stopped wanting to pilfer Babbo's drawers ("Who cares about his stinky stuff anyway?" she said) and stopped wanting to look for his girlfriend on the street. "Forget it," she said. "You'll never find her." She grew ruder than ever to Babbo. She refused to dust off his bowling trophies, and she gave him good-night kisses that barely grazed the surface of his cheek. One day when he came in, stripped off his socks, and calmly said, "One of youze get me my slippers," Lina's face turned red and she burst out, "Get them yourself!"

Babbo looked up from the sports page, surprised. Then his face turned cloudy and he clutched the newspaper by one end as if he were considering rolling it up and giving Lina a good hard swat right across her bottom. But Lina wasn't about to give him the chance. She raced upstairs and slammed the door to our room. Babbo was so angry he could hardly speak. "One of these days," he sputtered, "somebody around here is going to get what they call a *rude awakening*!" I sat frozen on the living-room floor, not daring to look at him. "Kids these days," he said. "Kids!" In his day, he said, none of this smart-aleck back talk would have been tolerated. Back then children did what their parents told them to do. "My father's word was law!" he repeated. "Law! And there was none of this horsing around. You got a slap right across the puss if you didn't listen!"

My heart pounded as Babbo yelled. As soon as I could, I slunk out of the room, ran upstairs, and fetched his slippers. I continued to get them every night, although the job had lost some of its appeal since I didn't have to compete with Lina for the privilege. Although I wanted to wear the Rey Corona ring, I no longer wanted to marry Babbo. But I kept on looking for his girlfriend, and my fantasies about her flamed up whenever I was bored: during math lesson or novena, or on Saturday mornings as I scrubbed the bathroom tile or pushed a dust cloth along the baseboards.

After a while—whether it was simply to follow Lina's lead or because I had grown tired of playing the game by myself—I stopped looking for Babbo's girl too. But the idea, imagined or otherwise, that Babbo would reach out to grab the woman of his dreams continued to comfort me. Nothing else he did managed to defy the normal order of things or upset the daily routine Lina and I had observed and recorded in our notebook. Up at five o'clock. Into work at six. Lunch: a hot dog and coffee in a Styrofoam cup from a sandwich truck on the shore at eleven-thirty. Home at four. Dinner at five. Asleep by eight. His grand passion was my great relief. For if he didn't have her—the slim lady in the suit and hat—what was the point of his life? Hard work? Sweat? An occasional strike at the bowling alley? He had all the wrong attitudes about the world, Lina and I felt. The be-all and end-all of life was not blisters on our ankles and cracked skin on our hands. It was not food on the table, clothes on our backs, and a roof above our heads. We would never be satisfied with just getting by. We were going to have more. We would do better. We would never say, like Mama and Babbo, *Well, what are you going to do about it?* or *That's the way it goes.* Only losers accepted their father's word as law; only the poor at heart took things the way they were handed to them.

※

Light-years later—after we were living in a world far removed from our childhood—Babbo died, and Lina and I went back to clear out the house. The key seemed to scrape louder than ever in the stubborn back-door lock. Once we were inside, I half-expected to find Babbo lying there on the couch. I could not believe he was lying in a coffin; I could not fathom that his body was sunk forever in the ground.

"This gives me the creeps," Lina said.

"Me too," I said. "Let's get it over with."

We both went straight up to his room, as if by sorting through and discarding his things we could drive his presence from the house. Yet once we were upstairs, Lina curled up with a pillow on what I still thought of as Mama and Babbo's bed, even though Mama had died a few years before. Lina stared at the cream-colored ceiling while I opened the drawers, inspected their contents, and stuffed the clothing into paper bags from the A&P. After a while Lina began to cry.

"Mama and Babbo never had terrible things happen to them the way we do," she said.

Lina did not have a happy marriage. I had no marriage at all. As Lina cried, I looked up into the mirror. The face that stared back at me—the faded skin unsuccessfully hidden beneath too-rosy blush, and the dark circles unbleached beneath the concealer crayoned on under my eyes—seemed to show signs of having undergone much more than Mama and Babbo ever had. Still, I couldn't stand listening to Lina's self-pity.

"How can you say that?" I asked her. "I'm sure they went through just as much as we have, and even worse."

Lina shook her head. "They didn't want things to be perfect, the way we do." She buried her head in the pillow. She cried and sniffed. Then she raised her face. "Ugh," she said. "This pillow smells like his *feet*." She tossed it angrily to the floor.

"Get a grip," I said.

"I don't want to." Lina's lips and jaw tightened, and for a moment she looked exactly like the girl who spent her teenage years picking senseless fights with Mama and Babbo: singing rebellious songs, tossing around the occasional *fuck* and *shit,* rearranging the furniture when Mama and Babbo weren't home, and contradicting them when they insisted that things were fine just the way they were, so why did she have to go and change them? Unlike me, who dealt with her dissatisfaction by curling up in a chair with a good book or lying in bed filling my head with dreams that occupied me for hours, Lina went wild. She turned boy crazy. Her rebellion came to a head when she was seventeen and announced her desire to attend music school in New York. Babbo wanted her to stay in New Haven.

"Why do I have to stay here?" Lina yelled. "Why do I have to *stay* anywhere? You always act as though people *gotta do* what they *gotta do*. It's not true. People have choices. You don't *gotta* be poor. You don't *gotta* drive a soda truck. You don't *gotta* have stinky feet. You don't *gotta* give the cigar ring to the loser!"

That loser, of course, was me, who grew faint to hear her say such things to Babbo, and who escaped from the house by the back door to avoid seeing how he would convince her—with the back of his hand—that a good fight didn't always get a girl whatever it was she wanted to get.

I looked down at the shopping bags full of Babbo's clothes. "Do you want any of this stuff?" I asked Lina.

"What for?"

"I don't know. Phil or the kids. I might take one or two of these shirts just in case I want to paint my apartment or do dirty work." I held up one of Babbo's gray polo shirts, then crumpled it up and stuffed it back into the bag.

"Are those stinky slippers of his still in the closet?" Lina asked.

"Probably," I said.

We were silent for a while. I knew Lina, like me, was thinking of how we used to raid Babbo's things like a pair of female pirates. Now we didn't want anything.

Finally Lina said, "If those pictures are still in that leather box, I'll take the one of Mama. You can keep the rest."

I opened the top drawer of Babbo's chest. I took out the leather box—there were still a few handfuls of change inside—and pulled out the photographs. I flipped through all the pictures until I came to the one of Babbo's supposed girlfriend, inscribed with the word *mine*, at the bottom of the stack.

Deep inside I always must have known that the slim, dashing young woman in the close-fitting suit and coy little hat was my mother. But I hadn't wanted to admit it. It seemed impossible— even obscene!—that the smiling girl blithely standing on the boardwalk could turn into the woman who pressed her grim lips together to mutter, "Out of my way, you!" as she marched off to novena or stormed past us to scour out the toilet. And so my dreams had gotten the best of me, leading me to hope that this young version of my mother—in the form of my father's lover— was still alive somewhere, standing in line at the movie theater, flipping through a copy of *Life* in the doctor's waiting room, or holding a melon up to her nose in the produce aisle.

"You told me she was his girlfriend," I said, half-accusing Lina of making me purposefully stupid. "You said she sold cigars, remember?"

"Exactas and trifectas," said Lina. "And perfectas." She stared at the ceiling. "That was just like Babbo, wasn't it, to bet on a bunch of horses and never take risks on anything else?"

"What makes your life any better?" I asked.

"How about yours?" Lina countered.

I bit my lip. I wasn't holding any winning tickets. Still, if I listened close enough, sometimes I could still hear in the distance the thunder of my horse's hooves pounding triumphantly across the finish line.

"Everyone has a dream," I told my sister.

Lina shrugged. She held out her hand. "Let me have that picture."

For a moment, I both hated and admired her, for wanting and demanding so much. I felt like putting the photo back in the box and burying it at the bottom of one of the bags beneath a pile of musty clothes. Instead, I surrendered it to Lina, but not without reminding her, "Careful. This was his."

ORPHAN TRAIN

I WAS TEN YEARS OLD before I realized my father's name, *in American,* meant Charles Wolf. Lina and I called our father Babbo. Mama called him Pop. Nonna called him Carlucci, and our uncles called him Looch or Lino. Only the utility bills in their stiff, forbidding white envelopes dared to address him by his full and formal name, Carlino Pasquale Lupo. Junk mail, in sharp contrast, came bannered with large bold type that announced, YOU'RE A MILLION DOLLAR WINNER, CARLA!

Babbo didn't take very kindly to having his sex changed by mail. "What do I look like, some kind of fruitcake or something?" he said, before he threw the Carla envelopes in the trash. When his back was turned, Mama rescued the envelopes from the wastebasket and eagerly ripped them open. She had three passions in life: funerals, church bazaars, and mail-order sweepstakes. She entered every contest that came her way, confident that it was just a matter of time before she won a trip to Waikiki, a snazzy red sports car, or a dream vacation home that looked like an Alpine ski lodge.

"You can't win if you don't play," she said, as she sat at the kitchen table, cutting out the Publishers Clearing House stickers with her best Singer sewing scissors, as if neatness would increase her chances of claiming the jackpot. With a prolonged swipe of her tongue, she licked the stamps and pressed them into place with her thumb, leaning forward with all her weight. "Cheap glue," she muttered as she crisscrossed the stickers with Scotch tape.

Lina and I scorned the whole business.

"You're not going to win," I said.

"Perchè?" Mama asked.

"Because you're not Carla," I said.

"So I'll go down to Fontina's and become Carla," she said, snapping her fingers, "just like that."

Fontina, a wizened man with rawhide skin, was the shoemaker. In the back of his shop he purportedly had a special machine that could manufacture false IDs.

"You won't win," Lina said, "because you're not ordering any magazines."

Mama pointed to the entry form. "It says right here, in plain English, you don't have to order."

"You don't get something for nothing," Lina insisted.

Mama shrugged. *"Tutti hanno i sogni."*

Everybody has their dreams. So the men in our family went to the track. The women entered raffles and went to bingo. Every Thursday night Mama's eyes shone as she sealed her red wooden chips in a fresh plastic bag. "I can just feel it," she said. "Tonight's my night." Two hours later she came home clutching yet another set of laminated holy cards or another plastic figurine of an apostle, a virgin martyr, or some obscure saint. The cash bonus at bingo—as well as the Easter ham and the Thanksgiving turkey—so far had eluded her. But she refused to give up. Contests were the American way.

When I asked her once what she missed most about Italy, she said, "Nothing! The streets smelled like mule poop. And imagine, there were no prizes."

When I put the same question to Babbo, he thought about it for a moment before he said, "Sunlight."

We lived in New Haven, where the murky green harbor smelled like raw mussels, and the sky, above the giant oil tanks that squatted onshore, seemed perpetually gray. Babbo worked as a delivery man for Dixon Park Soda, and it was at the company's distribution center that I first realized something was amiss about his name. Usually Babbo drove home from work in one of the company trucks and parked it in our driveway overnight, where it served as an advertisement to the whole neighborhood that Dixon Park soda was *Clean, Refreshing, and Oh So Bubbly Good!* But that night his truck had to be serviced, so Mama, Lina, and I went to pick him up.

We parked in the corner of the distribution center, far away from the huge trucks that were pulling in and out of the lot. Steep metal stairs led up to the loading dock. Exhaust fans from the warehouse made the platform vibrate.

Through the main door of Dixon Park came a man as short and squat as a fire hydrant. He pushed a handcart. He squinted at us, then shouted over his shoulder, "Cholly! Hey, Cholly! Family's here!"

"We're not here for any Charlie," Mama said, just before Babbo appeared from behind a flat of wooden crates, wiping his hands on a dirty rag. "This is who we're looking for—Carlino."

"That's Cholly in American, *capisce?*" The man laughed and pushed the handcart out to an open truck.

Mama pressed her lips together and her back stiffened. "Who's that character?" she asked Babbo.

"His name's Shorty."

"They ought to call him Lazy, talking so much on the job." She paused. "They call you Charlie here?"

Babbo shrugged. He tossed the rag down on one of the crates and motioned to Mama that it was time to go. Lina and I followed a few steps behind. With her mouth up to my ear, Lina whispered, "Go ahead. I dare you. Do it."

I was the family poet. Whenever we encountered a new word or something unusual worth poking fun at, Lina egged me on to make up a rhyme. *Cholly, holly, collie, polly* went through my head before I halted on the platform, stiffened my arms by my side, splayed my fingers, and launched into a tap dance and song:

> *Oh you're my Cholly-Pop*
> *My lollipop*
> *Don't drop the mop*
> *Or get stopped by a cop.*

We burst out laughing at the awkward rhythm and rhyme. Mama turned and shook a finger at us. Then she marched back to where we stood and pinched my ear. "Orphan train," she said.

Mama rolled the orphan train onto the tracks whenever we were acting naughty, sometimes as a two-word warning and other times complete with all the bag and baggage that accompanied her other *you better be grateful* speeches. Lina and I used to roll our eyes—and afterward make fake fart noises—whenever Mama started in like this: "Those were hard days—hard times! Right before we came over came the flu. It swept across the country and killed thousands of people. Children lost their parents, their grandparents. Imagine, they rounded those kids up and sent them on trains to all sorts of crazy places—Indiana, Nebraska, Wyoming. The kids, they had to work as slaves on farms—for Germans, no less. They had to speak English. They had to change their last names. They had to dye their hair blond."

The moral of this story: We had better cut out the funny stuff, or we would drive Mama and Babbo right into their graves and win ourselves a one-way ticket on the orphan train.

Little did Mama realize how the lowly chug of that train sounded like great and glorious music to our ears. Our lives were so dull and boring. We never got to see anything new; we never got to travel anywhere. The mere thought of embarking on such an adventure thrilled us to no end. "Mama and Babbo wouldn't have to die," Lina reasoned. "They could just . . . well, *disappear* for a year or two. Then they could put us on the orphan train by mistake and we could go away for a while and come back with new identities."

"I want to be honey blond," I said.

"I want to be so pale," Lina said, "that people will ask me if I'm sick."

I had inherited Mama's light complexion, but Lina had Babbo's olive skin. We both had hair so jet it shone like the hood of a freshly waxed Black Maria. Lina at least had cheekbones to make up for her big nose, but I had a face as round as a melon and a peasant's heavy chin. Neither of us wanted to look like what we looked like or be what we felt fate had determined us to be: nice girls who married our father's third, fourth, or fifth cousin's nephew, godson, or cousin-in-law. Marriage outside of the family circle seemed the only way out. Lina said she was going to marry a Swede so at least her kids came out the right color. I vowed to snag a Jones or a Smith.

All the way home from the warehouse, Lina leaned her chin on the open window of the car, staring at the storefronts we passed. She kept quiet. I could tell she was plotting something. At dinner that night, when Babbo was halfway through his bowl of *penne,* she said, "Why don't you call yourself Charles all the time? Or Chuck?"

Babbo grunted and kept on eating.

"We don't need any crazy names around here," Mama said.

"Charles isn't crazy," Lina said. "It's dignified."

"Chuck sounds good too," I said. "Friendly."

Mama glanced at Babbo. His face was turning red. "*State zitte* and eat," she warned us.

But Lina wouldn't let it go. "We should all change our names."

"What for?" Mama said.

"So we sound normal."

"You want to sound normal?" Mama said. "Then stop talking nonnormal."

Lina kept on going. "There's a saying that says, *When in Rome, do as the Romans do.*"

Babbo took one hand and gestured around the cramped, cluttered kitchen. "Does this look like Rome to you?" he said.

Lina shook her head. "That's my point. This isn't Italy."

Babbo pointed his fork at Lina. It was crusted with tomato sauce, and the piece of *penne* speared on the end wiggled precariously each time he jabbed it forward to punctuate his speech. "Let me tell you something," he said. "When I first came to this country, I stood in line with my father—for hours—waiting to sign in. There were two officers sitting at the table. The one on the left tried to spell people's names right. The other one, he said, 'Too many vowels!' You said LaRonda, he turned it into Leroy. Giacome he made into Jackson."

"Colored people's names," Mama said. "Imagine."

"So what if some people are colored?" Lina asked. "At least their names sound American."

"You think coloreds like their names?" Babbo asked. "Look at 'em, on TV, changing their names all the time so they sound like a bunch of Arab sheiks. Kareem Abdul-Jabbar. Muhammad Ali. What's the matter with Lew Alcindor, Cassius Clay?" Babbo took the container of parmesan and furiously shook a cloud of cheese over his pasta. "You want to know who changes their name? Crooks, that's who. The rest of us ought to be thankful we've got an honest name."

Upstairs, after dinner, Lina sat on the edge of her bed, twirling her hair around one finger. "Why should I be grateful for having a name that sounds like some weird kind of macaroni?" she said. "I can't stand being Pasqualina Lupo. I don't want a grandfather named Guido. I don't want an Uncle Luigi!"

"How about me," I said glumly. My name was Angelina, but everyone called me Angel. Lina couldn't even begin to imagine how difficult it was to live up to that.

Lina stuck out her tongue. "Italian names suck."

"Some of them sound dignified," I said.

"Like which?"

"Grimaldi. Rinaldi. Del Vecchio."

"Those are all right."

"And some of them actually sound kind of normal. The kind people can pronounce, like Romano."

"Everybody famous changes their name," Lina said.

"That's not true," I said. "There's an actress who has almost the same last name as we do."

"Ida Lupino is ugly," Lina said. "And she plays character roles. I don't want to be a character. I want to be a star." She flung herself down on the bed and kicked the bedspread. "If Babbo doesn't change his name, then I'm not calling him Babbo anymore."

"So what're you going to call him?"

Lina stared at the ceiling. *"You,"* she said.

Lina was worried. It was one thing to be Pasqualina in the Holy Redeemer Elementary School. But next month she was going to start junior high in a public school across town. She was convinced she wouldn't survive roll call the first day. The homeroom teacher would stand and read her full name off the list just as Saint Peter called out the names of those who were to step to the left or the right on Judgment Day. Lina would be damned.

Just as she expected, Lina was miserable in junior high school. The Irish girls shortened Pasqualina to *Squats* or *Mama Lina;* one day a boy pushed her up against a locker and said, "I bet your mother's a nigger." Lina often came home in tears. The only class she liked was Italian. The teacher, on the first day of school, went around the room and translated all the non-Italian names into

Italian. Mark became Marco, Joseph became Giuseppe, Vicky became Vittoria. Then, just for fun, the teacher translated all the Italian names into English. Pasqualina Lupo became Patty Wolf.

"Wolf," Lina said. "Isn't that a great name? Babbo—I mean *you*—I mean *him*—could be Charles Wolf. Mama could be Phyllis Wolf instead of Filomena Lupo. You'd be Ann Wolf."

"Sounds good to me."

"We could start a club," Lina said. "The Wolf Pack. No, I've got it. We're the Wolverines. We have to have a motto."

"Have no shame of your name," I suggested.

"Good. Right. We'll have meetings every night. We'll call them to order with a wolf's howl." Lina scratched her head. "What does a wolf sound like, anyway?"

The howl sound we came up with probably resembled more of a coyote's yelp, but we didn't care. "What's going on up there?" Mama yelled upstairs. "Sounds like a bunch of sick dogs or something." We closed the door. Mama and Babbo did not deserve to be privy to our secrets.

As Wolverines, our goal was to educate the common, unenlightened folk—our family, friends, and neighbors—that we lived in the United States now. At home, if Mama referred to the *carciofi* or the *collino*, Lina said, "I believe you mean the artichokes?" or "You must be referring to the colander" in a clear, semi-British voice that made her sound like Julie Andrews in *The Sound of Music*. If Nonna said *ciao*, I reminded her it wasn't time to eat. If we were sent to the market, we brought home A&P brand macaroni instead of di Cecco, and Sunbeam bread instead of the crusty loaves, wrapped in wax paper, from Manfredo's Bakery.

"I asked for Italian," Mama said.

"This is America," Lina said. "Americans eat white bread."

Mama squeezed the loaf of Sunbeam as if she wanted to wring the neck of the smiling blond girl in curls on the plastic bag. "And where's my *friselle*?" Mama demanded.

"I shouldn't *deign* to spend thirty-five cents on dog biscuits," Lina said.

Mama stuck out her lip and looked about as threatening as Muhammad Ali. Lina ducked out of the kitchen just as Mama reached for the wooden spoon. Mama used a Sicilian word for spanking, which I don't know how to spell to this very day. The sound of *polly-odda* would have been pleasing to my ear if the actual spanking hadn't been so stinging on the back of my thighs. The aftereffects of a good *polly-odda* could last for days.

❖

Although our goal as Wolverines was to promote the American way, our main pastime was listening to Lina's Italian language records, which she brought back from junior high school, neatly packaged in a burgundy box. Listening to the records proved that we needed to *learn* Italian, just like the Irish girls who called Lina names. We did not speak Italian naturally, like our parents; we were Americans and it was a foreign language.

The voices on these 45s sounded crisp and continental.

Buon giorno, Giovanna. Come stai?

Non c'è male, grazie.

Dov'è la stazione?

È cerca del museo.

Come si chiama il ragazzo?

Si chiama Paolo.

Ascolta e ripeta. Listen and repeat. One Saturday while we were doing just that, Babbo made an extremely rare appearance in our bedroom to paint the radiator, which was peeling gray flakes all over the carpet. Lina rolled her eyes at the effrontery of this man, this *you*, who could interrupt such an important session. She kept the 45 spinning on the record player for just a few more seconds before she yanked up the needle.

Beppino è di Texas.

È vero che tutti gli americani siano cowboys?

Babbo cocked his ear as he put down the paint can, then grumbled, "What kind of Italian is that?"

Lina looked knowingly at me and repeated the words of her teacher, Signora Testa. "Real Italian," she said. "Tuscan Italian. Italian pure as extra virgin olive oil."

Babbo grunted. "I don't understand a word of it."

Lina lovingly placed the 45 back into its jacket and slipped it inside the box. Downstairs, she told me the kind of Italian Babbo spoke sounded like somebody talking with their head stuck down a flushing toilet. Too many false *sh* sounds. Too many sucked-up syllables. Too many gargly, incomprehensible exclamations at the end that the listener had to interpret any way he or she saw fit.

Babbo was impossible, Lina said. An absolute *paesano*. If we couldn't have an American father, she reasoned, we could at least get ourselves an impostor. That afternoon, as Babbo nursed a headache from the fumes of the metallic radiator paint, Lina and I swiped his wallet and marched down to Fontina's. Lina knew the owner's son. Through some odd language that went beyond my ken of American, Italian, and Wolverine, she wheedled him into making a false driver's license, based upon Babbo's real one, for a Charles Patrick Wolf. When Fontina Junior came out of the back of the store and handed the laminated card to us, we slipped the real license into the usual slot in Babbo's wallet and put the false one behind, more as a sort of talisman than anything else, positive that Babbo never would find it.

Then Lina went into the back of the store, alone with the boy, while I waited.

※

Aqueduct, Belmont, Yonkers. These names sounded as magic to us as *bar* and *whorehouse,* forbidden places we would never be allowed to visit. So we sulked when Babbo went to the track, although we liked to eat the hot dogs that Mama invariably cooked for us. We appreciated that Babbo did not come home until far past our bedtime, so we didn't have to acknowledge him when we said good night. Lina and I stayed up late in our room, whispering, until we heard Mama turn in. Then we crept back downstairs and helped ourselves to the fudge ripple ice cream that Mama kept reserved for guests.

The next day we knew how Babbo fared at the track—usually by how fast and furious Mama's scissors flew through the Sunday paper, clipping the cents-off coupons for groceries, or (much pleasanter) by the arrival of a big truck in our driveway, which delivered something fancy to our run-down house: a used washing machine for Mama, or for Babbo, a brand-new La-Z-Boy recliner.

One night the phone rang just as we were finishing our ice cream, and Lina grabbed the receiver and said hello. The man on the other end of the line asked for Mrs. Carlino Lupo. "This is the Wolf residence," Lina said, and hung up, to my great amusement. The man called back again, and Lina repeated the same line, which broke me up even further. I don't know why, but I found the whole thing a real bladder-buster, and after three or four calls Lina and I had to push and fight our way to the bathroom so we didn't pee our pants in laughter.

The next morning the phone rang during breakfast, and when Mama finally got off she came into the kitchen and gave us a look that froze us harder than a fudge ripple ice cream headache. "Did you answer the phone last night?" she said to Lina, and when Lina hotly denied it, Mama came over and slapped her face. "Did you put a false driver's license in your father's wallet?"

"No," Lina cried, which earned her another *crack across the puss*. I thought it prudent not to mention Fontina Junior.

It turned out Babbo had been pulled over by a cop for speeding on his way back from the track. When he surrendered his license to the policeman, the fake license from Fontina's fell out. Unable to explain why he was carrying a fake ID, Babbo had been taken in for questioning. He had used his one allotted call to phone a cousin who was friends with a lawyer, and when the lawyer called our house, Lina gave him the line about the Wolf residence. The lawyer, confused about who Babbo really was, decided to wait until morning to clear up the situation. Babbo had to spend the night in the police station, and now Mama had to pay a lawyer *good hard-earned money* to clear Babbo's reputation. We had ruined his name, sullied it, and we would never hear the end of it.

"Wolf!" Mama kept hollering at us. "That's a Jewish name. Don't you tell a soul you made your own father into a *mata-Christ*. Don't you never tell nobody nothing about this."

Omertà, I later would learn this was called: keeping quiet to protect the family. And so, years later—just to be perverse—I would tell this story in intimate, whispered tones to my lovers, sometimes just to make them laugh, other times to make myself sound more interesting. But Lina kept the story close to her chest, and when I teased her husband once about going up to play the horses in the Green Mountains, I sensed Lina had never even mentioned the racetrack incident to Phil, although she had complained bitterly enough to him about everything else from her childhood. Did Lina keep the story under wraps because she would have to admit she had gone behind the curtain with Fontina Junior? Or because she truly was ashamed that she had changed Babbo from Lupo into a Wolf? Or was it because Phil and Lina had not been getting along with each other and Lina knew that someday she would have to leave him and reassume her maiden name?

"Didn't you tell him?" I asked.

"Tell me what?" Phil asked.

"Aren't you going to tell him?" I asked, and while Phil sat there, expectant—the air quivering with the tension of their impending divorce—Lina spoke the first word in Italian I had heard her say in years. *"Mai,"* she said, breaking one of Mama's cardinal rules.

"Don't ever say *never*!" Mama scolded us about a year after the false ID incident, when she came home with a twenty-pound ham, rippled with white fat, which was all hers for standing up and hollering *G-49* at the Easter bingo. The next week her name, spelled with two typos, appeared in boldface type in the parish newsletter, right beneath the marriage banns. She stabbed the newsletter with her finger to express her glee. Nothing made her happier.

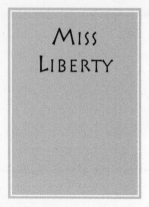

MISS LIBERTY

IT WAS DRIZZLING. Lina and I stood next to the bright red Salvation Army Dumpster, stomping our feet from the cold and touching our tongues against the minuscule drops of water that clung to our black wool mittens. The Church of the Holy Redeemer needed a paint job, so along with half the parish, we were shivering in the A&P parking lot, waiting for the bus that would take us on a fund-raising trip to New York City.

Uncle Luigino—Zio Gigi for short—had organized the trip. Gigi was our father's older brother, but unlike Babbo, he was a handsome man, with a thin, mischievous face and a prominent nose that crinkled upward when he smiled, which was often. People said he had a light in his eye. Mama said he shined it on nothing but girls. He was in his forties. Never married. After the war he had gone to college for two years on the GI bill. Now he worked in a bank processing loans, an occupation both Mama and Babbo found shifty. *A real politico,* Mama called him. He got too involved in the Knights of Columbus. "Every time you look at him," she said, "he's got a clipboard in his hand."

Anything that had to do with the written word made Mama suspicious, but it thrilled me. Zio Gigi seemed so sophisticated compared to my other relatives. They had three topics of conversation: death, money, and bowel irregularities. Gigi, on the other hand, was always putting his arm around me and Lina, quoting the great thinkers or telling us something about history. "Eaah," Babbo said, dismissing Gigi's brand of knowledge. "So he goes to the barber shop once a week and reads all the magazines."

Because Gigi was behind the trip to New York, Mama and Babbo were reluctant to go. Babbo stood on the edge of the crowd in the parking lot, his eyes shaded by his wide-brimmed brown hat and his hands sunk in the pockets of his tan raincoat. He jingled his keys. Next to him stood Mama, in her flat black boots and black coat. On the lapel she had pinned an uncharacteristic touch of whimsy—a rhinestone-studded Scottie dog with a fake emerald eye that she had won last year at bingo. In her arms she clutched a big brown paper bag that announced in red, *I Got It Cut-Rate at Railroad Salvage!* Inside were seeded rolls, a wheel of Auricchio provolone cheese, a foot-long stick of pepperoni, a serrated knife, a box of Ritz crackers, Band-Aids, aspirin, a flashlight, spare batteries, moistened washcloths wrapped in wax paper, a box of Kleenex, a bottle of fish-white suppositories, a roll of toilet paper, and complete changes of clothing for Lina and me.

Gigi pointed to the bag. "Planning to recross the ocean?" he asked.

"Laugh now," Mama said. "Eat on Staten Island later."

Gigi wrinkled his forehead. "We're going to the Statue of Liberty."

"On Staten Island," Mama insisted.

Gigi knocked his hand against his head. "What boat did you come on?"

"Same kind as you," Mama said.

"Don't you remember?" Gigi asked. "There was Staten Island, where the Americans lived. You got off at Ellis Island. And then, on the other island, was the statue."

"Staten Island, statue island," Mama said. "It's all the same to me."

Gigi turned to Babbo. "You remember, don't you?"

Babbo grunted. "I remember what I want to remember," he said.

Gigi took off his gloves and pinched Lina's cheeks with his cold fingers. He patted my head. "When we came over, your father was just a *bimbo,* smaller than you two," he told us. "He was scared to get on the boat."

"That was a long time ago," Babbo said. "When are these buses getting here?"

"Patience," Gigi counseled. He put his arms around our shoulders and squeezed us tight against his pant legs. "Your father said the same thing thirty-five years ago. He stood on the deck yelling, *Dov'è l'America?* As if America was going to burst through the ocean right before his eyes, like some lost continent resurrected from the bottom of the earth."

"Eaah," Babbo said. "What do you remember?"

"Plenty," Gigi said. "The name of the ship was *The Florida.*"

"I thought it was *The America,*" Babbo said.

"No, *The Florida.* I remember, because it caused a big commotion before we boarded. Some people refused to get on. The captain had to come out and tell them it was going to New York and not Miami." Gigi gestured around the crowded parking lot. "You think this is a lot of people?" he asked us. "Believe me, there were hundreds, thousands more that day. Your grandmother found a piece of rope on the dock and tied me to her, like I was a dog. I held your father's hand. What a scene when he wandered away."

"What kind of stories are you telling now?" Babbo asked.

"One minute he was right by my side, clasping my hand," Gigi continued. "The next minute we were on the deck of the steamer and he was gone. Mama started wailing that he had fallen overboard. Papa shook his fists. We had been waiting a week, you see, for the boat to come in. What if we missed it?"

"Don't listen to him," Babbo told us. "It's nonsense."

"You never heard such screaming and crying and carrying on," Gigi said. "I was so ashamed of the way my mother and father were acting that I untied the rope from my belt and stood a little bit off to the side. I didn't want people to think I belonged to such a *matta* family. That got Papa even angrier. He yanked me by the hand and we walked up and down the deck, searching the crowds. Finally, we found your father high above everyone's head. He sat on the shoulders of a sailor, wearing the sailor's bright white hat. He had *vomito*, throw-up, all over his shirt— seasick before we even put out to sea. He was howling. Papa took him down from the man's shoulder and gave him a huge hug before—*pow!*—he cracked him a good one right across the bottom."

Lina and I giggled at the thought of Babbo getting a spanking instead of doling one out.

Babbo jingled his keys and looked away.

"You see," Gigi said. "I remember plenty."

Mama shifted the Railroad Salvage bag in her hands. "I remember a few things myself," she said. "I was five years old. We waited for hours in that big hall. Did you go into the big hall too? The one with the wooden railing that ran all around the top and the huge flag hanging from the ceiling?"

Babbo shrugged.

"The noise in that hall was louder than any noise I ever heard," Gigi said.

"And the smell of the people's sweat—enough to knock you over," Mama said.

"I saw some Gypsies," Gigi said. "They had bells on their skirts and packs on their backs."

"I saw a colored woman for the first time," Mama said. "She had rotten teeth. Outside, I saw horses much finer than donkeys."

"I saw balloons," Gigi said. "And smelled hot dogs. Everything seemed so wonderful!"

Babbo grunted. "That's because it all cost money," he said.

Mama shook her head. "I had my first taste of lemonade for free. Some Red Cross ladies handed my mother a cup. It was steaming hot that day and my mother was thirsty, but she gave the cup to me. All the sugar had floated to the bottom and it tasted sour. But I kept on drinking, and by the time I got to the bottom it tasted sweet as candy." Mama clutched her bag with a start. "That reminds me. I forgot to bring the jug of Kool-Aid."

"Too late," Babbo said, pointing. Two buses, so splattered with mud I could hardly make out the name BLUEBIRD on the side, pulled into the driveway. Mama surged forward, hustling past the other people who were gathering up their things. She clasped her shopping bag and solidly stood her ground where she believed the first bus would stop. When it overshot her by six feet, she pushed forward and positioned herself in front of the doors. Then she rapped on the doors with her knuckles until the driver, a gray-haired man with bulldog jowls, yanked them open.

"Where's da fire, lady?" he asked.

Mama didn't condescend to answer. She muscled her way up the steps and placed her bag on the two seats behind him, then planted herself in the middle of the other two seats directly across the aisle. As the other parishioners boarded, she pointed out, "These seats are saved." She found herself in an uncomfortable position when Father Angelosi got on. Father was seventy-nine and had some kind of white fungus growing like mushrooms in his ears that had left him almost totally deaf. The fungus made him a popular priest. People from other parishes flocked to our church for Confession, because you could tell Father you had murdered your mother and for penance he would give you only three Hail Marys. Mama had to holler, "SAVED, Father, RESERVED, Father," four or five times before he caught her drift and moved toward the back of the bus.

"What do you mean, yelling at the priest?" Gigi asked when he got on.

"If you don't yell, he don't *capisce*," Mama said.

"Let him sit up front, why don't you?"

"Let him sit with the nuns," Mama said. "Better yet, he can sit with you. Two peas in a pod, both bachelors."

Mortified by the way Mama was acting, Lina and I tried to walk right by her and snag a seat at the back of the bus. But she caught us by the collar and pushed us down in the first row. Then she held up the line for two or three minutes while she stood in the aisle, positioning her shopping bag on the floor before she finally sat down next to Babbo directly behind the driver.

A sign posted on the bus reported that our driver, Vinnie Viscusi, was safe, reliable, and courteous. Mama suspected he was none of the above. As Gigi walked up and down the aisle, checking people's names off on his clipboard, Vinnie held a dirty green thermos to his lips and tilted it back. "I've heard about these crazy New York drivers," Mama said. "That better be coffee." A loud, wet belch was Vinnie's reply. Mama leaned over and sniffed until she was satisfied that it was only Chock Full O' Nuts that he was swilling. When Gigi finally gave the go-ahead, Vinnie put the bus in gear and took off with a jerk. Mama clutched her seat. "Watch out," she called. "We want to get there alive." Vinnie stopped the bus. He turned around, glared at Mama, then reached up and pulled down a green shade that separated him from the passengers. Then he burped and farted all the way to New York, causing Mama to recommend less *pasta e fagioli* and a lot more prunes. "I got a brother-in-law who's a plumber," she said to Mrs. Fenilli, who sat kitty-corner from her across the aisle. "Good as a doctor. And cheaper. He can tell you all the ins and outs of the bowel system."

The minute we hit the highway, Babbo fell asleep. After much fretting about the filthiness of the windows—"three dollars a ticket and you can't even see where you're going"—Mama pulled out one of her moistened washcloths and scrubbed at the panes. Then she handed the washcloth to Mrs. Fenilli, who did the same.

Mrs. Fenilli passed the cloth to Mrs. Rinaldi. Mrs. Rinaldi passed it to Sister Thomas and Sister Sebastian, who had to be told in Italian what to do with it. The sisters passed it to Father, who looked at it with a puzzled expression before he used it to wipe his face. His seatmate, Gigi, grabbed the washcloth away from him, put it on the end of his finger, and twirled it around. With great gusto, he sang:

> *Italian sailors*
> *Have a saying*
> *That goes without saying:*
> *The hell with London!*
> *The hell with France!*
> *There is nothing*
> *Like American pants!*

Gigi winked and nudged Father Angelosi, who began to sway to the music. Sister Thomas and Sister Sebastian clapped their hands; Babbo let out a big snore. Mama looked over at me. "What are you doing, crossing your legs? You gotta go?"

I shook my head.

Mama leaned down and seized the bottle of suppositories from the shopping bag, threatening me with the bottle.

"I'll go," I said.

Satisfied, Mama traded the suppositories for the roll of toilet paper. She took my hand and pulled me to the back of the bus, squeezing past some people who still were rearranging their things in the aisles. "Look out," she said. "Coming on through. This one here's got to go *numero uno*, maybe even *due. Bimbi*—can't hold it for two seconds."

At the back of the bus she huffed as she struggled to open the door of the bathroom. Once she pried it open, she pushed me in, then changed her mind and pushed me out, bunching up a wad of the toilet paper and swabbing down the seat before she stepped aside and pushed me back in again. "Go ahead, go," she said.

"Close the door," I said.

"What do I look like, some kind of *pazzone*?" she asked. "It took me five minutes to open it."

I pointed beyond the door to the other passengers. Mama glanced over her shoulder. Then she unbuttoned her coat and spread it wide, like a cape, as she stood in the doorway. "Just do your business and they'll mind theirs," she said.

It was senseless to argue. I pulled down my pants and squeezed out a meager tinkle. "That's all you got?" Mama asked. I nodded, grabbed the toilet paper, ripped off a shred, and wiped myself. Then I hastily pulled up my pants and tried to squeeze past Mama. She grabbed me by the collar and yanked me back. "*Lava le mani!*" she said. "Wash your hands."

When we got back to our seat, Lina stared out the window, refusing to acknowledge either me or Mama. I held my stomach because it felt queasy. Babbo continued to snore, and Mama, for lack of anyone else to talk to, turned around and started up a one-sided conversation with Mrs. Fenilli. "These modern kids," she said. "They gotta have their privacy. In the old days, there was no such thing. My parents, they had a *baccausa*, a wooden outhouse right by the tomatoes. Good fertilizer, my father said. We kids used to line up every morning. Privacy? Ha! Everybody knew everybody else's business, whether it was good or bad. The whole neighborhood knew after my grandfather went. He had the turds of an elephant. Enough to knock you over."

Lina leaned over my lap. "Stop it," she hissed at Mama.

Mama nodded at Mrs. Fenilli. "Listen to that one there. Too good for her own parents. She's embarrassed by what I got in my shopping bag. This morning she gets into a fight with me about the toilet paper. She wants to know why I gotta bring it. You know what I told her? I told her thank God she has the paper. In the old days, it was the Sears catalog, remember? Or the newspaper, if you were lucky. During the Depression, nothing but your bare hands." She reached across the aisle and poked my arm. "You," she said. "What's the matter with you?"

I opened my mouth to reply. My head felt fuzzy and my body felt like it was still lurching down the aisle of the bus. My stomach constricted and I burped a foul liquid. Lina just had time to shove me aside before I lost my cornflakes and milk all over my navy blue stretch pants.

Babbo woke up, looked over at me, and closed his eyes again. Vinnie Viscusi glanced back, swore a loud *dammit,* and told Mama to mop it up. "I'll mind the kids, you mind the road," Mama said. "Keep your eyes on it."

Mama shook her finger at Lina, Babbo, and me. "You see," she said. "You laughed at all the things I brought." She took up the Railroad Salvage bag, then grabbed my hand and once again pulled me to the back of the bus. She stopped only to display me to an alarmed Gigi. "You see why I don't like to travel," she said to Gigi. "The excitement is too much. And it's expensive. She loses her breakfast, I gotta feed her twice as much for lunch."

I recovered my equilibrium just outside of New Rochelle. Babbo continued to sleep. Mrs. Fenilli expressed the desire to do the same, and Mama, lacking a willing ear to listen, took her black rosary beads out of her coat pocket. "May as well get some prayers in," she said, and began mumbling to herself. When we began to inch across the bridge to Manhattan, Mama's eyes grew wide. She spoke her Hail Marys aloud as we passed under the steel spans. "Saints in heaven," she murmured, after we were safely on land again. "That's one big Atlantic Ocean."

Babbo woke up as the bus came out on FDR Drive. Mama immediately clutched her purse and pressed her shopping bag between her feet and knees, as if a herd of infamous New York pickpockets would storm the bus and steal everything we had. Lina kept her nose pressed to the windowpane, searching in vain

for anything that would represent the glamour of city life—a display of well-heeled mannequins in a department-store window, a
real-life woman in furs and a passel of chihuahuas on taut red
leather leashes, buildings that went up so high they ended in the
clouds. But all we saw were trucks and cars and buses, gas tanks
and water dirtier than the New Haven harbor. Babbo kept looking for Madison Square Garden. Several people claimed they saw
Times Square. Gigi swore he identified the building that King
Kong had climbed in the movie. It seemed to take longer to go fifteen or twenty blocks in New York than it took to get all the way
to New York from Connecticut. But finally the streets became
more narrow and less crowded. The bus pulled into a place called
Battery Park, twisted along a road, and finally came out along the
water. Lina said she smelled the beach. I sucked on my tongue
and imagined myself a stowaway on one of the big boats slowly
moving in the harbor.

The minute he stopped the bus, Vinnie Viscusi shook his head
and reached for his thermos. Gigi stood up and tried to call people to order. "Exit row by row," he called. But the parishioners
already were charging for the door. Lina and I squeezed in before
the nuns, leaving Mama and Babbo behind to quarrel about
Mama's shopping bag. Babbo insisted she leave it on the bus.

"What, are you kidding?" Mama said. "I've heard about these
New York thieves."

"What do you need that stuff for?" Babbo asked.

"You never know," Mama said. "You never know what you'll
meet in this world. Only one thing's for certain: you better be pre-
pared for it."

Lina and I dashed to the guardrail that circled the park. In the
middle of the choppy water stood the Statue of Liberty, holding
the torch aloft. My heart sunk. Although I had seen countless pictures of her before, somehow I thought that in person she would
look more soft and feminine, like Betty Crocker or the Clairol
girl. But with her perfect posture and blind gaze, she reminded me

of the ladies on the Playtex bra boxes, whose blank faces and massive, stiff breasts looked positively intimidating.

Lina turned away. "She looks like the color you puked up on the bus," she said. "Why'd they paint her green?"

Mama, who had come up behind us, swatted Lina on the back of her head. "Shame on you," she said. "It's a sin to say anything bad about that lady."

"That's right," Babbo said. "It's like saying something against the flag."

"Or against Mary," Mama said. She crossed herself. "Yes," she sighed. "I remember seeing her for the first time. The boat came just as it was turning dark. She was all lit up, like a madonna outside a church."

"You said the sun was shining," Lina reminded her. "You said it was hot and you wanted a drink and then you got some lemonade."

"What's that?" Mama said sharply. "Were you there? Don't make up stories."

Gigi joined us. He pointed out to the statue. "Isn't she gorgeous?"

"Anything in a skirt is gorgeous to you," said Babbo.

Gigi took out his pen and clipboard and began to round up the parishioners. "Stick together," he said. "Everyone on the next ferry."

Babbo looked panic-stricken. "You gotta take a boat over?"

"What do you think you do, swim?" Mama asked.

"I thought they would have built a bridge by now," Babbo said. He gazed across the water, where the ferry just was pulling away from the island. It bobbed in the water. Babbo's face turned green. "No, no, you go," he said. "I'll watch."

"What's to watch?" Mama said. "She's not going to put down her torch or blink her eye. Gigi. Talk to your brother. He paid good money for his ticket. Three dollars to stand on shore and freeze himself to death."

Mama scolded him; Gigi cajoled him. But Babbo stood his ground. He would not get on the boat. His cowardice made him generous toward Lina and me. He patted our heads, as if we were going away on a long journey, then reached into his pocket and pulled out two quarters for each of us. "Get yourselves a souvenir," he said.

Lina's eyes lit up with greed. I snatched the coins and jingled them together in my palm while we waited for the boat, until Mama warned me, "Hold on tight. Finders, keepers. Losers, weepers."

The *Lady Liberty* was a double-decker ferry, with narrow white railings stretching all around the edge. Lina and I wanted to stand on the top deck, but Mama insisted that we stay on the bottom, right beside the gate so we would be the first ones off. She plopped her shopping bag down and we had to obey her. A man dressed in a sailor shirt and hat untied the thick rope that anchored the boat to the dock. Then the boat began to bob and blow its foghorn as it eased out into the water. In the gray haze we saw the shadows of other ships—steamers, fishing trawlers, and low barges—moving silently in the distance. We saw Babbo sit down on a park bench, then the people on shore faded away.

Mama held on to the backs of our collars.

"Let me go," Lina said.

"You might fall overboard," Mama said.

"I know how to swim," Lina said, wiggling out of her grip and moving a good six feet away. I joined her. "She's so embarrassing," Lina said, her breath hot in my ear. "Like some old off-the-boat lady."

"Don't talk to her," I said. "Just pretend she's not our mother."

We glanced over at Mama. She stood as if her feet were glued to the deck. Her face was set so fierce and hard against us, she looked like the figureheads Norsemen used to put on their boats to drive the sharks away. She shook one finger at us. "No cahoots," she said. "I'm warning you." Lina and I linked hands to show our solidarity. With my free hand, I clutched the quarters that were in my pocket and rubbed them together, as if they were two pieces of dried wood that at any moment could kindle and explode into flame.

Mama was the first one off the ferry. Lina and I lingered on deck, smirking at her as she stood on the shore, gesturing with one hand for us to disembark. She squeezed her shopping bag so tightly with the other arm that the bag broke underneath. The flashlight, the batteries, the Kleenex box—all rolled out onto the brown grass that was wet with dew. Mama simply leaned over, brushed off the items, and recruited other parishioners to carry them. "Here, hold this." She shoved the toilet paper at Sister Thomas. "Father, have a pepperoni. Mrs. Fenilli, you got room in your purse for this provolone?" Mama glanced at the bottle of suppositories before she slipped them into her own coat. "Gigi," she called out. "How big are your pockets?"

Gigi ended up carrying the flashlight, which he used to shine on his clipboard as he gave us a brief introduction to the Statue of Liberty. We gathered around him at the base of the statue. He cleared his throat before he began reading from his brochure. "This marvelous symbol of freedom, which has welcomed so many immigrants to America's shore, was a gift of the French—"

"What's he talking about?" Mama said. "It was the Italians. Christopher Columbus brought it over."

"Sh!" Lina said.

Gigi continued. "Edouard de Laboulaye, a French historian, first conceived of a monument to symbolize liberty and the benefits of free government in the 1870s. However, the statue was not erected until 1884, after an intense fund-raising campaign on both sides of the Atlantic."

"And bet your boots we paid for most of it," Mama said.

"To show their good feelings, the Americans decided to build a monument of their own. On a bridge over the Seine River, they constructed—"

"The Eiffel Tower," Mama called out.

Gigi looked up and glared at her. He clicked off the flashlight, folded his brochure into little pieces, and tucked it into his pocket. *"Andiamo,"* he said.

"Where we going now?" Mama asked.

"Into the statue," Gigi said, as the parishioners headed for the entrance.

"You go into that thing?" Mama asked.

Gigi patted the brochure in his pocket. "It says here you take an elevator to the foot of the statue. Then you can climb a staircase into the crown."

Mama bent her head back and looked up at the top of the statue. Her face turned a pale verdigris. "You gotta be nuts going up that high," she said.

Lina and I began to fidget. "We want to go," I said.

"You could fall out the window," Mama said, "and break your necks."

"But you paid a lot of money for our tickets," Lina said.

That did it. Mama gestured with her hand. "Go, go," she murmured. "Gigi, watch them. Keep them out of trouble."

Lina and I bolted for the entrance, thrilled to get rid of both Mama and Babbo. We rode up the elevator with Gigi. When we reached the observation balcony on the top of the pedestal, I wanted to stop there and look out onto the skyline of Manhattan, but Lina was keen on going straight to the top of the crown. "Why not?" Gigi said.

The metal staircase was deserted. It wound round and round, with cramped landings to rest upon after every second or third turn. Our footsteps echoed against the cold, damp walls, deep and dark as if they were resounding within a cavern. Gigi gave the flashlight to Lina and the clipboard to me. He put his arms around us as he escorted us up the stairs. "So, girls, here we are," he said. "Inside the symbol of freedom, justice, and liberty. America is a wonderful country."

"I like it," I said.

"I guess it's okay," Lina said.

"It's more than okay," Gigi said. "In no other country in the world will you find such opportunities. In America, a man can say anything. Do anything. He can read books, go to concerts, attend lectures on religion and philosophy. He can get a good job. Go to school and get an education."

"What can girls do?" Lina asked.

Gigi bit his lip. Then he clapped her on the back. "Marry the men."

"Then what?" Lina asked.

"Make the *bambini*," Gigi said.

"That's stupid," Lina said, setting her foot squarely down on each step. "I'm never getting married."

"You say that now," Gigi said. "Ten years from now, we'll listen to the tune you'll sing."

"You're not married," Lina pointed out.

"I haven't found the right girl," said Gigi. "But I know someday I'll turn the corner, and she'll be there."

We breathed heavily as we climbed the stairs. My thighs and knees ached by the time we reached the crown. Only a handful of people stood up against the windows. When Lina and I pressed our faces up against the pane, we saw the city laid out like so many little building blocks. Clouds clung to the top of the silver skyscrapers. Gigi pointed out the Empire State Building and Central Park. I gazed down and tried to imagine where, in all those buildings, stood the places I had heard so much about—Radio City Music Hall, Carnegie Hall, Grand Central Station, and the United Nations. "There's water all over the place," Lina said. "And everywhere you look there's another bridge."

After a while other people joined us in the crown. Sister Thomas hiked her black skirt up over her ankles and sat down on one of the benches, huffing for breath. *"Bella, bella."* She nodded. *"La bella donna."* Father Angelosi gestured with the pepperoni as he pointed out what he thought was Saint Patrick's Cathedral. Mrs. Fenilli's purse kept popping open from the provolone, filling the crown with its pungent scent. "Well," she said to me, "we're here. What do we do now? Go down?"

I looked around for Lina or Gigi, but I couldn't find them. Leaving Gigi's clipboard on the bench, I stood behind some of the other people, trying to squeeze my way toward a window. Finally Father Angelosi let me in. But I didn't have a very good view of anything—just some of the boats coming into the harbor. I got impatient—and queasy from the height—so I kept looking back over my shoulder for Lina instead of looking out over the water. Finally Lina touched my arm with the flashlight and signaled for me to follow her. I pressed past Father Angelosi. "Where's Gigi?" I asked.

She curled up her lip. "Who cares about him?" she said, and walked out of the crown.

We began the long, slow walk down to the pedestal. Lina switched on the flashlight and cocked it against the walls, making wild patterns of light fly around the narrow stairwell. We met up with Gigi on the observation balcony. Lina walked right by him, her hair whipping in the wind. Gigi beckoned to me, looked me in the eye, and gave me a nickel to put in one of the big silver machines that you could use, like binoculars, to see things up close. The machine began to click. I pressed my eyes up against the lenses and pointed them toward the water. After a minute of searching through the waves, I located a tugboat. A man was hoisting some barrels along the deck. I spent another minute trying to focus on the bridge over to the right. The cars looked like little Matchbox toys scooting along the span. I wasted the rest of the time focusing on Battery Park, trying to spot Babbo on shore. But the machine was so unwieldy and the lenses so cloudy, I couldn't find him.

The machine stopped clicking. I put on my mittens and hugged my coat against me. Lina poked me in the arm. "Come on," she said. "Let's get inside and get warm. We can take the stairs down."

"We better tell Gigi," I said.

"Forget him," said Lina.

We sneaked off the balcony and went through the doorway that was marked for the stairs. After we had gone down two flights, Lina asked, "What'd you see that you liked the best?"

I thought about it for a minute. "A tugboat out on the water. What'd you see?"

She smirked and looked down on me, as if I were a crumb she was considering picking up and eating. She brought her lips close to my ear and whispered, "A man's dingdong."

"Where?" I asked.

I got so excited that I spit on Lina's coat sleeve. She coolly wiped it off.

"Back there," Lina said. "On the spiral stairs. While you were in the crown."

"What color was it?" I asked.

"Black and blue," Lina said.

"How big was it?"

"At least a foot. Maybe more."

"Did the man show it to you on purpose?"

"It wasn't a man," Lina said. "It was Gigi!"

I felt like a balloon that had just been deflated. "You big fat liar," I said.

"I swear to God," Lina said. "It's true. Gigi asked me if I wanted to go up into the torch. He said you had to climb a ladder and that we had to go down the stairs to get to the door. So we went down to the door. It was really dark and Gigi made me shine the flashlight on it. The sign said you weren't allowed up. So I said, *Let's go back up into the crown,* and Gigi didn't say anything. And then the next thing I knew, he was holding it out at me."

"Whatdja do?" I asked.

"I shined the flashlight on it," Lina said.

"You did not."

"I did," Lina insisted. "I wanted to get a good look. But then Gigi made a funny kind of face, like he just got caught telling a lie, and he put it back again." She smirked. "He had trouble pulling up the zipper. He swore the F word in Italian! He kept on saying, *Mannaggia, now I've done it*. And he told me not to tell Mama and Babbo."

"Are you going to?" I asked.

"I told him I wouldn't if he gave me a dollar."

"Did he?"

Lina smiled. "What do you think?" She patted her pocket. "I should have asked him for five. He looked like he was going to cry when he gave it to me. He said, *Someday you'll find out. Sometimes you can't help yourself*."

I looked over my shoulder. I felt scared, as if Gigi was lurking at every next turn, waiting to expose himself. But Lina walked on, not bothering to look either ahead or behind for any signs of danger. "You know," she said, "when you get up close to his face, Gigi isn't very handsome. He looks kind of old and ugly."

By the time we got to the bottom, I had gotten over being scared. I felt nothing but pure jealousy of Lina. Zio Gigi had singled her out. He thought she was smarter and liked her better. He was in cahoots with her and not with me. The funny thing was that Lina didn't seem to care about Gigi. She headed straight for the souvenir stand, where she spent ten minutes fingering all the items until she selected a miniature silver replica of the Empire State Building with green felt on the bottom. I chose a replica of the Statue of Liberty. With the dollar Gigi gave her, Lina bought a rhinestone pin similar to Mama's, only it was in the shape of an American flag.

We found Mama sitting outside on a bench, underneath the poem that talked about giving me your tired, your poor, and your huddled masses yearning to breathe free. We so rarely saw her relax that she hardly looked like our mother as she leaned back on the bench, her hands clutching her gloves and her rhinestone Scottie dog pin drooping. We seemed to wake her up from a dream. "What did you see?" she asked.

Lina silently handed Mama her flashlight. I reported on the clouds and the skyscrapers, the water and the bridges. "I felt like I was at the top of the world," I said. Then I bit my lip, remembering I had left Uncle Gigi's clipboard up in the crown.

"I've been thinking as I sat here," Mama said. "Remembering things I didn't think I'd ever remember again." She stood up and pointed across the water. "See that island there, you two, with the big building that looks like a castle? That's where we first landed. It was raining cats and dogs."

"You said the sun was shining," Lina reminded her.

"You said it was night," I said.

Mama gestured with her hand. "Sun, rain, night—what's the difference?" She pointed, once again, at the island. "As the boat came in, they let us all come up onto the deck. People held their breath. Some of the women began to cry. Even some of the men, can you imagine? They had to wipe a tear away. Then suddenly, out of the mist—yes, there was mist, and fog—we saw her, the Statue of Liberty, holding the torch. *La Bellissima!* my father called her. The most beautiful woman in the world. After the boat docked, we had to go below again. Then they came down and took the sick ones away. In the next room, imagine—a girl my age had died." Mama crossed herself. "They said she took her last breath just as we came into the harbor, too close to land to bury her at sea."

"What'd she die of?" Lina asked.

"*Chi sa?*" Mama said. "Who knows? There was so much illness. Some people never had a chance." She noticed our hands in our pockets. "Come," she said. "Show me what you got."

I held out my replica of the statue. Lina showed her miniature

Empire State Building. Then she reluctantly took out of her pocket the rhinestone American flag. Mama examined it. "Where did you get the money for that?" she asked.

"Gigi," Lina said.

Mama looked past Lina and located Gigi standing next to Father Angelosi. She pointed to the flag. "You're too good to them," she called out.

Gigi looked down at the pin and then over at Lina. I thought his face turned red. He shrugged. "What can I say?"

Staring at Gigi and Lina, I was suddenly seized with the urge to tell my mother everything. Instead, I whined, "Mama, I'm hungry."

Mama went straight into action. She rounded up Father Angelosi and Mrs. Fenilli. She took out her knife and began to skin the pepperoni and slice the cheese. "You see," she said. "You all had plenty to say at my expense. And now I should let you eat your words instead of sharing the food with you, eh, Father?"

Father cupped his ear. "What's that?" he said.

"*Madonna.*" Mama sighed. "FORGET it. Have a piece of CHEESE."

"It gives me the diarrhea," Father said.

Mama leaned close to his ear. "I got a BROTHER-IN-LAW who's a PLUMBER," she shouted. "He says you gotta eat it with BREAD. Soaks up the POISONS."

Lina chewed slowly, with a pensive look on her face. I stuffed my cheeks full before I swallowed in one big gulp, practically choking. After a while I dared to go up to Zio Gigi and touch his sleeve. He turned with a startled look.

"I left your clipboard upstairs," I said.

He waved his hand. "Forget it."

Lina was right. He did look old and ugly.

After a while Gigi began to count heads and round everybody up for the next ferry. To our surprise, Mama let us go up to the top deck. From there we could hear the flag on the top of the boat whipping in the wind and see the boat cut two lines of white spray as it cruised through the water.

Gigi stood far below us on the bottom deck. Lina made a face at him. Whispering in my ear, she threatened to spit on him and throw the rhinestone pin down into the water so it would drop to the bottom of the ocean. But Mama put a stop to that. She set down the remains of her Railroad Salvage bag, turned up our collars, put her arms around us, and drew us close to her rough wool coat. "When we land," she promised, "I'll get you something to drink. Lemonade or Kool-Aid. I'm so thirsty I can taste it already."

As we drew close, we saw Babbo standing on the dock, watching the boat pitch its way in. Lina raised her hand to wipe the salt spray from her eyes. Then she moved to the edge of the deck, watching the statue fade away. I jumped up and down and waved my hand at my father. Then he began to wave back, widely and with purpose, as if by doing so he could draw the boat toward shore and bring us safely home.

LA STELLA D'ORO

"STAR WATER" WAS Mama's solution to every mess. No fancy, expensive detergents for her—she dumped a capful of blue bleach into a metal basin full of hot water, watched it burst into small, glistening bubbles, and gave it her own brand name. She used star water to scrub the counters and stove, the tub and tile and toilet. She used it to soak out stubborn stains in anything from a tin pan crusted with burnt macaroni and cheese to a tablecloth spotted with grease. The smell of it—lingering in every room for hours after Saturday morning chore time was over—made Lina and me depressed. With its disgusting stink and beautiful name, star water seemed to epitomize the lack of glamour that pervaded our lives. Just a whiff of it reminded us that we were destined for nothing better than ordinary drudgery and chapped hands that reeked of ammonia instead of Chanel N⁰. 5, Tabu, or Jean Naté.

"When I grow up," Lina vowed, "I'm never going to touch a single rag, sponge, or scrub brush."

"I'm going to have a maid," I said.

"I'm going to send all my evening gowns to the dry cleaner,"

Lina said. "I'm going to throw out my underwear after the first time I wear it."

That sounded fine by me. I got stuck wearing everything Lina had outgrown, from the holiday dresses with the velvet cummerbunds and satin collars to her yellowed undershirts and underpants. I could hardly bear the shame. Lina's blouses lapped about my wrists, and her knee socks, which had lost all their snap, crept down to my ankles. The clothes that Lina wore became costumes on me.

I would have given anything for a closet full of brand-new outfits. But when I complained, Mama said, "You can do whatever you want with your cash when you're filthy rich." She never used the word *money*—she called it *cash* or *bucks*. And she never said *rich* without putting *filthy, stinking,* or *disgusting* in front of it, as if people who had more than a spare dime wallowed like pigs in a perpetual state of sin.

Because she despised money, Lina and I loved it. We planned on glittering with gold and dripping with diamonds, owning several houses, a stable of racehorses, and a fleet of yachts. I was going to be a famous writer. Lina was going to be a star—not in Hollywood, where most eleven-year-olds longed to be, but in Italy, where an opera singer could reign as queen. She had a clear, beautiful voice that even Mama, who was as parsimonious with her compliments as she was with her purse, called *a gift from God*. The key word there was *gift*. "Just remember where that voice of yours came from," she said, whenever she thought Lina was too full of herself. "And don't be getting too many ideas about where you're going."

Mama blamed Nonna for puffing Lina up. Mama's mother lived next door, in a neat little white house with a trellised rose garden in back and overstuffed chintz-covered furniture inside. After school, Lina would report home to Mama and then escape to Nonna's, where she was treated to a Stella d'Oro cookie frosted with vanilla and sprinkled with almonds. She spent the rest of the afternoon there, practicing piano or reading a book on the floor, leaping up and down every twenty minutes to either wind the crank of Nonna's cherry-wood Victrola or change the thick, scratchy 78-rpm records.

Nonna was what most people called *eccentric*. She sat perfectly straight, her wrinkled little hands in her lap, her left foot tapping out a tune on the carpet. Her right foot had been amputated, years before, because of gangrene. She hardly ever said anything, but her lips moved silently to the songs she listened to over and over again: Renata Scotto singing "Mi chiamano Mimi," Beniamino Gigli belting out "Celeste Aida." Lina loved this music too. On Saturday afternoons she sat faithfully by Nonna's left foot to listen to the Metropolitan Opera broadcasts. But if the opera was in German, Nonna switched it off. One of the few words she said in English was *Nazis*.

Nonna subscribed to *Il Progresso,* but she also had the *Register* delivered to her door. Lina took it off the front porch and brought it in. She read the headlines to Nonna, then the obituaries, Ann Landers, and the horoscope column, which was called "Omar Says." Nonna was a Virgo; Lina was a Leo. "A temptation may present itself this afternoon," Lina read aloud. "Beware of schemes to get rich quick. The evening hours bring unexpected news. A long-lost family member soon may visit!" Because Mama thought astrology was a bunch of baloney, Lina was thrilled with it. To visit Nonna was to embrace the possibility of handsome strangers and sudden turns of fortune. Omar promised her as much passion as the music.

Although Mama seemed to breathe easier once Lina was out of the house, I got the message, loud and clear, that I wasn't supposed to follow her even if it did hold the promise of a Stella d'Oro. "Those two are two of a kind," Mama said, as she handed me my consolation prize: half an apple and a couple of stale Ritz crackers spread with a thin layer of peanut butter. "Listening to the same songs over and over again, all about love and killing yourself. Driving yourself *matta* over nothing, is what I say." Accepting my silence as a sign that I was on her side, Mama looked out the window and glared at Nonna's house. "Just what we need, another rotten egg in the family."

That egg—rarely alluded to—was Lina's namesake, Mama's younger sister, Pat. Both Auntie Pat and Lina had been christened after Nonno Pasquale, ending up with the unwieldy *Pasqualina* for a name. We knew, from looking at old photo albums, that Lina had been called Patty when she was a baby. *Patty's first tooth,* the captions written on the white borders of the pictures said. *Patty on the potty.* Then something mysterious happened. Several photographs—probably of Auntie Pat—were missing from the album, the four dark corners used to mount them left behind. Auntie Pat had done something foul that caused her to be taken out of the book, and Mama and Babbo, anxious to forget the old Pasqualina, began to call the younger one by a different name.

Lina hated her name. "Sounds like a fat old washerwoman," she said.

"It's a nice Italian name," Mama said.

"I'm American," Lina said. When that failed to get a rise out of Mama, she added, "And I'm going to change my name when I grow up."

Mama clucked her tongue. "Be satisfied with what you've got."

"Why should I be?" Lina said. "You weren't. You were the one who changed it on me. Why'd you switch me, anyway?" When Mama didn't answer, Lina said, "It makes me feel weird. I feel like I'm two people in one, like there's somebody inside of me that wants to come out."

Mama pressed her lips together. "Get over here," she said, "and I'll clean that mouth of yours out with soap. I'll soak your crazy head."

Lina ran upstairs. Out of loyalty, I galloped after her. Behind our closed bedroom door, Lina vowed she was going to run away and live with Auntie Pat.

"But you don't even know her," I said.

"She lives in New York," Lina said, as if that told all. "On Jane Street. I wrote down the address from the box she sent me."

Auntie Pat was Lina's godmother. Every year on Lina's birthday she sent a box of books too educational for Lina's romantic taste. While Lina reveled in stories about young girls, usually orphans, who triumphed over adversity, Auntie Pat sent sturdy volumes that chronicled the true lives of women. Over the years Lina had collected a row of books such as *Marie Curie: Pioneer in Science; Clara Barton: Nurse to a Nation;* and *Maria Mitchell: Girl Astronomer.* Mama scoffed at the books and Babbo shook his head. After writing a thank-you note to Aunt Pat, which Mama carefully scrutinized, addressed, and mailed, Lina put the books on her shelf and forgot about them. I was the only one who read them, who was taken in by their tales of undaunted feminine courage. I guessed that Auntie Pat, when she was my age, had aspired to be a heroine. But now, according to Mama, she worked doing God-knows-what for some big-city publishing outfit. Nonna went to visit her in New York, twice a year, to see her favorite operas—*La Traviata* and *La Bohème.* Auntie Pat never visited her back.

"She looks like a racehorse," Lina said, scrutinizing one of the photos of Auntie Pat left in the album.

"She looks like Jo in *Little Women,*" I said, "after she sells her hair."

"I hate *Little Women,*" Lina said. "It's not written right. Jo should have run off with Laurie and been rich and famous instead of marrying that stupid old professor."

"I wonder why Auntie Pat never got married."

"She looks sort of ugly in the pictures," Lina admitted. "But I bet she's changed now. After all, she lives in New York. She's probably *stunning.*"

"I bet she has a mink coat," I said. "And diamonds and high heels."

"I bet she doesn't go to church on Sunday," Lina said. She looked closer at the picture. "She probably got into a fight with everybody over a man."

I liked that idea. "Maybe she wanted to marry someone they didn't like."

"Maybe she lives in sin with a man," Lina said. "Maybe he isn't Italian. Maybe he isn't Catholic. Maybe he's a foreigner. Maybe he's a Negro!"

We looked at each other, excitement in our eyes. Anything was possible when it came to Auntie Pat. The more Mama and Nonna didn't talk about her, the more our imaginations ran wild. Auntie Pat had been a lonely, misunderstood child (perhaps a victim of a baby switch in the hospital). As a girl, she had outshone our homely, ill-tempered Mama in every way; as a teenager, she ran wild; as a young woman, she sought her fortune in the city. She rose from the ranks, first working as a cocktail waitress, then a go-go dancer, before she graduated to a high-class call girl ensconced in a penthouse in midtown Manhattan. She was the epitome of slutdom, a bona fide brazen hussy whore who slipped rolled-up bucks into the slit of her cleavage. We loved her.

Lina liked to put on shows for me, and once she decided to present an imitation of Auntie Pat. After Mama had sent us upstairs to go to sleep, Lina ordered me to put on my pajamas, get into bed, and close my eyes. As I sat there with my eyes squinched shut, I heard her racing about the room, slamming drawers, rustling in the closet, and then shutting off the overhead light. "Okay," she finally whispered. "Open."

She stood at the other end of the room, her silhouette bathed in light from her bedside lamp, which she had muted by balancing a notebook on the shade. She was stripped down to her panties, a silver Christmas-tree garland wrapped around her shoulders like a boa. She thrust her right hip forward and then her left, manipulating the garland to expose first one slightly swelling nipple, then the other. She slit her eyes, licked her lips, and lowering her voice into a sultry, throaty drawl, she began to sing a popular song that Mama switched off every time it came on the car radio: "Big Spender."

I tried to whistle, but I hadn't mastered the art yet. I snapped my fingers, cooed at her, and by the time she reached the line *I don't pop my cork for every man I see,* I had cupped my hands to my mouth, forming a trumpet that continued to play the tune for her. Then Lina danced, a provocative bump and grind that made what little fat she had on her thighs and belly quiver. As I played my trumpet louder and louder, Lina grew bolder. She pinched her nipples between her thumb and forefinger and tweaked them at me. She straddled the garland and pulled it up slowly between her legs, purring with pleasure. She flung the garland to the floor, turned full circle, leaned over at the waist, and thrust out her behind. Slipping her thumbs into her panties, she began to inch them down over the mound of her buttocks. I giggled wildly.

Then the doorknob turned. My laughter went dead as Mama stood grim-lipped in the door. "What's going on here?" she demanded.

Lina pulled up her underwear. "I'm getting dressed," she said.

Mama stared at Lina. "Put on your pajamas," she finally said. "Cover up your filthy body right now. Right now."

I looked down at my bedspread. Out of the corner of my eye, I saw Lina walk over to our chest of drawers. Her back toward Mama, she got dressed.

Mama marched over to the lamp and snatched Lina's notebook off the shade. "Good way to start a fire," she muttered. Then, spying the Christmas-tree garland on the floor, she strode over and picked it up, crumpling it in her hand. "What is this?" she asked. When Lina didn't answer, she turned to me. "Speak up, or you'll get it too."

A year earlier I would have begun to blubber and blurt it all out, but now, intensely aware of Lina's threatening stare, I chose not to say anything.

Mama shook the garland at me and then at Lina. "Don't you ever let me find you up here"—she floundered for words—"waggling your *can* around like some sort of cheap I-don't-know-what. Don't you ever, ever again!"

Our real punishment was doled out at the breakfast table the next morning. "When you have to undress," Mama said coldly, not looking at either one of us, "you'll do it one at a time, in the bathroom or in the closet, or with the door open. From now on, no closing the bedroom door."

My heart sank. Now there would be nowhere to go, nowhere to hide, from Mama's tyranny. It was too dark to play outside after supper. The cellar was cold and damp. In the kitchen, in the parlor, in the dining room, Mama always found me. I couldn't even be safe in the bathroom. There wasn't a lock on the door, and in her relentless quest to have a clean house, Mama often called out "Knock, knock!" then let herself in to arrange towels on the shelf or scrub the sink. "Don't strain," she told me, as I sat on the toilet. If I was in the bathtub, she said, "Remember to wash *down there*."

Where could I escape? Lina, at least, had Nonna's house. I had only the public library. Twice a week I trudged back and forth to the library with an armload of books. Venturing into the adult section one day, between the high stacks that I thought contained every book ever written, I discovered a big, webbed chair in front of a tall window. It fit my body just right. I thought of it as mine. There, curled up with my feet tucked under me, I lost myself in marvelous tales of boats lost at sea, women roughing it in the Wild West, and children abandoned in the wilderness.

The library had many more biographies like the kind Auntie Pat sent Lina. I read them all—Harriet Tubman, Florence Nightingale, Eleanor Roosevelt, Helen Keller. I both loved the women and hated them. They were so bold and courageous, but they seemed to prove that in order to do something important, you had to look revolting. I couldn't bear to believe that, but the line drawings that graced the front covers of the books told the whole story. These women were too tall, too hefty, too self-righteous in their squared-off collars and heavy skirts. They had prominent noses and double chins. A disproportionate number wore glasses. They were ugly.

I vowed I would never let myself get like that. As the light began to fade through the library window and I packed up my books to walk home, I thought about who I wanted to emulate. But I could think of no one. Unlike Lina, I had no namesake to follow, no path to claim. I didn't have the guts or the looks to be like a TV actress or a model in magazines. Although I liked the librarians who smiled at me on my visits, they looked faded, dowdy, and dusty as books that hadn't been checked out in a long time.

The thought of becoming like Mama made me shiver. My teachers all were nuns, and I prayed to the very God I was rejecting that I would not get the calling. *Choose somebody else,* I whispered every night after I said my Act of Contrition. *Please, please.* The only teachers who weren't nuns were the gym instructors—large, imposing women who wore whistles on cords around their necks, sensible-looking shorts, and crisp white cotton anklets. I didn't like them because they gave me Bs. Even Lina, who excelled at gym, hated them. "Dykes," she said. Seeing the confusion on my face, she explained, "You know, *lezzers.* Women who look like men."

"Oh," I said.

"They stick together. They like each other, just like women like men." To create some suspense, Lina lowered her voice. "They do *unnatural* things," she said. "With vegetables. Cucumbers and zucchini. There's a girl in my class who's a lez. I heard she used a frozen hot dog and it thawed inside her. They had to take her to the emergency room to get it out."

I laughed. It seemed too fantastic to believe—and yet, coming from an authoritative source such as Lina, it had to be true. My giggles gave way to an uncomfortable feeling, then pure fright. The thought of anyone sticking anything up me seemed the grossest violation. I was sure it would split me in two and change me forever.

After that, I worried about myself. I was sure there was something wrong with me because I didn't like boys. The boys at school were always winking and nudging each other, deliberately burping out loud and cupping their hands beneath their armpits to simulate fart noises. My boy cousins I resented because they were accorded privileges Lina and I were not. They were allowed to play outside until it was time for supper, while Lina and I were called inside to set the table and help serve food. After supper, they ran back outside while we had to clear the table and wash the dishes. During summer, they stayed in the yard long after we had been called in, eating ice cream, playing hide-and-seek, and lounging on the hoods of their fathers' cars.

I was sure there was something wrong with me because I sometimes slipped the *National Geographic* off the rack in the library and sneaked the magazine back to my chair, where I traced with my finger the thick bellies and heavy gumdrop breasts of the naked aborigine women. And there was something wrong with me because I liked to look at Lina's body. Hadn't I hooted and clapped when she had danced in front of me? And wasn't one of the reasons I hated having the privilege of closing the bedroom door taken away was that now Lina sometimes undressed in the bathroom? Now I could no longer sneak as many glances at her out of the corner of my eye, no longer catch as many glimpses of her nubby little breasts or the tuft of hair that seemed to be growing in a perfect triangle where her body met her legs. Yes, I was a dyke because I could not stop myself from looking and because there were times when, after we had turned out the light, I could not stop myself from pressing my hands against my flat chest or cupping them over that strangely wet and warm place on my body, wondering when things were going to start happening to me.

But things always happened to Lina first. It wasn't fair, but it was the way. As Lina grew, Nonna began to call her *la signorina,* the little lady. Mama constantly fought with Lina over insignificant things, then tried to get me to side with her against Lina. But Lina won my loyalty. I couldn't help but admire her. She walked around as if she floated far above everyone. She sang a lot, spent hours folding the clothes in her drawers, and brushed her hair one hundred strokes every night. She confiscated an empty Dixon Park Soda crate off our father's delivery truck and parked it by her bed. Covering it with a flowered bath towel, she christened it her "vanity." On it she placed her hairbrush, a comb, and a tiny pocket mirror she had pulled from the grab bag at the St. Joseph's bazaar. Every night she knelt in front of her vanity as if it were a shrine, arranging and rearranging the same three items.

Mama commented on the makeshift vanity the moment she spotted it. "What's that?" she asked.

"It's . . . where I want to keep things," Lina said.

"What's wrong with your chest of drawers?"

"I have to share it with Angel."

"You're too good to share?" asked Mama.

"I didn't say that," Lina said. "I said . . . I wanted someplace of my own."

Mama looked threateningly at Lina. She stepped into our room, went over to the vanity, and one by one picked up the three items that sat upon it, inspecting them carefully. Holding the pocket mirror by the tips of her fingers, she set it back down on the crate. "Pretty girls and ugly girls," she warned, "all get the same when they're old women."

That spring a fourth item appeared on Lina's vanity. Nonna began to complain about pains in her stomach. She was tired; she didn't feel right. *"Stones,"* Mama said, in the same sour tone she used to order cod-liver oil or bunion pads from the druggist. Furtively, just as I gained all my other knowledge of the human body, I looked it up in the Funk & Wagnalls at the library. The picture showed an ominous cluster of pebbles nestled within the curve of a catsupy-red kidney. Mama forbade Lina to bother Nonna until her stones passed. But they would not budge, and Nonna went into the hospital to have them removed.

Before she went, she gave Lina a yellow tin of Jean Naté from her collection of talcum powders. She said it would help Lina remember her. Lina set the coveted tin beside the pocket mirror. The day of Nonna's surgery she must have twisted back the cap a hundred times to take a whiff. When Lina went out of the room, I was tempted to sprinkle some of the fine white talcum on my hand, but I knew Lina would smell it on me and get angry.

The following day—a Saturday—Mama grudgingly promised to take Lina to the hospital. Not being visiting age, I would have to stay behind. Full of envy, I sprawled out on my stomach on the bed, watching Lina get ready. After sorting through her clothes in the closet for what seemed like forever, Lina finally chose a white cotton blouse and a red plaid kilt that closed with an oversize gold safety pin. She set them on a chair. "I'm pretending I'm getting ready for a date," she said.

"Who's the man?" I asked.

"He's handsome, rich, and famous."

"Where are you going?"

"To the theater. To see the opening of a *fab*-ulous show. Afterward, we're going out for cocktails." Lina took off the top of her pajamas, then her bottom. She stood there in her undershirt and underpants, dreamy-eyed. "Then after that, we're going back to his penthouse." She reached down and picked up her powder. Sprinkling some in the palm of her hand, she rubbed a little under one armpit, then the other. She took off her undershirt and rubbed some on her breasts. Then she stretched out the waist of her underpants and sprinkled some powder down the front and rubbed a handful on the inside of her thighs.

She looked like a clown who had whitened all her secret parts instead of her face. After Lina had put on her clothes, Mama stopped in the door, wrinkling up her nose. Spotting the yellow tin on Lina's vanity, she held out her hand. Lina reluctantly surrendered the powder to her.

"I guess I don't need to ask who gave you this fancy stuff," Mama said. She held it to her nose and sniffed. I was sure she would confiscate the powder, but she handed it back to Lina with a short comment. "Soap and water will take care of your smells," she said. "Remember what I told you the other day."

After she left the room, Lina furiously wiped the top of the container and replaced it on her vanity. "What did she tell you?" I asked.

"Nothing."

"But she said she told you something the other day."

"She didn't tell me anything," Lina said. "Besides, you're too young to know."

"Know what?" I kicked the fringe on my bedspread. "It's not fair," I said. "You get to visit Nonna and have powder and do everything first."

"I'm older," Lina said.

"So I act better. Mama says so."

Lina lowered her voice to a whisper. "What do I care about Mama?"

"And I'm smarter than you too."

"So I'm prettier. That counts more."

"It does not."

Lina smiled to herself as she moved the safety pin that fastened her kilt an inch higher. "It does too. Just you wait and see."

Her smugness killed me. I was sure she was right. Pretty girls did seem to get all the attention. People always took notice of

Lina before they looked at me. The rule seemed to be that if you took two girls, or two sisters, one would be beautiful and daring and lusted after—like Auntie Pat and Lina—and the other would be shriveled as a dried-out sponge, her inability to be beautiful translated into an obsession with being right and being clean. I was sure this was my fate, and I hated Lina for usurping the better role from me.

Lina returned from the hospital with an even more haughty look on her face. "Nonna was connected to a whole bunch of tubes and wires, just like the monster in *Frankenstein*," she said. "And she had a long set of stitches that looked like a big black caterpillar crawling across her stomach."

I burned with jealousy. I had never seen a real scar. I couldn't wait to catch a glimpse of it. But Nonna stayed in the hospital one week and then another. Mama refused to take Lina back. She spent a lot of time on the phone, whispering with relatives about *complications*.

Complications needed no explanation. Many of our great-aunts and great-uncles already had suffered them—the hushed *turn for the worse* that sent Mama to church with a fistful of quarters. Each coin dropped into the tin collection box purchased the bright flame of a vigil candle. Vigils were the only item on which Mama would spend money freely. She kept a roll of quarters in a chipped coffee cup in the kitchen cabinet just for this purpose.

Lina and I surreptitiously watched the supply of quarters dwindle, only to be replaced by a fresh roll. Every day when we walked back from school we circled around another block so we could pass by Nonna's house, hoping as we rounded the corner that we would find the shades up and the lights on. Nothing doing. Lina's shoulders slumped as we crossed the yard and went back home to Mama.

One day, when we practically had given up hope, I spied a light in one of Nonna's side windows. We raced forward, Lina outstripping me and reaching the back porch first. She pressed her face to the glass and didn't take it away. When I got to the porch, breathless, I jostled her to the side and looked in too.

It was an awful sight. The overhead light in the kitchen was on, and the mark of Mama was everywhere: in the stringy gray mop and stiff broom that leaned against the wall, the metal basin and rags that lay on the counter, and the bottle of bleach and tin bucket that sat squarely on the floor.

Lina took her face away from the glass. "She's dead," she said.

Her flat voice sent a shiver down me. "Mama's probably been cleaning because Nonna's coming home," I said.

"They'll come back here after the funeral," Lina said. "For the party."

Although barred from funerals, we had been to many of those parties. The kitchen table was loaded with rolls and butter and pastries and cookies. The immediate family sat on folding chairs in the dining room, shaking people's hands and weeping softly as they accepted people's condolences. The air smelled like rotten flowers and fruit and coffee. The men were dressed in black suits and ties and the women in black dresses with delicate 14-karat gold crucifixes—worn only for Easter, Christmas, and funeral masses—dangling around their necks.

I looked up at Lina, wanting her to tell me what to do. I would not start crying until she did. She did not.

She put her hand on the door. "I'm going in," she said.

"What for?"

"I just want to go in."

"We better go home and ask Mama—"

"I hate Mama!" Lina said. She turned the knob and the door creaked, like in a horror movie, before it gave way. The smell of star water hit us immediately. The bright white counters, stove, and refrigerator created a glare, like snow.

"I don't think we should be here," I said.

"Nonna would want us to."

"There might be a ghost."

"I hope there is," Lina said. "I want to talk to her."

"I hear one," I said. "I hear somebody, Lina!"

The noise came from the stairwell, the sound of one foot on the stairs, then another, coming down slowly, to haunt us, kill us, spirit us away. "Let's go, let's go," I said, unwilling to leave without Lina. But she stood her ground, forcing me to stay.

The ghost got to the bottom of the stairs and crossed the living room. When she appeared in the door, she was tall and broad-shouldered and dressed in a black jacket, white turtleneck, and black knickers, like a horsewoman in one of those books about girls who want to be jockeys. Her black hair was cropped short, as if someone had shorn the hair to follow the contour of a cereal bowl plopped upon her head. She had eyes only for Lina. "Pasqualina?" she asked, holding out her hands.

Lina stepped back. Resenting not being singled out, I rushed forward and threw myself in her arms. "Auntie Pat," I said, "it's me, it's me!"

※

The party went more or less as I had imagined it. Lina and I watched as people filed by to hold Mama's hand. Auntie Pat stood behind Mama, refusing to sit in one of the folding chairs. *A beautiful death,* the relatives said. *She looked lovely.*

"They did a wonderful job with her," Mama agreed. I wondered how she could say that. Lying in the coffin, Nonna had looked like an old, sunken doll with too much red on her cheeks and lips, the sort of woman Mama would have referred to as *a made-up hussy* had she met her on the street.

"Lovely, my eye," Auntie Pat said later, as she parked her imposing form between Lina and me on the sofa. Lina moved a good three inches away. "Talking about her as if she were a bride. Putting so much paint on her you could hardly see the true character of her face. It was a travesty."

Because I had no idea what that word meant, I kept quiet. Lina did too. She looked especially uncomfortable sitting on the couch in the room where she had spent so many hours with Nonna. She kept looking around at the Victrola and the piano and the records, probably thinking about how her refuge from Mama was lost forever.

"So, girls," Auntie Pat said in her crisp voice, "we have a lot of catching up to do. Tell me about yourselves. What are your favorite subjects at school? What are your hobbies?"

By prodding Lina—she always turned to Lina first—Auntie Pat learned that Lina liked Language and Music best, and that someday she wanted to be a musician.

"You play piano, of course," Auntie Pat said, looking at the upright. Mama, who was sitting on the piano bench next to one of her cousins, looked back. "And I've heard you like to sing. Where do you take lessons?"

Mama glared at Auntie Pat.

"I don't have lessons," Lina said.

"Why not?"

"I don't know," Lina said crossly. "I just don't."

"You should have a teacher," Auntie Pat said, "someone to encourage you and give you advice." She looked at Mama. "Why don't you send her?"

Mama rubbed her forefinger and thumb together, as if she were feeling for a bill that didn't exist. "She takes music at school."

"But she should have private lessons."

The word *private*—like the word *money*—made Mama scornful. "She already has enough ideas in her head."

"And what's wrong with ideas?" Auntie Pat asked. "They're very good things to have."

Mama turned to her cousin and said, "Lina thinks she's going to be a stage actress."

"I do not," Lina said hotly.

Mama laughed. *"La stella d'oro,"* she said. "The golden star!"

Auntie Pat clearly didn't approve of Lina's ambition. You could tell she was struggling to decide whether to side with Mama or Lina. In the end, Lina won out. "And what if she does want to be a star?" Auntie Pat finally said. She turned to Lina. "Let me tell you right now, you can be whatever you want to be."

Lina sat there with her shoulders hunched, tears clinging to her eyelashes. "No, I can't," she blurted out. "I'll never be, I'll never be!"

The room went silent. All the relatives turned and stared. Lina stood up, ran across the room, opened the front door, and raced out of the house. Mama clucked her tongue and shook her head. Turning to her cousin, she said, *"Il bordo."*

Lina was *on the brink.* Not wanting to be the one who pushed her over, I avoided her in the weeks to come. It wasn't hard to do. After the party was over, after Auntie Pat took herself back to New York (where, Mama said scornfully, she would *rejoin her lady friend*), after the for-sale sign went up in the front yard of Nonna's house and the backyard became a playground for my cousins, Lina grew morose and withdrawn. She went for long walks by herself after school and pretended to be doing her homework for hours every night after supper. She wrote things in a notebook that she referred to as her diary, and every morning she put on gobs of the powder that Nonna had given her, so that even I, who liked the smell, got a headache.

One morning I came downstairs just in time to witness Mama slap Lina's face. "You're a woman now," Mama said. Lina stood there, her body stiff and rigid as Mama hugged her. She let Lina stay home from school. All day long I puzzled over this, but when I came back home and asked Lina for an explanation, she told me to mind my own business.

By then I was getting used to such remarks, hardened to that sort of treatment. Yet I was sick of being ignored, and even more tired of people trying to get me to take sides with them—Mama,

Lina, and Auntie Pat. I wanted to be on my own side, wherever it was, and whatever it might mean.

Summer was coming. I waited for it with high hopes, and when it finally arrived, I cleared out a small square of dirt behind the back hedge and pretended I had my own house. I played until the light began to grow dim and Mama called me in. I got ready for bed to the pulse of the crickets. Sometimes, from Nonna's yard, the loud voices of my boy cousins wafted into the bedroom. I watched them from the window. They were sprawled on the ground, plotting their futures as they stared up at the sky.

Every month Mama made Lina soak her bloodstained underpants in the bathroom. Looking into that water, watching the bubbles glisten and fade, I realized with a sinking feeling what the stars held for me.

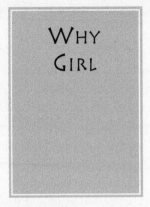

Why Girl

EVERY DAY BEFORE we set off for school, Mama warned us: *Don't go looking for trouble.* Lina and I listened. We steered clear of the boys, and at the start of gym period, we always lingered in the locker room and let the black girls go upstairs first so they couldn't step on the heels of our cheap W. T. Grant sneakers. When Lina and I finally climbed the steep metal staircase to the gym, Miss Bowman was in the middle of taking roll. She glared at us over her clipboard. She always called us *the Lupo sisters*. Because her chest was flat as a board, Lina and I called her *the Carpenter's Dream*.

The Dream's short red-and-white kilt swung back and forth, and the pom-poms on the back of her socks briskly bobbed as she moved through the crowd, dividing us into four teams of three black girls and two white girls each. Lina made Team C, but I ended up on Team D, which meant I got stuck wearing a pinny, a faded kelly-green apron that tied around the neck and waist, wet with sweat from the girl who had worn it the class before.

As I fastened my pinny, I stared at the pale face of Carpenter's Dream. The Dream had skin the color of a split baked potato before you put on the butter, and her dirty-blond hair was conspicuous in the halls of Roger Sherman High, which in 1976 was an uneasy mix of two black kids for every Italian. In the morning, all the doors to Roger Sherman were locked except for the front entrance, which was equipped with a metal detector. If the keys on a boy's belt or the beads on a girl's cornrow braids set off the red light, a fat ominous woman, a deaf-mute known only as *Matron,* made the culprits stand spread-eagled against the wall while she passed a large black wand over every inch of their body. Rumor had it that Matron took the wand home at night and spent hours hugging it between her own monstrous thighs. I was Catholic. I believed it.

Lina and I had ended up in public school because our father kept getting laid off from the Dixon Park Soda Company, and he no longer could afford to pay our tuition at Holy Redeemer. At first it had been a shock to go to Roger Sherman High, where plywood boards were the only view from the broken windows, rats fed on bag lunches left in the lockers, and the doors were removed from the bathroom stalls so the girls couldn't shoot up or get raped. But we soon got used to the grungy mud-colored classrooms and the way the students heckled the teachers during assembly and started food fights on Wednesdays—Spaghetti and Meatball Day—in the cafeteria. (No one ever started a food fight on Friday—Pizza Day—although once a major brawl erupted when fish sticks were served.) You never knew what would happen at Roger Sherman High. After the dreary monotony of Holy Redeemer, Lina and I sort of enjoyed the adventure.

Everyone flouted the dress code at Roger Sherman, which mandated no leather pants or skirts, no platform shoes or gold chains, and no bald heads on girls. Gym suits—baggy green and white affairs with an unflattering elastic around the waist—were required for Phys Ed, but after the first week Lina and I abandoned them. We had gotten our fill of uniforms at Holy Redeemer and were relieved to find that the only standard outfit appearing on the Roger Sherman courts consisted of thin ribbed tank tops—often worn without a bra underneath—and tight, faded cutoffs that covered the butt only—no thigh.

After getting Teams A and B started on the other court, Carpenter's Dream came over and supervised our tip-off. The girls exploded into action as fast and as loud as the M-80 firecrackers that blew off in the boys' bathroom from time to time. As usual, I lagged behind. Roger Sherman girls played for blood, and any girl who wasn't willing to scratch or kick her way to the basket had better hang back. I loped up and down the court, a useless addition to the pinny team, only touching the ball once, when it got slammed out of someone's hand and rolled back to me. I stood there for a moment, stunned to feel the orange leather beneath my palms. Then I turned and ran down the court, a solo flight that culminated in a call for *traveling* and a missed basket.

All the other pinnies groaned at me, and when Carpenter's Dream turned to focus on the other court, the black girls on my team began elbowing and shin-kicking me out of the way, running behind me, shouting taunts that ended with the phrase *white girl*, which sounded like *why girl, why girl*. Sweat flew off my face as I ran back and forth, trying to avoid their jabs, until I realized I should hang back in the center and not even follow them. I stood near the sidelines until Carpenter's Dream's shrill whistle declared that Lina had been fouled. Lina stepped out of the court to throw the ball back in. But instead of throwing it to someone on her team, she deliberately slammed the ball toward me, socking me right in the stomach.

I stood there, then threw the ball to another Italian girl—Mary Annetta Giunta on the non-pinny team, who threw it to Maria Feminelli, one of the pinnies. The rules of the game suddenly had changed. It took a moment for Carpenter's Dream to figure it out, but as we charged up and down the court, four white girls to six black, the Dream futilely ran up and down the sidelines, yelling, "Black girls! Black girls! White girls! Keep to teams! Pinnies with pinnies! Pinnies must play with pinnies!"

As her whistle shrieked, a crowd of girls fell in a heap under the basket, and a string of multicolored beads around someone's neck broke and burst in a hundred directions on the floor. Charlene Stewart went skidding into the wooden bleachers. When she sat up and put her hand to the back of her head, her fingers came away sticky and red. She fainted.

Charlene was taken to the nurse and the rest of us were sent to the main office, where after an hour and a half of stubborn silence on the part of us all, two black girls (Felicia Green and Terry Moore) and two whites (Lina and me) were sent to the new assistant principal's office for punishment.

Mr. Tyrone Oliver had played with the Green Bay Packers in the sixties, supposedly kneeling on the goal line and saying a prayer every time he made a touchdown. I had seen Mr. Oliver floating down the hall, head and shoulders above even the tallest of boys. He always wore pale yellow shirts and jeweled cuff links, a uniform that seemed to prove he was the coolest thing ever to grace the halls of Roger Sherman. But as Mr. Oliver leaned against his office desk, scornfully looking over our too-tight tank tops, painted fingernails, and hairy muscled legs, he suddenly seemed huge and frightening. All four of us girls looked set to crap our cutoffs until he opened his mouth, and we discovered with great glee that he had a southern accent.

He called us *guls*. He said we *guls* were a discredit to *Ra-jah Sher-man*. He said we were a discredit to New Haven. He pointed at Felicia. "You fixin' to scrub floors for the rest of yuh life?"

"No, *suh*," Felicia said. "I'm *a-fixin'* to sing backup for Diana Ross."

"You *gul*." He pointed at Lina. "How yuh mama gonna feel if you end up cleaning toilets?"

Lina shrugged, knowing that Mama valued a clean toilet bowl above everything except a good bingo game.

Mr. Oliver did not bother to interrogate me or Terry. He said something that I couldn't figure out about Abraham Lincoln and

George Washington Carver, and he gave us some jazz about Booker T. Washington sleeping for seven nights in a street gutter because Booker T. knew the value of a good *ed-u-ca-shun* even if we *guls* didn't.

Then Mr. Oliver said he was going to teach all us *guls* an old-fashioned lesson. We could just move on down to the locker room and clean the sinks and toilets until we had gotten a good taste of what our lives would be like if we didn't straighten up and hit the books. He would have Matron open the janitor's closet. "Now get out of my office," he said. "I don't want to see yuh ugly faces here again. And yank up yuh bra strap," he told Felicia. "It's showing."

With exaggerated motion, Felicia lifted the shoulder of her tank top and deliberately snapped the elastic of her black bra strap into place. Then we all left the office. Dangling from our fingers the blue paper passes that permitted us to walk the hall between classes, we sauntered down to the locker room, which was empty because fifth period already had started. We stood in the hall waiting for Matron, looking uneasily at one another. Like a model on the end of the runway, Lina threw her black hair over her shoulder, stuck out her hip, and pouted her lower lip. Terry looked down and twirled the raw-hide braid around her wrist. Felicia inspected her purple finger-nails, then took her hand and rubbed the skin below her neck, looking over the clots of dirt on her fingers before she brushed them away. Then she pulled back her shoulders and did a very accurate imitation of Mr. Oliver strutting down the hall. "He don't like my bra strap?" she grumbled. "Oughta be glad I got on a bra at all." She looked at Terry. "And what he talking about, us giving New Haven a bad name. Already got it one."

"Worse than Bridgeport," Terry said. "Don't even got jai-alai."

"Got the shitty old Coliseum, gonna fall down before the year 2000," Felicia said.

Lina finally ventured to join the conversation. "Got Yale," she said.

"Where that at?" Felicia asked, and we all laughed.

"Rich-boy school," Lina said.

"Smart-boy school," Terry said.

"Foreign country," I said.

After Matron opened the closet with a ring of keys that would outdo any jailer's, she handed us sponges, a can of Bon Ami, a broom, and two toilet brushes in plastic pails. Then she locked the closet and disappeared down the hall, her wand swinging against her hip like a cop's nightstick.

We went back into the locker-room bathroom. It stunk of mold and mice and almost enough cigarette smoke to cover up the odor of a backed-up toilet. We put all the supplies on the bench next to the first row of lockers.

Lina crinkled up her nose with disgust. "What're we supposed to do now?"

"I ain't emptying no cunt rags," Terry said.

"Only one thing certain," Felicia told Lina. "You started it, so you clean the most toilets."

Lina gave Felicia an icy look, then grabbed one of the toilet brushes. Felicia grabbed the other, and for a moment I thought they might start dueling. But then Felicia took her brush and went into one of the stalls along the left wall, followed by Terry. I trailed Lina into a stall on the right. Lina crinkled her nose again as she gingerly lifted the toilet seat and lowered the brush in, half-heartedly swishing around some of the water. None of us bothered with the Bon Ami.

Lina and I had gone through the motions of cleaning three toilets on the right when it started, as we all knew it would—the real standoff between us and them, not with shoves and punches and pushes, but with words.

From across the room I heard Felicia say, "Guinea girls think they too good to wash toilets."

"Dream on," Lina said beneath her breath.

"Don't pay any attention to them," I whispered. But it was hard not to.

"Guinea girls wear too much perfume," Terry called out loudly.

"Guinea girls go to hell, eat hamburger on Friday," Felicia said.

"Guinea girls got the mustaches," Terry said.

Felicia laughed. "Guinea girls put out big-time for black boys."

Terry whooped.

"My brother, he make it with a white girl," Felicia shouted. "Said it felt like fucking a frozen turkey." She laughed. "Then he do it with a guinea girl. She wearing so much gold he say he feel like he fucking King Tut."

"More like he fucking Big Butt," Terry said. "Guinea girls got them big butts."

Lina shoved past me and walked out of the stall. "So what?" she said. "Nigger girls got 'em too, and bigger. And they stink up the halls with their hair straightener."

Felicia and Terry dropped the brush into the toilet and came out of their stall. I peeked out at Lina, standing in the middle of the bathroom with her hands on her hips, and then I reluctantly came out and stood there too. Behind us were the toilets, and over to the side stood the sink, a huge bathtublike contraption that sprayed water like a sprinkler if you pushed the button. But we all knew the sink didn't work and that nobody intended to fix it. Nobody ever washed their hands after going to the bathroom at Roger Sherman.

Felicia and Terry glared at us, and we glared at them.

"You do drugs, girl?" Felicia finally asked Lina.

"What do you think?" Lina said.

"You got any?"

Lina sauntered over to the second row of lockers and twirled her combination. She opened the locker door with a bang and brought out her split-leather purse. Then she reached into a hole in the lining, waggled her finger, and drew out a Baggie sealed with a twistie.

Lina and I had smoked pot together only a couple of times before, mostly at family picnics, when we disappeared with our cousin Gus into the bushes at the base of the mountain at East Rock Park. It was one thing to smoke with your cousin, yet another to light up with your sworn enemies. But maybe this was Lina's plan. Nothing united Roger Sherman kids like doing drugs and standing up to teachers. If we got high together, we'd all stay out of trouble.

Terry cleared off the bench. Felicia produced matches and a pack of Zig Zag, and within a minute Lina had inexpertly rolled and lit up a joint.

"Hurry, hurry," Terry warned. "Matron gonna come back."

"Matron's off drinking coffee," Lina said.

"Matron gettin' off with her wand," Felicia said, before she took a deep toke and pulled in so much smoke she started to cough. "Where you get this good stuff?" she asked Lina.

"The Home Ec teacher," Lina said.

"She deal?"

Proud that she had pulled one over on Felicia, Lina smiled. "Yeah, and she promised to make us pot brownies at the end of the year. Send us home flying high."

We all laughed and leaned lazily against one another. We passed the joint until it burned our fingers to hold it. Nobody had a roach clip, so Lina had to grind out the joint on the bench and save the stub for later. I sat very still, closed my eyes, and listened to the hum of the fluorescent lights. The voices of Terry and Felicia and Lina sounded slow and far away.

"I hate this school," Terry said. "Shit-brown floors. Puke-green walls. Can't wait to get out."

"What are you gonna do?" Lina asked.

"Find a boy with a *big* dick," Terry said.

Felicia whooped. "You gonna find a boy who *be* a big dick."

"What's so great about dicks, anyway?" I asked.

Lina gave a loud yawn and said, "Seen one, seen 'em all."

"You find the right one, you get out of New Haven," Terry said. "You go to New York, Atlanta."

"I got a cousin lives in Atlanta," Felicia said. "She say the white girls got names like Ashley and Ruthie Sue. Say they got last names like *Titsworth.*"

Lina hollered with laughter, and I opened my eyes to keep from falling as we pushed and shoved at each other on the bench.

"What your tits worth?" Felicia asked.

"Five thousand," Lina said.

"Mine—five million," Felicia said. "Each." She stood up. "Any of you *guls* lesbos?"

After we all shook our heads, she lifted her tank top and yanked down the cups of her black bra, revealing her bulging breasts and dark, stiff nipples. "I should have showed these to Mr. Oliver," she said. "Could have gotten me out of cleaning toilets."

"You think he's good-lookin'?" Lina asked.

Felicia pulled up her bra and rearranged her tits beneath her shirt. "Dreamboat," she said. "But a dumb fuck."

"They say he from North Carolina," Terry said.

"What they got down there, besides firecrackers?" Felicia asked.

"Ku Klux Klan," Lina started.

"Baptist Church," I said.

"Preachers in pickups," Terry said.

"Cotton," Felicia said.

"Tobacco."

"Uncle Toms."

"Restaurants called Sambo's."

"Fried chicken."

"Barbecued beans that make you fart."

We laughed. Felicia squinted and then started to snap her fingers, her eyes seemingly growing narrower with each snap. She went over to the corner and dumped the contents of the wastebasket into the sink. Then she turned the wastebasket over her head. "Hey man. Nation of Islam, man."

"Huey Newton," Terry said.

"Bobby Seale," Felicia said.

"Malcolm X," Terry said. "Malcolm."

"You look like the Pope," I said, and Felicia took the pail off her head and pointed a purple fingernail at me.

"Why don't you guinea girls go to Catholic school?"

"Our father lost his job," I said.

Terry laughed. "Got kicked out of the Mafia."

Lina slitted her eyes and said, "You probably don't even know who your father is."

"I wish I didn't," Terry said. "Sick of him sticking his dick in my face."

"Bite it," Felicia advised.

"Chop it off," I said.

Terry snorted. "Then I gotta do the same to my brothers."

"I know your brothers," Lina said. "Your brothers stopped us one day on Division Street."

I was having trouble concentrating, but I finally bore down on my memory and brought up the image of the long dark brown car with a clicking muffler that had trailed Lina and me home along Division Street a few months earlier, soul music blaring. Then the car radio went dead and all we heard was the clanking muffler and the loud motor of the car. A boy leaned out of the window, whistled, and yelled, "Hey, spics!"

Lina turned and glared. "We aren't spics."

We kept on walking. The car slowed down more and continued to trail us. After a while the same boy called out, "Hey, guineas!"

Lina turned and put her hands on her hips. "What do you want?"

"Just looking," he said, and the boys in the backseat laughed. They began to call out taunts I knew were directed solely at Lina. I never was the object of male attention when Lina was around, and over the years I had learned not to turn when boys whistled so I didn't have to hear, "Not you, dogface, your *sister*!"

"Show us," the boys called out. "Come on, girl. Show us your white ass."

"I'm not white," Lina said. She pulled up her sleeve and held out her forearm for inspection. "I'm green. I got green skin."

"You got hairy arms, girl," one boy shouted, and another said, "You from the Planet Ape!"

"Same planet as you!" Lina hollered, and we laughed and broke into a trot, then ran home.

I looked at Terry. "We know your brothers," I said, even though I didn't have the slightest idea whether or not the boys in the car had been related to Terry. "Your brothers were the ones who set off the firecracker at the assembly."

We broke into raucous laughter.

The assembly had been called after the last cafeteria food fight and featured two speakers—a black lady and a white lady—from the city of New Haven social-work office. They stood up on the stage in the auditorium and talked into microphones that hummed and squeaked. They referred to themselves as *group facilitators*. Their goal was to *brainstorm* and *blue-sky* about eliminating *unnecessary racial tension* at Roger Sherman High. They told us if we just thought about it for half a second, we would see how stupid racism really was, since underneath we were all human beings. Then the white lady blabbed on and on about that experiment we were all so sick and tired of hearing about, about the brown eyes and the blue eyes, until somebody behind me grumbled, "Who care about eyes? It's the skin that counts."

Then the black woman stepped up to the microphone. "Let's

begin by brainstorming about the origins of racism," she said. "Any ideas about why we live in a racist society?"

Complete silence.

She raised her voice so she sounded like a television preacher. "I said, any ideas about why—"

"Some folks black, some white!" a voice in the audience rang out.

The woman nodded encouragingly. "Very good," she said. "Excellent start. Other thoughts?"

Silence, except for a few burps and laughter.

"Any thoughts on why racial tension is so prevalent in your school?" she asked.

"School run by the Mafia!"

"Principal's a nigger!"

"Lunch ladies white! Lunch ladies tell who to leave the cafeteria!"

The two speakers looked at each other, and then the white woman made a time-out sign with her hands and stepped up to the microphone. "We believe in conducting discussions in an atmosphere of mutual respect. Do you all know what Robert's rules of order are?"

"Fuck that Robert!"

"He an asshole!"

The black woman looked challengingly at the audience. "Do you think it's fair to call someone names if you don't even know him?"

"Show us."

"Bring Robert here."

"Take one look at his face and we say asshole or not."

A great roar of laughter and some scattered applause broke out, interrupted by a loud hiss from the back of the auditorium. We turned and saw a cascade of multicolored sparks burst off the back bench. Then came a pop, another shower of neon-green sparks, and a high-pitched whistle began to screech. It was the kind of earsplitting firecracker known as a Whistlin' Dixie, and it caused enough smoke and commotion to set off the fire alarm and send us all out into the courtyard, where we smoked cigarettes and passed joints until the fire department came and the *all-clear* finally sounded.

"Italian boy set off that Whistlin' Dixie," Terry said.

"How do you know?" Lina asked.

"Think a black boy would buy anything named Dixie?"

"Who cares who did it?" I asked. "I missed math. It was great."

Felicia yawned. "Those ladies at the microphone out to lunch," she said.

"Think we're stupid," Lina agreed.

"Think we're not supposed to see black and white when we look at other people," Felicia said. "They blind? They look at other people, what they see?"

I opened my eyes—half-closed with sleepiness from the pot—and looked at Felicia. For a moment I saw only the red veins in her eyes, and then the chocolate iris, which was almost identical in color to my own. Then the shrill bell that signaled the end of gym clanged, echoing for a moment afterward in my ears. We broke out the Visine and abandoned the sponges, the Bon Ami, and the toilet brushes as we wandered on to our next class.

Mine was Latin. Mama had made me sign up for it so I would have at least one class that wasn't completely full of black kids. The class was small and taught in the same room where they held Health. A crude drawing of a uterus, two long fallopian tubes stretched out as if to embrace and strangle the spectator, had been on the blackboard since the beginning of the year. Somebody had stolen the eraser.

We were translating a bunch of aphorisms from the worn-out textbooks. The first one, *Cogito, ergo sum*, fell to Raymond Williams. He looked down at his book and followed each word with his finger. "I'm thinking," he said slowly. "So I be." He looked up at the teacher. "Be what?" he asked.

The teacher looked puzzled. It felt like forever waiting for her to speak, and I wondered why I thought so much depended on her answer.

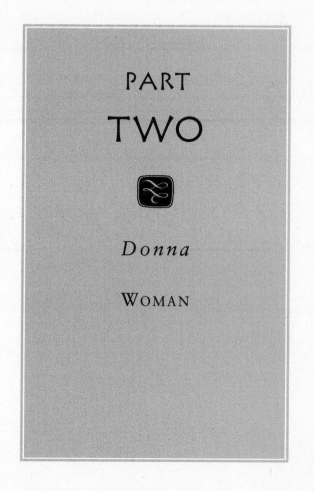

PART
TWO

Donna

WOMAN

TWO ITALIAN HITS

NOW LINA AND I had grown into what my parents called "dooie-donnies"—*due donne,* two women. I lived (regrettably solo) in a drafty apartment in Poughkeepsie, Lina and her husband, Phil, in a tony Wallingford suburb where the lawns shone emerald-green from 2,4-D. Whenever I went home—which wasn't often—our neighborhood looked more and more gutted, and the storefronts once known simply as *the baker's* or *the shoemaker's* were either boarded up or converted into pawnshops or twenty-four-hour Laundromats. My parents' home, which had seemed small to me even as a child, now seemed tiny as a miniature cottage placed beneath a Christmas tree. Because the foundation had settled unevenly into the ground, the whole house seemed to lean to the left, toward my grandmother's old house—recently occupied by a family of seven who came from (as Mama said) *Lord knows where.* I figured God knew where Haiti sat on the map, even if my mother didn't.

It was Babbo's birthday, and Lina, Mama, and I—exhausted from the unseasonably warm May heat—were slurping sour lemonade from twenty-year-old drinking glasses that once had been imprinted with hamburgers, fries, and golden arches, but that now bore only the big feet, Bozo hair, and toothsome smile of Ronald McDonald. Lina was chewing on her ice when Mama reported that some Yalie researcher was snooping through the neighborhood, hoping to interview some of the former workers at the now-defunct New Haven Pocketbook Factory—better known as *the Pockabookie Ladies.*

Lina spit her ice into her glass. "What's he gonna ask the Pockabookies—why they always wear black? Why they always shout *che si dice* across the street at one another? How many times a day they go to church, and how many whiskers they've got on their chinny-chin-chins?"

Mama said the researcher was a *she.* What's more—here Mama paused and lowered her voice—the researcher was *colored.*

Lina snorted. "That oughta go over big in this guinea neighborhood."

"It's going black now," Mama said.

To steer her off that well-worn subject, I asked, "How do you know what the researcher is like?"

"She went to Great-Zia Giulia's house," Mama told me.

"And Great-Zia probably slammed the door in her face," Lina said. "Probably thought she was peddling *The Watchtower.*"

"Say what you want," Mama said, "those Mormons have the faith."

Lina and I looked at each other and burst into laughter. "Jehovah's Witnesses, Ma," I said.

Mama rattled the ice in her glass. "I can't keep 'em straight."

Lina spoke slowly and carefully, as if she were addressing a toddler. "One kind is white and male. They have crew cuts and ride Schwinn bikes. The other kind is black and female. They walk and wear Easter hats."

Mama pushed out her lips in puzzlement. "Which kind can't dance?" she asked.

"Baptists," I said. "And the kind that can't talk are like the guy on the oatmeal box."

"Shakers," Mama said.

"QUAKERS!" Lina and I shouted back.

Mama frowned and crooked her finger at us—which prompted Lina to suggest she looked just like the ladies on the Ragú commercials—then disappeared into the kitchen to finish making dinner. Feeling lethargic, Lina and I took our inspiration from our father, who was lying on the sagging couch, fast asleep. While Mama rattled pots and pans, we propped our sweaty lemonade glasses on the worn carpet and lounged on the faded armchairs, pulling the dirty white stuffing out of the holes in the nubby fabric and then cramming it back in again.

"I feel guilty about not helping Mama in the kitchen," Lina said.

"Yeah, so do I," I said. "But not enough to actually get up and *do* it."

We sat there—*like two lazy bums*, as Mama would say—until Lina's husband, Phil, came back from the park with their two kids. Not even the noise of a toddler and a screeching baby could wake our father up from his deep sleep.

"Yo, Babbo," Lina said, snapping her fingers sharply in his face. "Yo, Birthday Boy—*svegliate*—wake up!"

When Lina finally roused Babbo from his sleep by kicking him once, in the shin, with her handmade Italian flats she had bought downtown on Chapel Street, Babbo lumbered over to the table and grunted with satisfaction to smell baked ziti cooling on the top of the oven. He then grunted with dissatisfaction as Mama detailed all over again, this time for Phil's benefit, the story of the researcher and the Pockabookie Ladies.

"Probably gonna write a book," Babbo said, ripping a hunk from the loaf of bread that Mama passed him. "Gonna force those ladies to say they were exploited by the factory."

Lina and I held our tongues—and were tempted to hold our ears—as Babbo went on and on about how, back then, the Pockabookies were damn happy to have a job. In those days people weren't too proud to pull a ten-hour shift putting handles on pocketbooks. It was honest work and put the *pasta e fagioli* on the table.

While we were eating our bruschetta and salami, Mama got up and fetched the ad that the researcher—*a sociologist,* Mama said, in a dubious tone—had placed in the weekly bargain newspaper, explaining the purpose of her study. After Mama read the ad aloud—pausing at phrases such as *work ethic* and *economic gain* and *division of labor*—Lina and I translated it for her.

"The researcher wants to know why the Pockabookie Ladies worked," I said.

"You work to eat," Mama said.

"She wants to know why some women worked and others didn't," Lina said.

"Easy—some husbands made more."

"She wants to know how it affected their families."

"Dinner was an hour later," Mama said.

"She wants to know how it affected their relationships with their husbands."

"*Fatti i fatti tuoi,*" Mama said. "As they say in America: MYOB." She pressed her lips together, and Lina and I laughed hysterically until Phil chided us. He didn't approve of the way we treated Mama.

"Bug off," Lina said sharply. "She's *our* mother." Which made us laugh even louder to cover our shame and our guilt that we—such modern, crazy girls—could have come from such an old-fashioned, dressed-in-black mother, who did not differ very much from the Pockabookie Ladies themselves.

❖

Here they come—*eccolè!*—the Pockabookie Ladies! The factory whistle blew at 3:59 each afternoon, and the drivers dumb enough to come down the avenue at 4:00 had to stop their cars for the long file of ladies streaming out of the factory. The Pockabookies did not believe in crossing at the light. They cut across the avenue wherever it suited them, like a horde of water buffalo charging across a river. If you sat in one of the waiting cars—or followed behind the ladies on the street—you heard nothing but a babble of Sicilian, the squish of their flat, padded shoes, and the fat swacks of their hands, which they used to slap and poke and prod one another to drive home the point of their stories. The Pockabookies wore nude-colored knee-his that plastered the black hair on their legs against their skin, sleeveless paisley muumuus in lurid color combinations, and, always, black crocheted sweaters on top. Each had her own black leather purse to carry, courtesy of the factory. The ladies appreciated such largesse. Who were they, anyway, to expect decent treatment from their employers? Just plain old Pockabookies!

When Lina and I were young, we looked upon the Pockabookies with absolute dread. Never mind Michelangelo, the Medicis, Mona Lisa, and all the folks we someday would learn about during our college art-history classes. For us, being Italian meant being *Pockabookie-issima*. Horrors!

Lina and I wanted to look and act like Marilyn Monroe—before she killed herself, of course—with sultry bedroom eyes, lush big lips and tits, and a rear end that curved like the back end of a Studebaker. Marilyn had *all-American* looks, said the magazines. We read *Life* in the waiting room of the dentist's office, and we believed it.

After a short conference with some of her older girlfriends, Lina told me the way to avoid becoming a Pockabookie was to drink a lot of ginger ale, a beverage that in our house was considered highly American. Lucky for us Babbo worked for a soda distributor, and we could swill all the Dixon Park ginger ale that we wanted. Unable to figure out why we suddenly had lost our taste for orange soda and root beer, Babbo brought home case after case of ginger ale. Then, after another conference with her girlfriends, Lina broke the bad news. "Not only do you have to drink tons of ginger ale," she said, "but you can't eat anything along with it."

I squinched up my face. "Sounds like Lent," I said.

"I think it's called a liquid diet."

Lina and I thought about the *cannoli* and *cornetti* that Babbo brought home from the bakery, the spumoni we got whenever we visited our aunties, and the frosted cookies that we ate at Communion parties and wedding receptions, and decided the Pockabookie Lady Diet could *vaffanculo* for all we cared. We didn't have a scale anyway and were weighed only at the beginning of the school year in the nurse's office, where we also had to bend our head forward to be checked for lice and listen to the nurse exclaim about how our hair was so *dark* and *thick* compared to the blond locks on the Irish kids at Saint Aidan's.

Looking for latent signs of Pockabookie-ism, Lina and I undressed in front of each other and reviewed our body parts. "You've got a fat *culo*," Lina said, tweaking my buttocks, and I said, "So you've got a flabby back" and grabbed a roll of fat above her shoulder blades until she yelped in pain. We both decided we had hammy upper arms, and to remedy the problem Lina swiped two moldy old volumes from a Funk & Wagnalls set that was rotting on the shelf in the church basement. Every night in our room we furiously swung *S–T* and *J–K–L* up and down in butterfly movements and jumped one hundred jacks, until Babbo shouted at us to stop shaking the whole house—unless we wanted to end up without a roof over our heads.

"You mean *floor*," Mama hollered. "Your father means the floor. We want a floor beneath our feet."

"Screw the *floor*," Lina said. "And who cares about the *roof*? Sky's the limit, baby."

Lina and I were going to be movie stars. Right next to the Pockabookie Factory stood a Mark One Theater, and every weekend the management catered to the local population by showing matinees imported from Italy. On Saturday mornings the manager climbed a tall ladder and rearranged the letters on the marquee to announce:

OGGI! OGGI!
DUE FILMI ITALIANI!

Then, in English—although we didn't have the vaguest idea why real Americans needed to know that the Mark One intended to play Italian movies—the sign was translated in smaller letters:

TODAY! TODAY!
TWO ITALIAN HITS!

The Mark One played anything and everything Italian they could get their hands on: spaghetti westerns and potboilers that featured B actors, an Italian version of *Dracula,* artsy films with Roberto Rossellini and Marcello Mastroianni, two-handkerchief sentimental dramas with Claudia Cardinale and Gina Lollobrigida. Sometimes they played American movies dubbed in Italian, like *Some Like It Hot* and *The Singing Nun.* Once they even ran *The Bridge on the River Kwai,* which made Lina and me wonder how they translated all that whistling into Italian.

People came from all over New Haven—in big dented cars with duct tape patching the vinyl seats—to crowd the theater. After the success of *The Godfather,* some of them sported the popular bumper sticker: MAFIA STAFF CAR: KEEPA YOU HANDS OFF! Lina and I were mystified by this. We had heard *The Godfather* was a movie where a man slept with a horse. We wondered why and how but were resigned to never finding out, since this movie had been banned by the Church and was listed under the heading CONDEMNED by our archdiocese newspaper.

Desperate to get to Hollywood, where we hoped to act in the very movies that *The Catholic Transcript* was so quick to condemn, Lina and I made halter tops out of the same red bandannas we had used for our Annie Oakley Halloween outfits. We rolled the cuffs of our shorts to the tops of our thighs and pretended we had on white go-go boots instead of our fuzzy pink slippers. In our room we practiced a song-and-dance routine that we intended—someday—to take on the road. We called ourselves "Two Italian Hits," a name that seemed vaguely reminiscent of the phrase Mama used to disparage women who put more than powder and lipstick on their face. *Bombshells,* Mama whispered in a fierce, urgent voice, as if these women were on the verge of exploding right in front of her like latent grenades. It was the same way she said *Sexpot* when the radio announced, that long-ago day at the beach, that Marilyn Monroe had committed suicide.

The Two Italian Hits fizzled out faster than fireworks. Only Lina made it on the stage, by acting as Fiona and Eliza Doolittle in the high-school productions of *Brigadoon* and *My Fair Lady,* roles that won her a scholarship to Hartt School of Music. But her schooling—and her career—was cut short when a Trinity College boy got her pregnant. So she married Phil. And had Pammy. And then, three years later, Richie. I went off to Vassar—back then, a former women's college that was not Catholic, which led Mama to suspect I was a dyke—then stayed in Poughkeepsie to work for a major greeting-card company.

Back home, on the day the Pockabookie Factory closed for good, the final whistle pierced the air at 4:00 P.M., and the ladies came out in a mob, one last time, each carrying a white vinyl box purse with a gold clasp in addition to the standard black leather pocketbook. For years afterward you could always spot former Pockabookies out in public by looking for that white vinyl purse, which became their trademark.

The factory stood vacant for a long time. Weeds grew up around the cement building, which was plastered with signs that stated THIS BUILDING IS CONDEMNED, and then the flimsy plywood fence surrounding it became covered with obscene half-

Italian, half-English graffiti. The Mark One Theater closed for good. And one day—shortly after I realized I would never return home for good again—the tractors came and demolished both buildings.

�֎

Mama's birthday came in June, just one month after Babbo's, and when I went back to help celebrate, Mama reported the researcher had made some progress. "She got some of the Pocka-bookies to *talk*," Mama said, her lips pressed tight together as if to indicate that she would never do such a thing.

"For fifty bucks an interview," Lina said, "who wouldn't?"

"They shouldn't *talk*," Mama said.

"They might need the money to eat," I said.

"Don't they have family to feed them?" Mama asked.

"Don't you read the newspaper?" Lina asked. "Old people these days are eating dog food."

Mama paused. "I see those oldsters in the grocery store, buying Chef Boy-ar-dee."

"Canned spaghetti: the equivalent of Alpo," I said, and Lina made bow-wow noises until Mama shook her head.

"I have Great-Zia Giulia over for dinner almost every other Sunday," Mama said. "But still she went on the interview. She asked me to drive her. Downtown of all places. I refused. But I heard she got someone else to take her."

A smile spread across Lina's face.

Mama looked at Lina sharply. "I might have known you'd be the one! And before, you couldn't be bothered giving Great-Zia the time of day."

Lina shrugged. "So what? I was curious. When we got down to Yale, I told the secretary Great-Zia didn't speak English very well, so I would have to go in and translate."

"So?" Mama demanded. "What was this researcher lady like?"

"She had a southern accent," Lina said. "She actually said *y'all.*"

Mama nodded her head. "Just like they do on TV."

"And she kept on using words like *gender* and *economic disparity,*" Lina said.

"So Great-Zia really *did* need a translator," I said.

"She acted like she needed a bodyguard," Lina said. "The whole time we were in the researcher's office, she kept her white Pockabookie purse on her lap, like the woman was going to steal it. After it was all over and she collected her cash, Great-Zia shook her head and asked me, *What was the point of all that?*"

"Didn't they issue checks?" I asked.

Lina smiled wickedly. "After the first day of interviews, the researcher found out that checks wouldn't cut it for the Pockabookies. They wanted cash on the nail, or they wouldn't cooperate. Great-Zia stashed her bills, and out on the street she hung on to her pockabookie for dear life, like a mugger was on every street corner."

"I've always wondered what the Pockabookies kept in their purses," I said.

"Rosary beads," Lina answered. "House keys, but never car keys. Laminated holy cards. A list of the Sorrowful Mysteries. A key chain from the Statue of Liberty."

"Freud says a purse represents a woman's vagina," I said.

Mama gasped. "Watch your mouth."

"Oh, they never stuck anything in *there,*" Lina said, "that didn't belong to their husbands. And even that, infrequently."

Mama gasped again.

"Close your eyes and think of England," I said.

"Or see Rome—and *die,*" Lina suggested.

Mama crossed herself as we burst into raucous laughter.

❖

The next time I came home was the Fourth of July, for a family picnic that Mama—because of the mosquitoes—insisted on holding out in the garage, with stinky citronella candles burning on the folding tables. Mama sat sentinel under the garage door, a turquoise flyswatter poised in her hand, ready to crush any bug that dared to enter. Pammy whined about not having toasted marshmallows for dessert, Phil complained of a headache, Babbo ate too many B&M beans, and the corker came when Baby Richie plopped his pants, and Lina discovered she had gone through the last diaper.

Lina stuck Richie into his car seat and asked if anyone wanted to come along on a diaper run. "I'll get a little exercise—why not?" was Mama's response. She got up from her chair, walked five steps over to Lina's new minivan, and sat down in the front seat, her flyswatter still in hand. Lina gave me a pleading look. I sighed, got up, and climbed into the backseat next to Richie. I cracked the window as Lina drove to the 24-Hour Store, which stood on the corner where the Pockabookie Factory used to be.

Because it was a holiday, the 24-Hour Store was crowded. Customers were in every aisle, from the car supplies to the dairy case. Mama clutched my arm. "Don't look now," she said, in what she probably thought was a quiet voice, "but we're the only white people here."

"No shit," I said, just as loudly. Then I looked over at her and realized, with dismay, that she still had the turquoise flyswatter in her hand.

"Leave that flyswatter in the car, Mother," I said.

She looked at me threateningly, the way she used to when I was a kid and she stood over me with a wooden spoon in her hand. "You never know," she said, slapping the flat part down on her hand. "You never know when you might need to use it."

I walked away. I went over to the candy aisle and selected an Oh! Henry bar. Even though I had been eating hot dogs, hamburgers, eggplant parmigiana, and lasagne all day long, I felt like I needed chocolate to get me through the rest of the evening.

As usual, Lina played the fussy consumer. In the next aisle over,

Richie was bawling and Lina was on the floor on her hands and knees, sorting through the big bales of Pampers and Huggies and loudly complaining, "They're all girl diapers. All's they have is girl diapers in his size." She stood up and looked angrily at the big black guy, dressed in a too-small red smock, who stood behind the counter.

"These are all girl diapers," she said. "Don't you have any boy diapers in size Large?"

The man stared back at her and smiled.

Lina squinted her eyes at him. "Lee?" she asked, in a much nicer tone of voice. "That you?"

"Lina. Hey, what's happening?"

Mama looked over, her flyswatter raised. She frowned when she saw Lina had left Richie on the ground to move closer to the counter. Mama went over and swooped Richie up. By then the smell of his diaper had gotten so bad I had to move two aisles away.

After an initial blank of memory, I recognized Lee as a guy from Lina's high-school class. I suspected, from the way they greeted each other, that Lina had done drugs with him—smoked pot behind the bleachers in the football stadium or snorted coke out in one of the wooded areas that students needed a car to get to, like Lighthouse Beach or Fort Nathan Hale Park.

After she had chatted with Lee a while, Lina finally asked, "You married?"

Lee shook his head. "Got myself a kid, though."

I looked over to see Mama's reaction. But just at that moment Richie howled and screamed in Mama's arms, which prompted her to smack him a good one, right on the butt, with her flyswatter. I opened my Oh! Henry bar, in spite of the fact that I hadn't paid for it, and began to nibble at the chocolate before I opened my mouth wider and gnawed on the nuts. Lina opened her Dooney & Bourke purse and ended up paying for both my candy and a package of girl diapers.

When we got back to Lina's minivan, Richie continued bawling. He didn't want to get into his car seat. "Get in!" Lina shrieked, in a nasal voice—as if she were holding her breath—while Richie arched his back and struggled. We all rolled down the windows on the way back, even though Mama said it wasn't safe to do that anymore in this neighborhood.

"Why do they—" Mama said, and I rolled my eyes, because I knew *they* always signified either blacks or Jews. "Why do they always say *what's happening?*"

"Why do guineas always say *che si dice?*" Lina asked.

"Because that's what you're supposed to say when you see someone you know," Mama said. "Someone you recognize."

"What does *che si dice* really mean, anyway?" I asked.

"I don't know," Mama said.

"You say it, and you don't know what it means?" Lina asked.

Mama shrugged. "Why do I have to know what everything *means* all the time? Why do I have to think?"

"Because you're not an animal," Lina said. "You're a human being."

Mama raised the flyswatter. Lina reached over to grab it. The steering wheel slipped and the van veered.

"*Madonna mi!*" Mama gasped. "Do you want to get us killed?"

Better dead than red was one of the slogans someone had spray-painted on the side of the old Pockabookie Factory. Next to it, someone else had scrawled, *Better dead than Italian.* As Lina struggled and then gave up trying to pry the flyswatter from Mama's hand, yelling, "Go ahead! Just go ahead and act like an old guinea lady, but leave me out of it!" I knew she was thinking along the same lines. The very Italian-ness, the Pockabookie-nish of Mama—her need to shake the throw rugs out of the second-floor windows and her obsession with cleaning the lint out of the dryer—was exactly what drove Lina and me crazy, because we knew we had inherited some of it, and the whole thing made us feel nuts ourselves.

Over the years, to deal with Pockabookie-ismo, Lina and I had tried turning it into a joke. For Christmas one year, I got Lina *The Mafia Cookbook* by Joseph "Joe Dogs" Iannuzzi, a former chef for the mob. Lina bought me videos of *The Godfather I* and *II* and a book called *How to Speak Italian Without Ever Talking.* This book showed black-and-white photographs of dark, swarthy men with spread collars and gold chains and women in calico aprons wielding rolling pins and wooden spoons, gesticulating to get their points across. Among the messages they conveyed in Italian sign language were *Go fuck yourself! Your mother's a whore! Holy Mother of God, why did I have to have such kids like you? Cool it, creepo!* and *Don't bust my chops, bonehead!*

When we got home and walked into the hot, steamy house, Phil was resting on a chair with a cold washcloth over his eyes, Pammy was stacking alphabet blocks on the floor to spell out SHUT UP, WISEGUY, and Babbo was snoring on the couch.

Lina gestured toward our father. "He's asleep again," she said. "I can't believe it; he's always asleep."

Lina dumped Richie on the floor and I listened, sickened, as his diaper squished. With the toe of her $125 flats, Lina kicked Babbo's leg. "Yo, Dad," she said. "Yo!"

Babbo came to, startled, with a snore.

"What means *che si dice*?" Lina demanded.

Babbo rubbed his bleary eyes and looked blankly at us— his two girls, with our slicked-back hair, thin thighs, and stick-like arms—as if he hardly recognized who was speaking. *"Chi sa?"* he said. "Who knows?" And then, as if the question had taxed his brain far too hard, he instantly fell back into slumber.

When I got back to Poughkeepsie, I looked up the expression in the nonverbal Italian dictionary Lina had given me. The photo showed a real *goomba*, his hair slicked back with Vitalis, gesturing with characteristic Italian friendliness at a Pockabookie lookalike who was crossing a street.

Che si dice? Hey, che si dice?

And the translation beneath: *How's it going? How you doing? With instant recognition, two Italians hail each other on the street.*

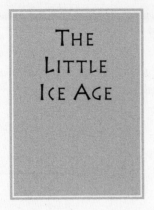

THE
LITTLE
ICE AGE

WHEN I GOT HOME for Mother's Day, forest fires were raging in southern California, a blizzard had buried the Midwest, and my father was snoring on the couch with the Weather Channel blaring on TV. During the week Babbo lugged crates of bottles through the rain, slush, and snow for the Dixon Park Soda Company. On the weekends, he experienced the great outdoors by watching the weather station for hours on end, gathering information on cold fronts, heat waves, hurricanes, and floods that never would reach his corner of Connecticut. *Just look at that,* he'd comment. *That's some frost they got there in Florida.* Or *Holy Mo, get a load of those houses. Twister smashed 'em to bits.*

He always smiled and folded his hands over his stomach as he reported the news, happy to have avoided another disaster. Then he sat back and let the weatherman take him to places he never had seen and never would visit: the Texas Panhandle, the Great Plains, the High Sierras, the Rockies. I liked to think he had a secret craving for adventure that hadn't been satisfied by his annual Knights of Columbus bus trip to Yankee Stadium. Lina said he was just too lazy to get up and change the channel. She got him a remote for Christmas once. He never figured out how to use it.

The morning of Mother's Day, Babbo's heavy body sagged the couch cushions, and his belly rose and fell as he snored. I crept past him to get a drink of water. Stepping into my mother's kitchen was like entering a time warp. For years the decor had been as static as a diorama in a natural-history museum—but instead of moth-eaten buffalo, desiccated tortoises, and black snakes that had lost their shine, the kitchen was full of tasteless ceramic objects, none of which would bring more than fifty cents at the local flea market. The refrigerator was studded with Pope John Paul and Pizza Hut magnets. On the stove were planted empty salt and pepper shakers in the shape of two ears of corn. On the counter loomed four majolica canisters in the shapes of a winter squash, an artichoke, an eggplant, and a pumpkin. All of these worn and chipped items were the object of a game Lina and I used to play called Name That Ugly Thing. Lina began by identifying one of the least offensive knickknacks in the house. I countered with yet another more hideous thing. Then the race was on to top each other.

The pink porcelain baby shoe with the purple pincushion in the middle.

The condiment dish shaped like a Venetian gondola.

The plastic Pietà on top of the TV.

The crucifix studded with seashells.

The coconut with the painted face that says, Welcome to Miami Beach!

The lamp that has a great horned owl on its base.

The Last Supper plate with the heads of the apostles worn off!

Most of the ugly things had been gifts—souvenirs from relatives who had dared to venture beyond the borders of New Haven to pay pilgrimages to shrines, visit fourth and fifth cousins in Florida, or take a Perillo tour (transportation, lodging, and meals included) to Italy. Every Saturday, Mama used to dust these reminders of other people's travels, always ending with a peach-colored conch shell from Sanibel Island that sat on top of the radio. She held it to her ear to listen to the pounding of the surf (nodding as if satisfied that the sound was still there) before she blasted it with Lemon Pledge and swabbed out the dirt.

I took a glass from the cabinet and drew some water from the tap, then swallowed the water in one gulp. I put the glass down in the sink. The house always had been spotless before. Now dust covered all the knickknacks, coffee stained the counters, and white mineral deposits dulled the faucets. Upstairs, the shower curtain was spotted with mold, and the hardwood floors were littered with dust bunnies. Babbo refused to get a cleaning woman after Mama had the stroke. "Phil and I offered to send someone over," Lina said, "but he wouldn't go for it."

"Maybe he's afraid someone will walk off with the family heirlooms," I said.

Lina snorted. "More like he thinks I should clean it."

Lina lived in Wallingford, only twenty minutes out of New Haven. I lived two hours away in Poughkeepsie. Although I drove home only once a month, I usually ended up scrubbing the floors and wiping down the bathroom tiles. Part of it was due to boredom. Babbo and I had nothing to say to each other, and after five minutes of watching those cheesy-smiled weathermen chatting about air currents, wind speed, and relative humidity, I was ready to *do* something. But more than anything, guilt inspired me to get out the mop and broom. *Mama would die if she saw this mess*, I thought.

Babbo was still asleep. I bypassed the broom closet where Mama always kept the buckets, disinfectants, and scrub brushes. I went upstairs and took the hall phone into the bedroom Lina and I used to share, curled up on my twin bed, and dialed Lina's number. She answered on the first ring.

"Oh, it's you," she said.

"Who were you expecting?"

Lina paused. "Is it springtime in the Rockies over there?"

I got up and closed the door to block out the sound of the TV. "Yes, and the Southwest is suffering from drought," I said.

"So," Lina's voice turned suggestive, "what was the temperature like in Florida?"

I had spent the previous weekend in Captiva with a company sales rep. "Oh, you know," I said, "the kind of hot and heavy that quickly turns to chilly."

"In other words," Lina said, "you hate this guy's guts now that you've slept with him."

"Bingo," I said. "I got a terrible sunburn too. My face feels paralyzed it's so tight."

"What did Babbo have to say about that?"

"He's asleep."

"Better expect thunder," Lina said.

"I've got my umbrella." I twirled the phone cord around my hand, then let it go again. "What's the outlook on your home front?"

"Phil took the kids to the park," Lina said. "That's my Mother's Day present, not to be Mommy for a day."

"What does that say about mommyhood?" I asked.

"Not much."

I clicked my tongue at her.

"Oh, I don't care," she said. "I'm sick of frosting cupcakes. And I'm tired of reading bedtime stories. I don't care if Curious George flies a kite or rides a bike. I wish he'd throw himself off a bridge."

"Then the Man in the Yellow Hat would get lonely," I said.

Lina paused, then assumed Mama's stiff, disapproving voice. "It's about time somebody put an end to that weird relationship. A man and his monkey. What kind of fool example is that for kids?"

I kept up the imitation. "Crazy nuts."

"Kooks," Lina said.

"Sick heads."

"Perverted turkeys."

We laughed. Lina and I always had mimicked Mama, but we had been doing it more and more since she had the stroke. It was as if someone had designated us to do the talking for her now that she had been robbed of her voice.

"Babbo and I are going to see Mama in about an hour," I said. My voice turned wheedling. "Meet us there?"

"Sorry," Lina said. "We already went this morning. We have to take Phil's mother out to brunch."

"You stink."

"I'll have a Bloody Mary for you," she said.

"Have two," I answered, thinking of the long afternoon ahead.

"Cheer up," Lina said. "The whole place is decked out for Mother's Day."

"What did you get Mama?" I asked.

"I made Phil go to the florist and pick up some mums. I couldn't handle doing it myself." Lina paused. "What's the use? She can't even see or smell them. She doesn't even know we're there."

"You don't know that for sure," I said.

"She doesn't even bat an eye when you sit down next to her," Lina said. "She just sits there in her wheelchair like—like a stuffed owl, her body all stiff and her eyes all glassy."

To me, Mama looked like a photograph of a nearsighted woman who had taken off her glasses. She didn't seem to be really there. Her face was as flat and impenetrable as the face painted on a mummy's coffin. Her body seemed as cold and hard as a whole chicken removed from the freezer, one that would take hours to defrost.

"It's creepy," Lina said. "I get scared looking at her. I know it's stupid, but I'm afraid if I touch her I'll turn to stone. After I visit her I want to run away and do everything I've ever wanted to do before it's too late." She hesitated. "Can you keep a secret?"

"Who do I have to tell it to?" I asked.

Lina's voice swelled with self-importance. "I'm having an affair."

I looked around the bedroom, suddenly reminded of the time I sat on this very bed and Lina swore me to secrecy before announcing she had smoked her first cigarette.

"Well?" Lina demanded, when I didn't answer.

"Well what? With who?"

"He's a lawyer."

"What kind—divorce?"

"He specializes in health-insurance claims," Lina said.

"Maybe he can help us with Mama."

"Fool," Lina said. "He already has. How do you think we met?"

I hadn't gotten very involved in the family finances. But I knew the insurance company had been holding back payments on some of Mama's hospital bills, and Babbo—who never questioned authority—practically had wiped out his savings trying to cover the charges. When Lina found out, she insisted on seeing a lawyer about the unpaid claims. Babbo was dead-set against lawyers. He called them *lupini,* a pack of wolves. But Lina went anyway, apparently ending up with one who was more of a wolf than Babbo ever could have imagined.

Lina spared me the complete story. Breathless as a teenager, she said she would save the *specifics* until she could talk to me in person. The gist of it was, she met the lawyer twice a week, at motels off the highway. He was on his second marriage and had a teenage boy who lived with his first wife.

Lina didn't mention—and I didn't ask—his name. I didn't want to know it. A name went with a face, and I didn't want to imagine him any more than I already did. I saw him as the kind who had a prominent collarbone and weathered neck, broad shoulders, heavy arms, and a stomach that quivered on the borderline of flabby. The whole thing made me feel sick.

"What about Phil?" I asked.

"What about him?"

"Don't you love him anymore?" I asked.

"Of course," she said. "On one level."

"Then how *can* you?"

Lina clicked her tongue impatiently. "You don't know. You can't even begin to imagine what it's like being married. How boring it all is, how much you feel like you're in a cage!"

"You should try to work things out," I said.

Lina was quiet for a moment. Then the tone of the experienced older sister came back into her voice. "You just don't understand. Phil doesn't *do* me the way Bob does."

Bob. I immediately pictured heavy cheeks that smelled of after-shave, a thick mustache going gray, and a full mouth that called my sister *baby*. Then I saw the darkness of the motel room, the cut-glass ashtray on top of the TV, the Gideon's Bible—never opened—in the nightstand drawer, the rumpled white bedsheets, the turquoise and orange bedspread, the shaft of light that came from under the bathroom door. I was sure Bob was the kind who didn't close the door all the way, who thought the whole world was delighted by the sound of his pissing.

"You better be careful," I warned. "Phil isn't stupid."

"That's what I wanted to tell you. I slipped up last week."

"Lina!"

"Relax, it wasn't Phil. It was Babbo. He caught me."

Lina left the Howard Johnson's off I-95 around two-thirty. Just to be safe, she always parked in the back of the motels and came and went through the rear door. But as she crossed the lot to her car, a Dixon Park Soda truck rumbled up the driveway. Babbo was making a delivery.

For a moment, Lina was paralyzed. She stood in the middle of the lot with the car keys in her hand. Babbo had to stop the truck to keep from running her over. He stared at her. Then he turned the wheel sharply and pulled the truck parallel to the rear door of the motel. He continued to stare at her through the truck window.

"So what'd you do then?" I asked.

"What the hell could I do? I got in the car and drove away."

"Why didn't you make up some excuse?"

"Like what? Hi, just dropped into HoJo's to buy the kids some saltwater taffy?"

"Anything would be better than letting him think—"

"Oh, what's the point," Lina said. "He knew. He knows. I just wanted to warn you. Things are pretty ugly between us."

"Did Babbo say anything to you?" I asked.

"That's not his style. It's the old freeze-out, remember? The stonewall effect?"

I remembered it well. Both Mama and Babbo met most everything they didn't like with the icy silence of disapproval. When Lina and I were young, our primary goal in life had been to *get away with things*. If we got caught, as we often did, Mama and Babbo turned their backs on us, like God was said to turn away from unworthy souls at the final judgment.

I didn't know what to say to Lina. The whole thing sounded seedy and gross to me. Before I knew it, I found myself lapsing into Mama's voice.

"You kids are rotten to the core," I said.

"Heading for trouble," Lina said.

"Gone to hell on a handcart."

Lina laughed bitterly. "Bad eggs," she said.

❖

After I hung up the phone, I lay on the bed for a while, staring up at the ceiling. Lina had so many things that I wanted—an old-fashioned house so quaint it looked like it should be dusted with glitter and stuck on a Christmas card, sharp-looking clothes, and two cute little kids whose faces, throughout the course of the day, reflected a fascinating gamut of emotions, from contentment to greed, disappointment to sheer bliss. Phil made enough money so Lina didn't have to work. Twice a week she went to the gym or took classes while someone else watched the kids and cleaned the house. She went on swell vacations—to Hilton Head, Lake Placid, and Nag's Head—once a year. Why anyone would want to throw all that away for an hour at Howard Johnson's was beyond me. But when I thought about the kind of person Lina was, it wasn't surprising. Although everything eventually had *worked out*, as Mama and Babbo put it, Lina had married Phil for one reason: because she was pregnant. From the moment the hasty wedding arrangements had begun, we all had been holding our breath, waiting for something like this to happen. It wasn't in Lina's nature to box herself in, and it was beyond our expectations that once there she would be content.

Wallingford was no place for Lina. The women who lived there frosted their hair and painted their nails. They walked the malls in split skirts and crisscross sandals and did lunch in pairs at least once a week. Their husbands wore lime-green polo shirts and khaki pants and played eighteen holes every Saturday. Phil, in part, fit that mold. After graduating from Trinity and studying nights for his master's degree, he had become a hospital administrator. He often worked late. Weekends he spent puttering around the yard. *The Lawn Doctor,* Lina had referred to him last time I visited.

"Keep your eye on that man," she said, as we sat on the back porch, watching Phil trim the hedges. "I fear for his soul. All that 2,4-D is going to his head. He donates on a regular basis to his alumni association. The doorbell rings after dinner, and he buys candy bars and raffle tickets from every goddamn kid. The other night he actually went to a Rotary Club dinner."

Phil stopped trimming. "I didn't say I would join."

"Let me know when you do," Lina said, "and I'll go stick my head in the oven."

"Sweetheart," Phil said mildly, "you wouldn't dare mess your hair."

Phil let Lina's barbs bounce off him. He was incredibly easy-going—the sort of decent, affable guy people always were *fond of*. Unless, of course, they happened to be in love with him. Which, for the past few months, I had happened to be. *Just a little*, I told myself. *Just a little*. I told myself it was a passing thing, some sort of wild crush that spun itself out of boredom, spiraled like a funnel cloud, mashed you flat, and then whipped away just as fast as it came. It was as ridiculous as the desire in summer for a fire and hot cocoa, a lust in winter for bare legs and lemonade.

I lay still on the bed, trying to forget about how much my sunburn itched and how tight I felt inside my own skin. I remembered the dream I had, just a couple of nights ago, in which Phil and I were making love on Lina's new lawn furniture, or the one from a while ago, when we were rolling over and over on the grass—in slow motion—against a sunset as drippingly pink and yellow as the ones pictured on the condom packages. I had those dreams once every few weeks. They made me feel warm and wonderful inside. Then my alarm went off, and I woke up in my dark, stuffy apartment, having to face another day at a job I hated, or staring at the bare back of some man I hardly knew, hoping he wouldn't stick around for breakfast.

It made me want to laugh with despair to think of how much trouble Mama and Babbo had gone through to raise us as good girls. Was it because of that, or in spite of it, that we had turned into the types who went into bars and hotels, ordering double drinks and double rooms for the afternoon, without the slightest hint of guilt or unease?

Just look at the two of them, I could hear Mama saying. *One carrying on with a lawyer, the other a hot pants over her own brother-in-law. Madonna, what a crazy family.*

I got up from the bed. Thinking about how low Lina and I had sunk made me want to scrub down the house. In the hall closet, I found a jumbo can of Lemon Pledge and a box of rags Mama had fashioned from Babbo's worn-out underwear. Mama never had believed in wasting good money on paper towels. Once a year she used to gather up all of Babbo's worn-out boxer shorts, cut snips in the legs, and pull the shorts, with great loud ripping sounds, into neat little rags. She wore a tiny, grim smile on her face. "Jesus Christ," Lina once said, "what in the world could she have been thinking of while she did that?" I didn't want to know, so I didn't answer.

I couldn't handle using my father's old underwear to dust the house, so I grabbed an extra box of Kleenex. I started to clean Mama and Babbo's bedroom, which had been forbidden territory when we were growing up. I still felt like I was breaking rules by going in there. The shades were down, making the room look as musty as it smelled. I popped them up to the top of the windows, flooding the room with sunlight, and opened one of the panes a crack. Outside, robins dotted the lawn and the smell of lilacs pervaded the air. It would be a perfect Mother's Day, I thought, for any mother who went out to enjoy it. But Mama never went outside now. And Lina had passed up her chance to go to the park, waiting for her lawyer to call.

Oh, it's you.

Who were you expecting?

Before I could begin dusting Mama's chest of drawers, I had to clear it off. Like almost every other surface in the house, the chest was covered with a lace scarf, and on top of that sat about ten of our favorite candidates for Name That Ugly Thing. There was a statue of Mary standing on a globe (the infant Jesus in her arms, her bare foot crushing a serpent's head) and a multicolored mosaic box, some of the tiles missing, in which Mama stored her holy cards and rosaries. There was a night-light, in the shape of Jesus standing with a lamb, that you could plug directly into a socket. An abalone shell sat next to a piece of petrified wood. I picked up the wood. It was cold, heavy, and glazed. My mother's cousin Vincenza had brought it back from the West Coast as a souvenir, along with a wax statue of a bear from Yosemite Park and assorted postcards showing Old Faithful at sunrise, full light, and sunset.

Once, when I was seven, I stole the petrified wood and brought it to school for a report I gave on the Ice Age. With a thorough butchering of history and geography, I claimed that the wood dated back millions of years to Neanderthal man and that the wood turned to stone when Asia and North America split into two and the glaciers came sliding down both continents. I also claimed it was a souvenir from my summer trip to California, a fact that Sister Saint John of the Cross duly reported to my mother after church the next Sunday. Mama blew her top. "Liar!" she said to me. "Thief. Sneaking behind my back, stealing my things." That petrified wood was an antique, she said. A real relic, worth a lot of money. I could have cracked it or broken it. I had the nerve. What did I have to say for myself?

I hung my head. "Nothing," I said.

Mama shook her finger at me. She'd teach me the meaning of saying *nothing*. For the rest of the day I was not allowed to talk to anyone, and Babbo and Lina were forbidden to say anything to me. The radio, TV, and phone were strictly off limits. If I had anything to say, I could just tell it to God. He would always hear my voice. He was always listening.

The silence that day was excruciating. Lina, bless her, wrote me a few notes, which she passed to me when Mama's back was turned. But other than that, I felt as cut off from the world as someone deaf and dumb. My lips kept moving silently, like the little old ladies in church who hunched over the altar, mumbling the rosary. From that moment on, I resolved to keep everything hidden from Mama. She did not deserve my confidence.

I used up a quarter of the box of Kleenex dusting the knick-knacks. After I knocked all the dust off the bureaus, the nightstands, and the headboard of the bed, I got out a laundry basket and threw in all of Babbo's clothes that were slung over the chairs. The clothes were rank and stiff with sweat, and I held each piece by my fingertips before I let it drop into the basket. Then I went to strip the bed. I paused before I took off the pillowcases. Underneath the pillow that had been Mama's, I knew I would find her nightgown—neatly folded and tucked away, just as it had been the morning she had the stroke and every morning of her life before that.

The first time I had come into the room to change the sheets, I found the nightgown beneath the pillow. It shocked me to find something that was so obviously *waiting* for Mama to come back. I didn't know what to do with it, so when I remade the bed I simply tucked it back under the pillow, deciding to let Babbo deal with it. But Babbo never moved it. Even though I was sure he continued, from force of habit, to sleep on *his* side of the bed, with his head on his pillow, and his body taking up only half of the mattress, he must have known the nightgown was underneath the pillow. Several times when I changed the sheets I left it peeking out from under the pillow, to give him an opportunity to move it. He still kept it there. I wondered how much of that decision stemmed from hope, and how much from habit.

I, too, was guilty of habit, of keeping my things in the same old place. Even though I hadn't lived in my parents' house for years, I still carried the key with me every day. It was attached to a silver key tag that depicted the Vatican. The inscription said *La Città Eterna*. The key ring sat at the bottom of my purse, along with all the rest of the junk I needlessly toted around: compacts that spilled powder, breath mints that had fallen out of their foil liner, a tube of Vagisil, pens that had run out of ink, my birth certificate laminated in plastic, a St. Christopher holy card that said on the back CATHOLIC: *In case of accident, call a priest.* Mama had given me the card when I went away to college, acting as if I were embarking on a long journey around the world, instead of a two-

and-a-half-hour drive across the Connecticut state line to Pough-keepsie. *You never know,* she said. *You never know what will happen.*

Once a week I tried to clean out my purse, dumping the contents onto my nightstand and vowing to put them somewhere else. But then I left them there for days, until I got sick of looking at them and threw them back in. Mama did have a point. You never knew what you would need or what would happen. Or at least I liked to think so, because my life had become so overwhelmingly predictable.

For the past five years I had written verses and supervised production of the Catholic greeting-card lines at Special Moments Stationery, Inc. Lina poked fun at my job every chance she got. "Special Moments!" She snorted. "Sounds like a feminine-hygiene product to me." She lowered her voice into a whisper. *"For those days when you really need to feel fresh. When douching just isn't enough . . ."*

Mama always hushed her. If I had to work, Special Moments was a good place, because I got boxes of greeting-card samples, which I regularly surrendered to her. "Just look at this," she said to my aunts, fanning out the assortment of cards as if they were a winning hand in pinochle. "Look. Birthdays, weddings, showers, funerals. They even put her in charge of the cards for Catholics." Mama rearranged the cards in a neat stack. "Do you believe some people pay a buck seventy-five for just one of these things?" She put a rubber band around the middle of the stack and snapped it with satisfaction. "Free," she said.

On my birthday, Mama always sent me one of the cards I had given her. She did the same thing on holidays like Thanksgiving and Easter. After her stroke, I missed getting mail from her. For in addition to the cards, every week she sent me a letter. She wrote it on Sunday night, and Babbo, who must have suspected a bomb sat in every corner mailbox, personally delivered it to the post office on his way to work on Monday morning. The letter, written with a nineteen-cent Bic stick on plain white tablet paper, arrived at my apartment every Wednesday. *I went to the Feast of Saint Paul dinner. The manicotti was good, but the sausage and peppers—too oily. The Rosary Society is making potholders for the Holy Redeemer bazaar. Father John wants more $ to fix the organ. Last year he wanted more $ to fix up the vestibule. It's always something. I hardly see that sister of yours these days— too busy with her own life, I guess. Babbo's on the couch, sleeping. The mass for Nonno and Nonna is this Thursday. I'll go out to the cemetery after and plant some geraniums. Somebody stole the flowers off Zio Tuilio's mother's grave. What's the world coming to? What a shame. And isn't it something about Gino? So young! You never know when God will call your number.*

When I turned over the envelope, a newspaper clipping usually fluttered to the carpet. Mama sent obituaries with almost every letter. Some of the names I barely recognized—third cousins of my parents, a bank teller who had waited on Mama for twenty-five years, a church usher. Others I knew well—nuns, neighbors, the lay helper from my catechism class. *They gave her two columns and a photo—quite the spread,* Mama wrote. Or, *Look at this, only a couple of paragraphs. He really got gypped.*

Mama seemed to thrive on other peoples' deaths. The minute she heard the thump of the newspaper hitting the front porch, she went out, fetched it, and turned straight to the obituary page. If she recognized one of the names listed, she immediately called my aunts, arranged a car pool for the wake, ironed her black dress, and planned for an early supper. Then she went down to Frankie's Newsstand and purchased another copy of the newspaper. "Today I knew somebody," she proudly told Frankie as she handed him her quarter.

She carefully clipped the obituary from her newspaper and put it in a faded red Macy's gift box whose cracked seams were reinforced with Scotch tape. Just before All Souls Day she went through her yellowed clippings to see who she should remember in her prayers. The clipping from the spare newspaper she sent to me, expecting me to put it in my own box. I refused. The pictures of the dead people—always dated from years before so they looked as if they had passed away in the bloom of youth—creeped me out so much I immediately crumpled the clippings. The newsprint left stains on my hands like the black smudges the priests ground into the foreheads of the faithful on Ash Wednesday.

After I finished gathering up the laundry, I pried the window open all the way and shook out the scatter rugs. I thought about how Mama and Babbo had visited me only three times total in all the years I lived in New York. Once while they were there, they got into a dispute over the name of Babbo's cousin's mother. Mama insisted she was called Ziata, short for Anunziata. Babbo stuck to his guns. "Her name was Ziela, short for Graziela," he kept repeating.

"You're wrong," Mama said.

"She was related to me, not you," said Babbo.

"So what?" Mama asked. "Does that improve your memory? You got a head like a sieve for names." She turned to me. "Go get that clipping I sent you," she said. "That'll prove it."

"I'm not sure you sent it to me," I said.

"I send you everybody who dies."

"But I don't think I have Ziela."

"*Ziata*," insisted Mama. "Go get your box and I'll find her."

"I don't have a box," I finally admitted.

Mama's face grew stony. "I send you those clippings special," she said. "And what do you do? You throw them out."

I shrugged and kept quiet. Unlike Lina, I had never stood up to Mama. I had listened to what she said and then done the opposite thing the moment she turned her back. And for the most part, Mama assumed I followed her instructions. For instance, she kept on sending me clippings after she found out I had no box, simply adding more detailed commentary in her letters to convince me of the person's worth. *He always gave Babbo a fair deal,* she wrote. *She was a nice person—I never understood why she didn't get married. This one on the Monsignor is worth saving. Imagine, he knew three different languages!*

As much as I hated the obituaries and the harping on religion and death, I still missed Mama's letters when they stopped coming. On Wednesdays, no matter how many catalogs and bills filled my mailbox, I felt something was missing. I found myself calling Lina more, to find out what was going on in the neighborhood. "How the hell should I know?" she said. "I don't have time to read the newspaper."

"What's the word from Babbo?"

"Since when does he ever talk?"

"Do you ever see Aunt Marga or Aunt Fiorella?"

Lina clucked her tongue. "Those dried-up old cunts," she said.

Lina hated our aunts. She was still bitter because some of them hadn't sent her a wedding gift when they found out she was pregnant. Feeling only slightly more generous, Mama cashed in six books of S&H green stamps and presented Lina with a two-slot Hamilton Beach toaster.

❊

Babbo woke up just as heavy thundershowers were lumbering across Alabama and Georgia. "I thought I heard you moving around up there," he said.

"So why didn't you call out and say hi?"

"I figured you'd come down soon enough." He winced and held his leg as he sat up. "Darn arthritis has got me again." He squinted at me. "Your face is red as a lobster."

"I went to a tanning salon."

He glared at me. "That's good money down the drain."

I shrugged. "It's a nice day," I said. "Is it supposed to last?"

"How should I know?" he said.

"You're watching the weather news," I pointed out.

"You got to wait half an hour before they give the local conditions."

The blare of the TV suddenly was too much to take. I went over and snapped off the power.

"When do you want to go visit Mama?" I asked.

"Now's fine," Babbo said. "They're probably done giving her lunch." He slowly got up. "I got your mother a geranium."

"I saw it on the kitchen table."

"Did you bring me a card for her?" he asked.

"It's in here." I motioned to my purse.

Babbo frowned when I took out my keys. "You've been driving all morning," he said.

"So I'll drive some more," I said.

"My car is bigger," he said.

"There's only two of us," I pointed out. "Besides, I'm blocking you in."

We went through this tussle every time I visited. I refused to ride with Babbo, because he drove ten miles an hour in a forty-five-mile zone. Babbo hated to be driven by anyone, especially a woman. He was suspicious of my Toyota. When he bumped his head putting the geranium in the backseat, he said, "Why don't you buy American?"

"Because the Japanese make them better."

"They're taking over the country," he grumbled.

"Last time you said the blacks were doing that," I said.

"Them too, with their civil rights," Babbo said. "What rights did we have when we came to this country?"

I held my breath, waiting for the old melancholy tune that both Mama and Babbo liked to bang out, like some rusty percussive music on a tin bucket and washboard. *It was raining cats and dogs when the boat got to New York. We stood in line for six hours with nothing to eat or drink! When we finally got to the desk the immigration officers spelled our name wrong! We were too scared to correct them! We weren't proud in those days! We*

lived twelve people in a three-room apartment above a bakery!
We ate day-old bread and were thankful for every crumb we
could get! My father worked on the wharves from three A.M. to
three P.M. We kids shoveled snow, delivered newspapers, and did
whatever we had to do to earn a penny! I braced myself for the
torture of hearing this family saga one more time, but Babbo
spared me. Still, what did it matter? I had already heard it, and
rehearsed it all, in my head.

I started the car and backed out of the driveway. The minute
we were on the road, trouble began. Babbo was a backseat driver.
All the way to the convalescent home he pointed out every peril
that stood in our path: blind driveways, sharp turns, members of
the animal kingdom from dogs to squirrels to birds, drivers who
didn't know where they were going. "Watch it," he called out on
the corner. "They come around that curve like a hurricane, one
hundred miles an hour. Stoplight ahead."

"I see it," I said.

"That yellow turns to red in the blink of an eye."

"So I'll brake," I said.

When he wasn't playing traffic cop, Babbo took on the role of
tour guide. He acted as if I had moved halfway across the globe
and the neighborhood I had grown up in had been destroyed by a
nuclear bomb and rebuilt from scratch. The truth was that everything—from the run-down houses to the shabby storefronts and
boarded-up movie theaters—looked exactly the same. "That's a
new deli there," he pointed to a store that was at least five years
old. "You can get some good pastries at Luccino's. A couple of
crooks held up that jewelry store."

"You told me that last time."

"Puerto Ricans," he said. "From Bridgeport. Dope addicts. It's
just not safe anymore. Nowhere is. There's a character on every
street corner. Pothole ahead. Watch it."

By the time we got to Saint Ronan's, my nerves were jangling.
The convalescent home, a four-winged complex surrounded by

open fields, sat at the bottom of a hill. The parking lot was crowded, and Babbo insisted on getting out and directing me into the last tight space. I hardly had enough room to get out of the car and reach into the backseat to take out my present. On the other side of the car, Babbo struggled to get out the geranium plant. He looked forlorn standing there, the flowers bright red against the gray of his worn-out polo shirt. The petals were starting to shatter.

We crossed the parking lot. The pollen from the neighboring field made me sneeze. The moment we entered the lobby we were hit by the smell of rubbing alcohol and boiled broccoli. The front hall was decked with brightly colored posters like a pediatrician's office. Red crepe-paper ribbons and white fold-out bells hung from the fluorescent lights. On the back wall a cord was strung with multicolored construction-paper letters that spelled out *Happy Mother's Day.*

Babbo set the geranium down on a table outside the nurses' station.

"What are you doing?" I asked, even though I knew.

"You're supposed to check in," he said.

"Nobody else ever does."

Babbo pointed to the sign, heeded by no one but himself, which commanded visitors to register their names in the guest book and obtain passes before entering. He parked himself in front of the window while the receptionist, obviously on a personal call, twisted the phone cord around and around in one hand, smiling and laughing. Finally she took the phone away from her ear, cracked the window open, and asked Babbo in a brusque voice what he wanted.

I turned away so I didn't have to listen to their inevitable argument. The receptionist told Babbo he could go right on in. Babbo insisted on following the rules. Finally she crammed a piece of paper through the window, asked him to sign it, and dug up two laminated cards. Babbo clutched the passes as if he were a five-year-old boy about to gain admission to an amusement park. He held one out to me.

"We don't need those," I said. "Just put them in your pocket." I started to stalk off down the hall.

"Where are you going?" he asked. "It's to the left, not right." From the tone of his voice, I knew he was accusing me of not visiting often enough. I clutched my present and followed him. He came to Saint Ronan's every day after work and spent Saturday and Sunday afternoons with Mama. He sat next to her in the easy chair, reading the sports page from end to end. Then he read the front page and the want ads—God knows what for—before he put down the paper and fell asleep. Lina told me that when she came to visit Mama she often found Babbo snoozing in the chair. "Just resting my eyes," he said.

Mama's room was at the end of the second wing, across from the showers. Her roommate, who also had suffered a stroke, was named Evelyn. She always lay on her back in bed, her white hair brilliant against the faded pillowcase, her arms like withered sticks on top of the bedspread. There were no flowers or cards on her nightstand. "Nobody ever visits her," Babbo said as we walked by her bed.

Mama—or a strange, silent shadow of who she used to be—sat in the exact same position as the last time I had seen her. The nurses always strapped her in her wheelchair and turned her parallel to the window, with her good side toward the doorway and her bad side—with the drooping eyelid, sagging cheek, and crooked mouth—hidden. She was dressed in a navy blue robe. Her hands hung in her lap like weights, and her feet looked like they were glued to the wheelchair rests.

"Hi, Mama," I said. The false cheerfulness in my voice made me sound like I was talking to a two-year-old. I took a deep breath before I went up to her, leaned over, and did what I always dreaded: deposited a dry kiss on her surprisingly soft cheek. She blinked. Babbo handed me the geranium. He moved a water pitcher, a paper cup, and a box of tissues off the nightstand and onto the windowsill. He pushed the big pot of yellow mums to the side.

"Those must be from Lina," I said.

He grunted. He put the geraniums directly in front of the mums, then sat in the easy chair facing Mama. I went over to Evelyn's side of the room and got another chair. The cushion made a soft farting noise when I sat down on it.

I bit my lip. Sometimes I wished we could just sit there with Mama and respect her silence. But we had to talk. The conversations were inane when we tried to include Mama and equally ridiculous when we ignored her.

"Well," Babbo said loudly as he looked at Mama, "we got ourselves a gorgeous day here. Pretty as a picture. The sun's out and the air is just right. No traffic at all. Coming here was smooth sailing."

I bit my lip. *I got so mad at Babbo I almost hit a truck,* I felt like telling Mama. *Babbo was braking so hard on the passenger side, I'm surprised his foot didn't go straight through the floorboard.* The fact that Mama probably wouldn't understand anything I told her made me feel giddy. I knew I could say any number of horrible things to her and she would just have to sit there and take it. Fortunately, Babbo was there to keep me in check.

"Babbo brought you a geranium," I said to Mama.

"A nice-looking geranium," Babbo said, louder.

"She doesn't need a translator," I said to Babbo.

"She has trouble hearing."

"She's not *deaf.*"

Babbo glared at me. I ignored him and looked at Mama. "And we brought you some cards," I said.

"Nice cards," Babbo said loudly. "She wrote them all by herself." He gestured at me. "Show them to her. Read them to her."

I got up to get my purse. "I'll just show them," I said.

"Read them," he said. "And while you're up, fix her glasses."

Mama's eyeglasses—silvery-gray frames with thick lenses—had slipped down her nose. I carefully pushed them up again. She didn't even blink. I sat down next to her and opened the cards. The one I had brought home for Babbo had the words *A Prayer for a Mother* embossed in gold on heavy white stock. A red rose on a long green stem decorated the page. Inside was my typical chingy-changy rhyme scheme, ending with:

> *and all the mothers everywhere*
> *may God this good day bless*
> *but you alone are special to us*
> *—miles above the rest!*

I read it aloud to Mama in a soft, self-conscious voice. Babbo had forgotten to sign the card, but I still said "Love, from Babbo" at the end, as if his signature—crooked and not very familiar-looking to me, since he rarely wrote anything—was present.

Then I read my card. I hadn't written it. I had picked it out at a Hallmark shop. I must have stood in front of the rack for fifteen minutes, rooting through the selection, bypassing all the ones that would imply that Mama was the best mom a daughter could ever have, the ones that would call her warm, wonderful, and compassionate, the ones that would baldly state I loved her. My card showed a robin sitting on a tree. The verse was short and sweet.

> *A little bird has come to say*
> *Warm wishes for Happy Mother's Day!*

After I read the cards, I handed them to Babbo to put on the nightstand. Babbo took the one with the robin on it and turned it over. "Hallmark bought you out now?" he asked.

I shook my head.

He held up the card. "You paid money for this?"

"Obviously," I said. I turned around and got out my present. Babbo frowned as he took in the size of the package, the red and blue paisley foil wrapping, and the extravagant red ribbon and bow.

"Where'd you get that fancy wrapping?" he asked.

"Macy's."

"They gift wrap for free?"

"Not anymore," I said.

"What's in there?"

I pointed to Mama. "It's supposed to be a surprise."

Babbo sat back and watched me open the box. Inside was a navy blue velour robe with white piping on the collar and cuffs. It wasn't all that different from the robe she had on, but it had been the only thing in the entire lingerie department that was appropriate for Mama. Her wardrobe, before she had the stroke, consisted of a black dress worn to mass, novenas, and funerals; a flowered dress for weddings; and for everyday wear, a black pilly cardigan sweater, several pairs of sleeveless shirts two sizes too big for her, stretch slacks, and low-heeled Cobbie Cuddlers. Lina and I had been in despair over her clothes for years. As teenagers, we had hung back from her or marched on ahead, embarrassed by her dowdiness. As adults, we gave her new sweaters and dresses that hung in her closet with the tags still attached. She acted as if only sluts paid attention to what they put on in the morning. "Fancy duds," she said, "for fancy ladies."

Picking out the robe at Macy's had been almost as excruciating as picking out the Hallmark card. I made the mistake of responding to a saleslady's *May I help you?* not with a noncommittal *Just looking* but with the specific *I'm looking for a gift.* That was just the opening the woman was searching for. *A gift for whom? What size did my mother wear? What colors did she like? What kind of material did she prefer?*

I couldn't stand to be put on the spot like that. "I'm looking for something sensible," I told her, rudely turning my back. Ordinarily I loved everything about shopping—the screech of hangers being pushed aside as I combed through the garments, the hum of the lights, the *ding-ding-ding* of department-store bells, and even the innocuous Muzak that, inappropriately, failed to crescendo when you found just the right item for just the right price. But because I had been looking for a present for Mama, I found myself shopping like Mama. I was brusque with the saleswoman, suspecting her of trying to railroad me into buying something beyond my means. I grabbed at the garments and inspected the price tag before asking if there was a clearance rack. I made my choice and grimly pressed my lips together as I reached into my purse to pull out my wallet. I even paid with cash, not a credit card. Then, ashamed of my behavior, I took the escalator upstairs and shelled out ten bucks to have them gift wrap the present.

I held up the box and displayed the robe to Mama, then passed the box to Babbo.

"That's just like the one she's got on," Babbo said.

I shrugged. "So now she has another one."

"What does she need two for?"

I pressed my teeth together in the back. "It's supposed to be a present!"

He fingered the robe, then put the box on Mama's bed. "Tanning salons," he said, with just enough of a sneer in his voice to let me know he hadn't believed my story for a second. "Cards that cost two dollars. Gift wrap. Expensive presents. You better learn how to save for a rainy day."

Every day of my life is rainy, I felt like telling him. *So why save for it?*

"I make good money," I lied.

"For now, maybe. But what about the future?"

"What about it?" I asked.

Babbo gestured at Mama. "Something like this costs a lot of money. You got good health insurance? You got savings?"

"Just because Mama had a stroke doesn't mean I'm going to have one."

"They say—"

"Who says?" I asked.

"The doctors," he said. "That it runs in families."

I shrugged.

"That one with the beard, the Jewish one in the hospital, he even told that sister of yours she better watch her step, cut back on the red meat, and not take those birth-control pills—" Babbo's face grew red, from both anger and embarrassment. "So what does that sister of yours do? She laughs at the doctor. She laughs at this Dr. Klein, so even he says to her, 'When you're young, you think nothing is ever going to happen to you.' He says to her, 'Just remember what happened to the dinosaurs!'"

I laughed, a little shrilly. "What do dinosaurs have to do with it?" I asked. "They've been extinct for millions of years."

Babbo shook his finger at me. "That's right," he said. "Because they couldn't see what was coming. Selfish. Stupid. Living like there was nobody else in the world to think of but themselves. You want to be the same way?"

Babbo rarely looked me straight in the face. But when he fixed his eye on me with the intensity of an animal about to jump upon its prey, I could tell he was trying to figure out how much I knew about Lina and *this affair of hers*, as he would call it. A blush spread across my face and gave everything away. He looked disgusted, as if I were in cahoots with Lina, or as if I were the guilty party.

"Hey, look," I said. "Just because you're mad at Lina doesn't mean you have to take it out on me."

He sat back in his chair, triumphant. "Who said anything about her?" he asked.

"It's always the same thing," I said. I unconsciously looked over at Mama, then looked away. "Whenever Lina did something wrong I got punished for it. She stole from the drugstore, so I couldn't play outside for weeks! She stayed out too late with boys, so I got locked up in the house!" I kept on talking, all wound up with self-pity, like some blond-out-of-a-bottle actress on the three o'clock soap opera. "I'm sick of it!" I said. "I'm not Lina. And I'm not Mama. I'm not going to have a stroke! So why don't you let me live my own life?"

Babbo glared at me. "Who knows what your life is?" he said. "You come and go, here and there. You got your own agenda. So follow it."

I fingered my car keys in my pocket. "I'm going for a walk."

"Fine," Babbo said.

"I'll be back soon."

"That's perfectly all right."

I despised myself for keeping on talking. "Do you want anything from the vending machines?" I asked.

Babbo stared straight ahead at Mama. "I came here to visit," he said.

I pushed my chair back, walked past Evelyn (whose eyes were now closed), and went down the hall. The overworked, overweight nurses were making their rounds, pushing their carts in and out of the rooms. I couldn't stand their brisk and efficient movements, their loud voices, and their ugly watches with round faces and black bands, which they consulted every time they dispensed medicine or wrote something on their charts. It was always *time* for something with them. Now it's time for juice, they said. Now it's time to get changed. Time for showers. Time for bed. It wasn't that I didn't appreciate the care they gave Mama. But the fact that they saw my mother reduced to this— that they bathed and diapered and fed her, washed her bottom and wiped the applesauce that dribbled down her chin—made me want to look away from them in shame.

In the old days, Mama would say, *daughters used to take care of their mothers!*

I started to seethe inside. I got so angry I almost answered her out loud: *This isn't the old days!*

I walked down to the end of the hall, where the south wing met the east. In the activities room, the more-alert patients came to visit with their families. The room was long and flooded with sunlight. Floor-to-ceiling windows looked out upon an open meadow. Beyond that lay an apple orchard, where the gnarled trees already were covered with healthy white blossoms.

The room was more crowded than I had ever seen it. The older people here didn't look as if they were permanently fixed in their wheelchairs, but as if they had just sat down to take a short ride. Some of the patients grasped metal walkers. All of the generations were here: grandparents, parents, teenagers, toddlers, even crying babies. A man in a straw boater was playing a medley from *The Sound of Music* on the piano. As he launched into "My Favorite Things," I thought about how much the whole scene reminded me of a wedding. On a table in the corner of the room, a plastic tray of cookies sat next to the ever-present dull silver coffee tank. I went over, took a Styrofoam cup from the stack, and filled it with the evil-looking black liquid. Whoever made the coffee at Saint Ronan's believed in doling out strong doses of bitter brew. I drank it anyway.

From my chair in the corner, I surveyed the room. The decorations on the bulletin boards, like those in a kindergarten classroom, changed from season to season. Mama had been here long enough to run the entire calendar: Valentines made from doilies, green leprechauns, Easter bunnies, witches and jack-o'-lanterns, turkeys and pilgrims, snowflakes cut from white construction paper, and nimble little elves and reindeer that pranced from floor to ceiling. The central bulletin board sported a large multicolored sign that declared TODAY IS THE FIRST DAY OF THE REST OF YOUR LIFE! Beneath it sat a frail old woman in a wheelchair. A corsage was pinned onto her dress, and in her lap sat a photo album. A middle-aged woman—obviously her daughter—was flipping the pages and pointing out the pictures.

I watched them jealously. I wished I were anyplace else but where I was. I wished I were sitting next to Phil at a restaurant, my foot grazing his underneath the table. Lina had all the luck, I thought, and none of the ability to appreciate it. But she could hide her ingratitude pretty well when it served her purpose. She would be drinking her Bloody Mary right now, laughing with Phil's mother and teasing the kids, as if the world were one big hunky-dory place in which nobody had the need to keep secrets or the bad taste to fuck or puke or get sick. Why couldn't I belong to such a world, where on Mother's Day, families gathered at all-you-can-eat brunches to sip champagne and orange juice and nibble on croissants and ham and eggs? Everyone would be polite and perfumed and civilized. Nobody would talk about bad drivers or bad weather, nobody would use the words *buck* or *kook*, nobody would put a price on things, nobody would harbor grudges that went back years and years, nobody would dredge up the past or make dire warnings about the future.

I shifted uncomfortably in my chair. My back itched from sunburn, and what Mama always had referred to as *down there* felt suspiciously sore. I nibbled on the Styrofoam edge of the coffee cup. This is it, I thought. I finally got it, the big fat clap. Gonorrhea, Florida style. Herpes, à la Captiva. All thanks to a little-known sales rep for Special Moments Stationery, Inc. Why had I gone on that trip? Before we even left, I knew that I had nothing in common with him, except that we were both on the make. By the third day, I was frying on the beach while he stayed inside the hotel bar, drinking Dos Equis and watching tennis on the wide-screen TV.

Was I that lonely?

Me and thousands of others. Yes, yes.

As the piano man in the straw boater launched into "Climb Every Mountain," I looked around at all the families, trying to convince myself that they were stuck together with just as fragile a glue as the kind that held together my own family. Then I looked down at my hands. The webs of my fingers were covered with shreds of flaking skin. I'm getting old, I thought. I'll never meet anyone. I'll never have children. Babbo's right, I might have a stroke. Then who will take care of me? Lina, at least, had Pammy and Richie. They may grow up to despise her, but they still would look after her. No one would look after me.

I grew overheated and restless as I drank the coffee. The pounding finale of "Climb Every Mountain" sent me out of the recreation room and back into the hall, where I had to press myself against the wall to avoid bumping into a nurse's cart. I went back to Mama's room. Mama sat as rigidly as ever in her chair, like a plastic figure permanently glued on a piece of doll-house furniture. Babbo sat just as motionless, his eyes shut and his hands braced on the armrest, as if he were on a plane that was about to take off. Someone passing by the room who did not know their situation would be hard-pressed to say who had had the stroke. Mama's wheelchair would be the only giveaway.

Babbo let out a little snore as I sat down. I sat there for a long time, just looking at Mama, at the brittle gray and black curls that surrounded her forehead, the lenses in her silver glasses that glared in the sunlight, and her crooked cheek, which hung like a dog's jowl. Her skin was pale and translucent as the glaze on a doughnut, and her lip was stretched on one side, as if to reflect her dissatisfaction. I had to bite my own lip to keep from crying. I should be good to Mama, I thought. What if she never recovered? What if she died? What if I never saw her again? There was so much to say that had never been said, that would get lost, forever, if we didn't connect right now.

I thought I would tell her that I loved her. Instead, I remembered her tight voice, the petrified wood, and the gritty bar of Lava soap (made with real volcanic ash) that she used to thrust between our lips. *I'll wash your mouth out,* she hollered, whenever she caught us lying or swearing. I was sure that bar of soap still sat in one of the kitchen drawers, the corners all gnawed and full of our sharp teeth marks, and I felt rage, dark and bitter as the coffee I had just drunk, boil up within me.

I leaned forward and brought my mouth close to my mother's dumb, still ear. *Mama*, I started to whisper, *my mouth is a volcano. My crotch is on fire. I remember everything. You slapped my face so hard when I got my first period you almost gave me a black eye! The time you fitted me for my first bra, you pulled the tape measure so tight you practically strangled me! This is how I've turned out, Mama: I hate my job. I feel like some crazed bird cooped up all day in the office. But when I get home, I'm lonely. I shop too much. I overeat. I take a Sominex and go to sleep with the TV on. I screw guys I can't even stand! In the morning I look in the mirror and can't believe how old and ugly I'm getting.*

It was all right there, on the tip of my tongue, and I could have shot it all out like a spitball through a straw. But not a word got said. Because Mama blinked. But she did not open her eyes right away—she closed them, as if to shut herself off from me, and from her mouth came a wild bark, a harsh, garbled sound that seemed to come out of the bottom of her soul. It sounded like the desperate noise of an animal pinned down on a veterinarian's table, the rough growl of an evil spirit or incubus, the crazy cry a man might grind out of you in bed. I could not have imitated it if I tried. But because my mouth was open and I had been set to speak, it made me wonder if it had come from deep down inside of me.

The noise frightened me so badly I instinctively turned to my father. "*Babbissimo*," I whispered, just as I had called him when I was a child and jumped into his arms at the first sound of thunder. *Daddy, dear big Daddy, protect me.* But Babbo's eyes remained closed. The only indications that he even was alive were the long breaths that whistled out of his mouth and the short bubbly breaths he took back in.

I looked back at Mama. Her face, once again, was as blank as a clock without hands. Then the fan snapped on, breaking the silence. As the air from the ceiling vent began to ruffle Mama's hair, a close, cloying odor filled the room. I stood up—looking one last time at Mama and Babbo—before I fled the room.

As I walked down the hall to the nurses' station, I tried not to look through the doors at the other patients. But it was like being in a locker room: No matter how hard you tried to avert your eyes, you still caught glimpses of embarrassing parts of other people's bodies. Instead of pendulous breasts, flabby butts, and stippled thighs, I saw feet stiffly positioned on wheelchair rests; brittle, shaking hands; twisted faces; and pink scalps shining through thin gray hair.

At the nurses' station I rapped on the window, and a woman with frosted blond hair and thick pink lipstick opened the glass.

"My mother just soiled herself," I said.

She took down Mama's name and room number and closed the window. I turned away and slowly walked back to Mama's room. I stood in the hallway, just outside the door. After a few minutes, a Filipino nurse—small and sympathetic, dressed in a pressed white uniform that made her look like a tiny angel—came down the hall. "You need some help with your mother?" she asked.

"God," I told her, "you can say that again."

NOTHING GOOD IS EVER GOOD ENOUGH

ONE CHILLY, RAIN-SPECKLED night in March, I responded to a personal ad. I'd like to blame a bag of Chee·tos for this rash act. But I have only my lonesome self to censure. After a dreary week of scrawling sentimental greeting-card jingles, I smuggled my Chee·tos (beneath my coat) into the entry of the three-story home where I lived. No use letting the neighbors know I was turning into a junk-food pig. While I checked my mailbox (empty), I heard moaning—female—melt from beneath my landlord's door. I paused on the landing and wondered, for a moment, if that lamentation did not come from some vast and lonely cave within myself.

Two breathless flights of stairs later, I discovered my bathroom ceiling was still leaking and my heat was on the fritz again. Since I didn't dare return downstairs and chew out the landlord, I shivered, then huddled beneath a smelly, mustard-colored wool blanket on my fold-out couch. My muscled lout of a landlord gave me goose bumps in more ways than one. To avoid indulging in my latest lame fantasy *(he came upstairs to fiddle with my thermostat and ending up fiddling with . . .)*, I ripped open the bag of Chee·tos and hunkered down with the want ads.

I vowed to limit myself to one salty Chee·to for every APT FOR RENT ad I read. Fortunately, the rental market in Poughkeepsie was booming. Chee·to Number 106 had just passed my chapped lips when I idly turned from all the apartments I could not afford to the men I felt I could no longer live without.

MEN SEEKING WOMEN

I kept eating. And reading. Why? Because my sister had a house and a husband and I did not. Because I was pushing thirty and no closer than a baby to understanding the answer to this question: What did men really want?

One thing and one thing only, my mother had warned me— and Love Connection's long cattle call for Free Spirits, Uninhibited Ladies, and Sensual Sun Goddesses seemed to prove her right. Although serious lip service was given to candlelit dinners, long motorcycle rides, and walks on Poughkeepsie's nonexistent beach, the subtext was loud and clear. *Friendship first,* claimed these European Gentlemen and Bad Boy Poets. None of these big spenders bothered to shell out the additional fifty cents per word to add the obvious: *fucking second.*

The only ad that emphasized brains over bodacious bodies came from a college teacher who claimed to enjoy architecture and literature *(you know who Rilke is—and like to read him. In 750 words or less, tell me why).* As I considered responding, I sucked the Chee·to between my lips so dry it resembled the ghostly white bratwurst-on-a-stick sold at church carnivals. Surely somewhere in the Hudson Valley sat some reasonably unugly guy who could outshine this dreary word-counting pedant. Maybe I didn't have the nerve to tell my landlord to jack up the heat instead of the rent, but couldn't I at least say what I wanted in the romance department?

I licked the orange powder off my fingers and took up a Paper Mate pen.

LIGHT MY FIRE! *(Or at least help me get up the gumption to tell my landlord to fix the furnace.)*
My name is Angel, yet (according to my mother) I'm any thing but.
Boys always 1) looked at my sister; 2) looked at me; 3) then quickly looked back.
I spent the night of my senior prom watching Escape from the Planet of the Apes.
In college I slept with three of what we laughably called Vassar men. One actually wore a black beret.
While doing it!
After college I took the first job offered, chirping insipid verse for a gagulous greeting-card company.
My biggest professional challenges: staying awake and pretending that intercubicle flatulence doesn't exist.
Last year I was seduced and abandoned (with bacterial vaginitis) by a Special Moments traveling salesman. One round of killer antibiotics later, I still suspect I smell like a day-old prawn on melted ice.
Sometimes I wonder how I've evolved from the girl who deemed Waiting for Godot *the most meaningful piece of literature in the Western world to the woman who goes to the mall and tortures herself by looking at the diamond engagement rings.*
(Just for the record, I prefer platinum over gold, and emerald cut over marquise. Also oral sex over penetration.)
But enough about me! You are:
Non-beret wearing.
Gainfully employed.
Do not suffer from irritable bowel syndrome.
29–33.

Own interesting real estate.
Fond of Italian food.
Willing to go down on me.
Blond.
Possess parents who herd reindeer in the Arctic Circle.

I put down my Paper Mate. Counted my words. Even with the first twenty words free, this tall order would set me back $114.50. But I had just spent my last $1.83—in the form of eight quarters, one desperately recovered from the floor of my '81 Toyota—on this bag of Chee·tos that was making my heart as well as my stomach feel sick.

I spent the rest of the evening writing the college teacher a five-paragraph essay complete with truthful introduction *(Warmth is something lacking in my life . . .),* three main points *(I liked* Sonnets to Orpheus, *Frank Lloyd Wright, and . . . and . . . salty food!),* and lame, apologetic conclusion *(I've never done this before, so please forgive. . . .).* Since I was on word 749, I left off the object of *forgive* and signed my name as *Angelina.*

After I ran out in the rain and dropped the thin white envelope in the mailbox, I wanted to thrust my arm down the chute and retrieve every one of the 750 words. What if he liked to read aloud poetry—that didn't rhyme? What if he turned out to be the Vassar philosophy instructor who'd given me a mercy C-minus and scrawled on my final paper, *See me for problems with cause and effect?*

Dr. Symbolic Logic had a near-illegible hand. The letter I received was written in precise blue cursive script that could only come from the nib of a fountain pen, and was signed *Dirk. Dirk Diederhoff!* Instant fifty points off—until I remembered I was christened Angel, a name ordinarily associated with midget Hispanic jockeys. Still. This *Dirk* taught German and liked to visit historic houses. As I carefully memorized his suggestion to meet at a local coffeehouse, I wondered how I would last through even an espresso with such a man—me who didn't have the foggiest how to pronounce Rainer, who barely knew Le Corbusier from Palladio, whose knowledge of German culture was gleaned from watching *Hogan's Heroes* and listening to Wayne Newton sing a song I thought was called "Donkey Shame."

On the other hand, Dirk had not requested a photograph. My heart pounding as if I'd already swilled sixteen cups of espresso, I grabbed the phone, dialed his number, and at his severe hello I stopped myself just in time from introducing myself as *Angelina Diederhoff.*

"It's Angel," I said. *Shit.* "The one you wrote to." *Retard: He'd probably written back to twenty!* "I'm free all day this Saturday." *Loser!* "Around three?"

"Three then," he said. "At Java."

"Wait," I said. "How will I know it's you?"

"I'll stand just outside the door."

"What if it's raining?"

There came a chilly silence. "I own an umbrella."

※

March was long, cold, and rainy. Dirk Diederhoff did indeed stand under a black umbrella, which he solicitously held over me as he shook my still-gloved hand. Although I had pictured him like Friedrich the smooth-faced boy soprano in *The Sound of Music* or the impoverished, rough-bearded Professor Bhaer from *Little Women*, Dirk resembled neither. Pale, honey-blond, gold-bespectacled, he could have been the cover model for a Junior Year Abroad program—posed for contrast between a petite, solemn Japanese girl and a too-tall smiling Nigerian. I had to press my thighs together for fear he'd hear my crotch singing a joyous version of *"Deutschland über alles."*

Dirk collapsed his umbrella and we went inside. At the counter, he unzipped his dark green tundra jacket and reached into the back pocket of his gray cords. "This is on me."

I wanted hot chocolate with whipped cream and the biggest slice of cheesecake in the case. "Just a plain cup of coffee," I told the purple-haired girl behind the counter.

"House Blend," she corrected me, in such a superior tone that I wanted to yank all six silver rings from her snotty snoot.

Dirk (I found out later) did not approve of her Ferdinand-the-Bull look either. He got a cup of the Kenyan and we retired to a window table splattered with sugar. As if preparing a line of cocaine, Dirk folded an ecologically-correct napkin (soft as sandpaper) into precise quarters and pushed the sugar in a straight file to the edge of the table.

Before the coffee had cooled enough to sip, Dirk gave me the opening lines on his *curriculum vitae*—undergrad at University of Minnesota, master's and Ph.D. from Michigan—then backtracked and told me: born on a wheat farm fifty miles from St. Cloud. Two brothers, both farmers, both married with kids.

Dirk was on a one-year—*renewable*—appointment at Vassar. Where, he added, he was very disappointed in the caliber of the student body.

"I went to Vassar," I said.

His pale cheeks turned pink.

"Do you know anyone in the philosophy department?" I asked, and when he shook his head, I said, "*I* always did my homework."

"Don't get me wrong," he said. "Some of the students are bright. The rest are resentful if I correct their spelling. And wear—like that girl behind the counter—earrings in inappropriate places."

Apparently tongue studs did nothing to help these students' already poor pronunciation. After Dirk told me he gave out a lot of Fs, I sat up even straighter. I could see why the bowels of his students would loosen when he strode into the classroom and set down his briefcase. He seemed impatient to hear the wrong answer when he asked, "What languages do you have?"

The sip I took of my House Blend burned my lips. "English. A smattering of Italian. And French."

"How many years of French?"

"I started in seventh grade."

"And you were inspired by?"

"*The Undersea World of Jacques Cousteau.*"

"Really."

"That was a joke," I said, even though it wasn't. "The real reason was because I'd heard about this novel, *Madame Bovary.*"

"Overrated, don't you think?"

I nodded. Vigorously. After I had outgrown *Heidi* and *Little Women*, I had pulled Flaubert from the public-library shelf, expecting to find one dashing man after another mounting the insatiable Madame (who lay splay-legged on a fainting couch, moaning something vaguely reflexive like, *M'amuse me, oh m'amuse me!*). Instead, the book opened with some stupid schoolboys squabbling about a hat.

"*Madame* was disappointing in English," I said, and as an alternative to *incomprehensible,* I told Dirk, "and . . . well, just plain *dense* in French."

My initial meeting with Dirk proceeded much like my interview with Vassar's admissions officer. Thankfully, Mama—her black box purse grimly clutched between her gnarled hands—was not squatting in the waiting room, ready to greet Dirk with this sole question: "*Quanto* is this going to cost me?" When prompted by Dirk, I described my favorite authors, my strongest and weakest subjects, and my short- and long-term goals. After half an hour of nimbly fielding his questions, I looked down and saw that I had squeezed my empty coffee cup so hard it had collapsed.

"I guess I'm not getting a refill," I said. When he didn't laugh, I asked, "Tell me—why did you write that ad?"

Now it was his turn to sit up even straighter. "Why did you respond?"

"Ever since my mother died, I feel lonely a lot," I said. "I mean, it's hard to meet others in my line of work."

He nodded. "It was puzzling at first. But now I've accepted I'll never meet anyone at Vassar."

"Aren't there other young professors?"

"Either they're married or—" He paused, and I thought he was searching for some more mature way to describe those female profs that we callow undergraduates had portrayed as *hailing from the Isle of Lesbos* or *belonging to the Family Van Dyke.* "Or they're tenured."

"What does that have to do with it?"

"I'm not on a tenure-track line."

Since I could never remember whether it took a long or a short A, I avoided *caste* like the word itself had leprosy. "What does that make you, then," I asked Dirk, "an Untouchable?"

"*Persona non grata,*" Dirk said. "That means—"

"I work in a cubicle," I said. "No need to translate."

I could tell Dirk wasn't used to being interrupted. He started to take another sip of his coffee. But his Kenyan was kaput.

Dirk then launched into what seemed a carefully planned pitch explaining why he had advertised in the personals. He did not do bars or work out in a gym. Although plenty of other faculty did not share his scruples, he thought it reprehensible to prey upon his students. He sought an intellectual equal. I nodded, thinking, *Good thing I didn't ask him what interested him most about architecture: the floor or the ceiling.*

"You haven't told me much about your family," he said.

I thought about Mama frozen in her wheelchair and now even colder beneath the ground. I remembered Babbo sweating out the summer in front of a nonoscillating fan, nursing a warm can of Old Milwaukee as he watched reruns of *McHale's Navy.* Then I thought of Lina—currently house-hunting and quarreling with Phil about whether or not they really needed two Jacuzzis.

"Do you have a pen?" I asked.

Dirk pulled a fountain pen from his shirt pocket. I uncapped it and reached for one of the brown napkins. "Since you enjoy architecture," I said, "here's a blueprint of my parents' house."

I drew for Dirk the cramped kitchen where Mama had stirred her sauce on Sundays, the living room stuffed with dusty knick-knacks where Lina and I had spent winter afternoons fashioning dollhouses from shoe boxes, the dining room where Babbo presided over Easter and Christmas meals, and the sloped ceilings under which we all slept. "When there was a lot of snow," I said, "the eaves creaked and it felt like the roof would collapse at any minute."

Dirk examined my crooked drawing. "I'll show you the meaning of snow." He unfolded one of the napkins all the way, took the pen, and drew me his parents' farm—the house, the outbuildings, and all the fields—in scale, with each square inch representing fifty acres. "Imagine all this in a blizzard," he said.

The thought of so much land—never mind so much white stuff—was staggering. My eyes must have widened, because Dirk said, "Of course, I'm the third son."

"Like in Grimm's fairy tales?"

"Exactly. I've chosen not to farm, so none of this will be mine. Except"—he pointed to the northwest corner of the napkin—"twenty acres here, mortgage-free, where the wind blows the hardest." He took another glance at my drawing and pointed to the front porch, where I had sketched the curlicued-metal screen door marked *L* for Lupo. "What can you tell me about the family inside?"

"A lot," I said. "But maybe some other time."

Obviously I had made some cut in the selection process, because Dirk reached into his shirt pocket, pulled out his Academic Planner, and wanted to know if I was free to get together two Thursdays from now.

Imagining the long list of women he had to interview, I rudely asked, "Why not next Thursday?"

Dirk flushed. Next week was spring break. He was going back to Minnesota—which was enjoying a thaw—to help his father paint the barn. White, not red.

❊

When he came back, I found out that Minnesota had been snowed under. Rainer was pronounced *RHY-ner*. Heine was not pronounced like that childish euphemism for a man's gluteus maximus, and Günter Grass's last name had nothing whatsoever to do with a lawn. I learned all this—and much, much more than I ever wanted to know—about Teutonic literature. According to Dirk, one of my great attractions was my ability to really discuss things. "You have no idea how stultifying it is," he said, "teaching bored undergrads how to say, *Where is the exit?*"

"How *do* you say that?"

"*Where is the exit?*" Dirk smiled. I waited a couple of weeks, only to find out that this was as close to telling a joke as he would ever get.

Armed with farm-boy thrift—and a salary not much larger than my own—Dirk also had to count his nickels. We hung out in coffee shops, and when the weather finally broke we went for long walks in the park and visited Lyndhurst, Boscobel, and Van Cortlandt Manor. While admiring the roped-off rooms of former robber barons, Dirk spoke strongly against conspicuous displays of wealth and rampant materialism; meanwhile, I mourned the death of my platinum-and-diamond engagement ring.

As we stood in Frederick Vanderbilt's suggestively carved and molded bedroom, Dirk told me, "You know, Angel, you're the first woman I've met in Poughkeepsie who drinks the tap water and isn't ashamed to admit it."

"I can't afford Evian," I said. "But just for the record, I wouldn't mind drinking it. Or living here. Or sleeping there," I said, gesturing to the eminently fuckworthy four-poster bed.

Dirk immediately turned to his guide. "*The posters of Freder-*

ick's bed are modeled after the baldacchino of Saint Peter's Basil-ica in Vatican City. But what's the matter, Angel? You look extraordinarily pale."

"I need some fresh air," I said.

We stepped out onto one of the many porches of the Vander-bilt Mansion. As we looked out onto the wide, brown Hudson River, Dirk asked, "You don't really want to live in such a place, do you?"

"Beats a garret," I said. Then I shrugged and laughed and told Dirk about how Lina and I used to lie beneath the sloped roof of our cramped, depressing bedroom, constructing our Dream House room by room in our imagination. Greedy Lina wanted a Venetian palazzo, a chateau in the south of France, and a pent-house with a view of Central Park.

"I would have settled for a Swiss chalet," I said. "You know, like the kind on a cuckoo clock?"

Dirk nodded. Approvingly. And said something about a *Haus* that was *klein.* Or *kleine.*

House. Small. These simple words I could understand. But in spite of Dirk's patient drills in the rudiments of German grammar, I still mixed up the feminine and the masculine, and I could not tell the *who* from the *how* and the *where* from the *why.*

❊

In gradual progression—as if mastering the solid pronouns before tackling the juicier verbs—I held Dirk's hairless hand, I kissed his peach-tinged lips, I leaned into his muscular chest to receive his embrace. I always greeted and said good-bye to Dirk at the bot-tom of the stairs—right outside my landlord's door—where I hoped overhearing some heated activity transpiring inside would spur Dirk to pursue me two flights up to my garret, where together we would make the leaking rafters shake. But as April slid into May, I wrote in my diary: *I'll bet Dirk waits until he turns in his final grades before he fucks me.*

Dear Diary: I was right. At the end of spring semester, I knew sex finally was on the syllabus when a bottle of white wine rested on the passenger seat of his Volkswagen hatchback. It was Thursday—two-dollar night—and Dirk was taking me to the kind of movie theater where no popcorn was sold in the lobby. After we sat down in Dirk's favorite place—the exact middle of the theater—I whispered, "I crave salt."

I don't know what I expected in response to this statement. But my fleeting, ludicrous fantasy (that he'd strip off his twill shirt and chinos and offer up his whole body, like a salted celery stick, for me to lick) got dashed to the ground when he said, "That's your Mediterranean blood speaking."

"Huh?" I said. "I mean, *Wo bitte?*"

"*Wie bitte.*"

"Pardon me?"

Dirk looked over his shoulder—a not-so-subtle hint that I could stand to lower my voice. "I meant nothing offensive. I just think you're genetically coded to live in warmer climates. You crave salt because it helps the body retain fluids."

"In other words, I look bloated?"

Dirk gave me a puzzled look. "Angel. You're acting like . . . *a woman.*"

"Imagine!"

Dirk's milky cheeks flushed. "Does high blood pressure run in your family?"

"No," I said. "But PMS does."

Dirk raised his eyebrow. "*Ich nehme das Wetter, wie es kommt.*"

"Translation?"

"I take the weather as it comes. You, of course, obviously fight it."

"How do you know?"

"From that story you told me. About your mother and the lemons."

How I wished I never told Dirk this tale: that on summer days—when emotional temperatures in our home pitched past the boiling point—Mama parked the peevish, quarreling Lina and me on the front porch with a plateful of salted lemon slivers and made us suck on them until our lips burned. Lina and I actually liked this punishment, which only proved Mama's point: We were always looking for an excuse to make a sour face. *If it's hot, you want cold,* Mama said. *If cold, then hot. For you, nothing good is ever good enough!*

Dating Dirk made me think she was right. As the theater filled with other two-dollar, tap-water-drinking types, I tried to damp down my dissatisfaction with Dirk. Although I liked the way I could complain about my childhood to him, his response seemed so *middle American.* Clean and sturdy as winter-hardy wheat, he made me feel like some tropical agricultural product that had to undergo rigorous inspection before it could be permitted beyond the U.S. border. I regretted every second I spent trying to adjust myself to pass his scrutiny and every hour (and there were many) that I devoted to grading his behavior and obsessing over this question: Was he The One? I may have bombed symbolic logic, but I'd had enough disappointment in my life to realize that if A wasn't B, then at some point C would have to become good enough.

The lights lowered and the credits rolled up on this German art film called *Das Haus ist blau.* Since all of the movies we saw were foreign, I'd grown accustomed to sitting next to Dirk during brief scenes of nudity (they bothered me only insofar as the breasts shown looked firmer and higher than my own). But less than ten minutes after the screening, it became obvious that *Blue House* was going to show a lot, lot more than two suckable nipples. Here was a moist vagina. Then came a highly improbable long pole of a penis. Then close-ups of the man's firm, clenching buttocks and the woman's gritted teeth were accompanied by the now-moot subtitles:

I'll fuck you into the ground.

Give it to me. Again. Again. Again!

Dirk leaned over and whispered in my ear, "Are you as embarrassed as I am?"

I was aroused. So badly I thought people sitting two rows ahead and behind probably could smell my vaginal odor. But I simply nodded. Dirk took my arm, and before I knew it, I was being ushered out. We were not sitting on the aisle, and for the rest of my life I knew I'd remember the hiss of a man's voice—"Sit down!"—and the sick squish that sounded forth when I stepped on a woman's Doc Martens in my haste to reach the exit.

On our short walk through the lobby, I kept my eyes so studiously averted I memorized the worn pattern on the once-red Oriental carpet. Out on the street, it was cold and raining.

"I left my umbrella inside," Dirk said.

"Just leave it."

Dirk put his arm around me. "Angel. I apologize. Deeply. I failed to do my homework. I had no idea what sort of film that was or I never would have taken you to see it."

The flecks of water on my face felt clean and good, and as we walked across the slick parking lot, the thought of the wine awaiting us in the car washed away some of my peevishness. "You don't have to keep saying you're sorry," I said, even though Dirk had said it only once.

"I should have read the reviews. I had no idea it would be so . . . tawdry."

My sole consolation: At least Dirk had not gone up to the cashier and asked for his four dollars back. He unlocked the passenger side of the car. When I got in, I bent down to retrieve the wine bottle from the car floor, and as I fastened my seat belt, I cradled the bottle between my legs.

He pointed to the cork. "That's for us."

"I figured as much."

"If—when we get back to your place—you'll invite me up."

"I will."

As a former Eagle Scout—and farm boy at heart—Dirk carried a Swiss Army knife at all times. "I have a corkscrew on my Swiss."

"I own a corkscrew," I said. "And two wineglasses."

But I didn't own much else. That became apparent the moment I opened the door to my drafty studio, futilely jacked up the thermostat, and invited Dirk to sit down on the only item in the room that had a right to be called furniture: my Castro convertible couch. Dirk immediately gravitated toward my books, stacked on Dixon Park Soda crates my father had swiped from the warehouse. Dirk proved himself to be more of a man than I originally thought by bypassing Chekhov and Nabokov and picking up the framed photo of Lina that sat on top of the crates. The picture showed Lina standing—without Phil—on the porch of her new house. Homeownership agreed with her—or at least it improved her posture. In any case, Dirk seemed all eyes for Lina's thrown-back shoulders and her proud and provocative breasts.

"So this is your famous sister," he said.

"Mm-hmm."

"You say it like you don't want it to be so."

"I told you. She always got all the attention."

"Why isn't her husband in the picture?"

"He's very good-looking," I said. "I'd find him a distraction."

Dirk put down the photo. "Why don't you visit them more often?"

"They're busy. Settling down into their new house. Which is bigger and better than the big huge one they had before."

Dirk fell silent. For all his lofty talk about intellectual versus material wealth, he, too, was eaten away inside by real-estate envy. Although he never said as much, I suspected that Herr and Frau Diederhoff—being *of the land*—considered their scholarly youngest son mentally deficient because he didn't want to till 1,500 acres.

I sighed. "It's so dreadful to be poor."

"You're not poor," Dirk said. "You have a roof over your head."

"I was quoting," I said. "One of the opening lines. Of *Little Women*."

"I've never read it."

"There's a German professor in it."

"How is he portrayed?"

"As the love interest of the heroine."

"Maybe I'll look at it sometime."

My throat went dry. I swallowed, and my throat felt even more parched as I imagined Dirk reading this line: *Mr. Bhaer could read several languages, but he had not learned to read women yet.* "I'm sure you'd think *Little Women* was very sentimental," I said. "The characterization of the professor is . . . well, hokey. I mean, he lumbers around saying doofus things like, *You haf no umbrella! Gif me your ear! That is not our omniboos!* and *That ist gut!*"

"*Das,*" said Dirk. "*Das ist gut.*"

"And he keeps correcting the heroine's grammar."

"I see." Dirk paused. "Well? In the end, does she finally get it right?"

Personally, I loathed the way Jo March settled for promenading with the Professor on muddy roads while her prettier sister Amy and the highly desirable Teddy Laurence took conjugal strolls over velvet carpets. Nevertheless, I said, "It's considered a happy ending."

"That means marriage," said Dirk.

"How do you know, if you've never read it?"

"It's written by a woman," Dirk said, and before I could wedge in a word of protest, he added, "and it's a nineteenth-century domestic novel, probably written in the tradition of Jane Austen, for an audience that would consider spinsterhood a very unsavory prospect. Thus the little woman undoubtedly marries the professor."

"There are four little women," I said. "Three of them get married and the other one drops dead."

"What of?"

I wanted to say *heartache*. But I couldn't remember whether Beth March suffered from pneumonia or consumption. Louisa May Alcott was so metaphorical about death, I told Dirk, that the first time I read the novel, I did not understand that the phrase *the fire was out* was meant to mark Beth's passing. "I figured someone had forgotten to stoke the coal," I said, "and then I was confused, for the rest of the book, why the dead sister never was mentioned again."

According to Dirk, I had grown into a much more sophisticated reader. But I certainly owned the lowest grade of kitchen implements. Dirk rejected my corkscrew and took out his Swiss Army knife. He got ten points for not breaking the cork, and another ten for pouring me a huge gobletful of wine. We clinked glasses. *"Prost,"* said Dirk—and fool that I was, I asked for an exact translation.

An interjection. Third person singular. The subjunctive of *prodesse,* to do good.

"To your health," I said, and swallowed an unseemly mouthful. I was no wine connoisseur, but I could tell this white from the Rhine Valley was good stuff—hardly the rotgut red I bought, which was cultivated and bottled in strange places like Chile and Yugoslavia.

On the couch—an uneasy six inches between the right leg of my Gap jeans and the left leg of his L. L. Bean chinos—I found out that the U.S. government sometimes paid subsidies to Dirk's father for letting his fields go fallow, that from 1976 to 1979 (when the crop was sold at a decent price to General Mills), I may have ingested Diederhoff wheat each morning at the breakfast table, that *Elective Affinities* was written as a way of sublimating the author's love for a girl forty years his junior, and that *Caspar Hauser or The Sluggishness of the Heart* was based on the true story of a teenage foundling who displayed normal intelligence in spite of having no record of ever having communicated with other humans. As Dirk held forth, I kept drinking and thinking I could not possibly spend the rest of this evening—or my entire life—listening to this man gas on about the great Goethe and his heirs to the literary throne. I have my landlord to thank for saving me from such a sad fate. In the midst of expounding upon the Germanic Romantic hero—often feminized and displaying behavior more traditionally associated with the Mediterranean temperament, hence Werther practically pistol-whipping himself into hysterics over Charlotte—Dirk stopped and said, *"Es friert."*

"What?"

"Angel, it's very cold in here."

"I *told* the landlord."

"Told him what?"

"That the thermostat is broken."

"Tell him again."

"I don't want to tell him again." When Dirk looked at me like I was irrational, I added, "I guess it's a woman thing. I don't like to go down there. He makes me shiver—"

"So you'd rather shiver up here?"

Knowing I had to put a stop to this caviling—or the night would be lost forever—I clutched the stem of my wineglass and told Dirk, "There was a time in March when I considered writing him a nasty letter." I paused. "But I wrote to you. Instead."

Who could claim now I didn't understand cause and effect? As if he were replacing the chalk on the ledge after a lecture, Dirk put his glass down on my plastic Parsons table, leaned over, and pressed his lips on mine. By then I'd had enough wine to find myself entirely responsive to the gesture. I put down my goblet, and within a moment my arms were around his neck and my tongue was exploring the curious lack of cavities—or rather, silver fillings—in his mouth.

"I want to sleep with you," Dirk murmured in my ear.

My fingers were already going for his belt buckle when he added, "But only if you think it's right."

"It's right."

"Let's go into your bedroom."

"You're sitting on it."

Dirk broke away and gave me a puzzled look.

"This couch," I said. "It folds out."

Dirk rose and held both wine goblets while I moved the Parsons table. One of the legs fell off and it was all I could do to keep from muttering obscenities as I pushed the severed leg back into place. I removed the couch cushions. Probably figuring it took a man to do what this girl accomplished on her own every night, Dirk stepped in to pull out the creaky springs and thin mattress. All this hoisting about of furniture did nothing to stoke the flames of romance. However, it did afford me the necessary break to—as Dirk hesitantly put it—*take precautions.*

I ran the water in the bathroom sink so Dirk couldn't hear me squirting the soon-to-expire spermicide into the too-brittle cup of my four-year-old diaphragm. I really was out of practice. I put too much jelly on the rim, and twice when I squatted to insert the diaphragm, it slithered out of my hand and ripped across the room like some berserko flying saucer, once even hitting the duct tape that the landlord had put up to patch a ceiling leak. When I finally got it in, the diaphragm felt twisted and cold and clammy as the voice of the uptight, would-be-liberal woman whose pained lecture on birth control was the high price I paid for getting examined at the Free Clinic. "If you girls . . . *want it* . . . again," she said, her lips pursing purple at such a thought, "you must insert more spermicide."

I suspected Dirk was a one-time-only man. I thought about

giving myself a quick whore's bath, but I did not take Dirk for the go-down type of lover and I didn't want to keep him waiting. When I resurfaced from the bathroom—still fully clothed because I didn't want him to see me stippled with gooseflesh—I found the lamp dimmed and Dirk beneath the sheets, his chinos and twill shirt and even his underwear neatly folded beside him on the floor. He had deprived me of the pleasure of undressing him. But this meant I could concentrate on the pleasure I got as he switched off the lamp—*smart guy!*—and undressed me.

I must admit I liked the way he handled me. He was good with buttons. Even did a tolerable job with the bra. The too-studious way he sucked on my breasts (he seemed to be timing it, giving equal attention to the left and right) was forgotten by the time he slid his hands into my jeans and gradually worked them down my thighs, tossing them (without folding) onto the floor. When I wrapped my legs around his hairless thighs, I wished I'd done a better job with a razor that morning.

"Do you have trouble?" he whispered.

"What with?"

"*Coming.*"

"Not if you use your mouth," I said, instantly regretting my earlier do-not-wash decision.

Although I suspected Dirk had learned his technique from (where else?) a book, the source of his knowledge soon ceased to matter. I found I could forgive a lot of a man who was willing to spend a good quarter of an hour with his head between my thighs and who had the self-control to thrust into me for many minutes beyond that.

After it was over, I leaned my head onto the pillow instead of his shoulder so the pillowcase would catch my inevitable, inexplicable postcoital tears. Dirk waited a respectable three or four minutes, then (probably following the same medical manual's advice) he got up to clear the toxins from his bladder. I lay on my back listening to his urine, then to the sound of running water in the sink. Dirk washed his hands so long I knew that if I followed him into the bathroom, I'd find the faucet would be too hot to touch.

He came back to my sad, creaking bed, his face and hands scented with my soap instead of my salty odor.

"Angel," he said, "your bathroom ceiling is leaking."

"I know."

"This is unacceptable. In the morning, I'll go downstairs and tell your landlord about both the heat and the ceiling."

I smiled. "What makes you so sure I'll let you stay until morning?"

With horror, I heard him reach for his parka. Then he tossed it over me and climbed back into bed. "You'll let me stay," he said. "Unless you want to freeze to death." He stroked my hair and my shoulders. "Was it good for you?"

Truth to tell, no man had ever bothered to ask me before. I knew I should have been happy that someone should care, even if something anxious in Dirk's voice made it sound as if he expected to be graded using the plus/minus system. But suddenly I felt confused and embarrassed. Dirk had penetrated me. But it had been my landlord's long wet tongue licking me, over and over again, in my imagination.

"*Das*," I said, "was . . . good."

"*Gut.*"

I lay on my back and regarded the sloped ceiling. Then I closed my eyes and snuggled closer to Dirk. From across the room, plenty of guys could look hot enough to give you goose bumps. But when you were really freezing, only the guy willing to hold you in his arms could stroke away the cold. Only he could lie next to you in a garret and make you feel—for a moment, at least— that a fire was blazing in your very own Swiss chalet.

Sometimes
I dream
In Italian

THE MINUTE I STEPPED inside the South Seas Restaurant, I knew my sister had invited me there just to be facetious. The lobby was so red it hurt my eyes, and the gold plastic dragon on the wall looked more like a deranged poodle than some fierce mythological animal. The menu posted on the cash register boasted authentic Polynesian and Chinese cuisine, but the man behind the counter obviously was Vietnamese. His name tag read:

YOUR HOST
MR. V. TRAN

Inside, Lina waited by the back wall, at a tiny bentwood table for two that was topped by a red and black umbrella. The fabric on the umbrella looked spray-painted, and I suspected that if we stripped it we would find the tricolors used to decorate pizza patios, and maybe even a bold advertisement for CINZANO.

"Where in the world did you find this place?" I whispered.

Lina smoothed a lock of her shellacked black hair. "Bob used to take me here."

Bob was Lina's old lover. He had given her genital warts, a

topic I didn't care to discuss just before lunch. I sat down and opened the red laminated menu.

"Forget the food," Lina said. "This joint is known for the drinks."

I looked at my watch.

"It's Saturday," she reminded me. "Besides, if you eat a lot of rice, it'll wear off by one-thirty."

When our waiter—a Mr. T. Tran—appeared, Lina felt compelled to state her order twice, in the loud exaggerated tones our parents used to use whenever they spoke English to someone who wasn't Italian. To make up for Lina's condescension, I mumbled my order and had to repeat it twice.

Lina got a mai tai. I got a frothy drink called a grasshopper, which reminded me of the seafoam-green punch my aunts had served after my mother's funeral.

Lina reached over and stole the tiny paper umbrella out of my glass. "Pammy loves these things," she said. "I'll save it for next time she starts whining. Did you know Pammy's a whiner?"

"Yes," I reminded her. "I've baby-sat."

"Phil sends his love," Lina said. "To you."

"My love also," I said, sipping the grasshopper.

Lina's plum-colored lips raised slightly, as if she had just confirmed what she had suspected for years: that I once had harbored a strange crush on her husband. "You've got a foam mustache," she said, and I wiped my lips with a red paper napkin.

Lina took a long drink of her mai tai, folded her plum-tipped fingers together, and leaned across the table. "All right, let's get down to business."

Ostensibly Lina and I were meeting to settle the question of what to do with our father. For months now, Babbo had let everything go. The house was draped with cobwebs; the car growled because it needed a new muffler; the laundry sat gray and stiff in the corner; and Babbo, who refused to bathe, smelled gamy as a stuffed skin that the taxidermist hadn't treated quite right.

"He's a mess," Lina said. "The other day I went over and the faucet in the kitchen sink was streaming water because he forgot to turn it off. The toilet was clogged with poop—"

"Spare me the details."

"—and Babbo started talking at me in Italian."

"What did he say?" I asked.

"How the hell should I know?" And when I frowned at her, Lina said, "Like I'm supposed to remember? Use it or lose it, as they say. Anyway, I kept yelling at him, *Non capisco, I don't kabeesh you, Daddy*, and I kept on repeating it until a mouse—a real live mouse—zoomed out from under the couch, looked at me, and then zoomed back in."

I shuddered. "I hope he's not home when I get there—"

"Oh, Babbo never goes anywhere—"

"No, the *topolino*."

Lina wrinkled her nose. "You could feed him the three-month-old *formaggio* that's been sitting in the fridge."

"Stop. I'll be sick."

Lina straightened her silverware on the table. "Phil says we should put Babbo in a home."

I hesitated. Then I said, "All right. Keep on talking."

"But the whole thing gets me depressed. It's like Mama all over again." She swallowed the last of her mai tai. "Do you ever think about Mama?"

I felt like telling Lina, *I dream she's coming at me with her fingers pinched together, ready to pick the nits out of my hair. I dream someone opens her coffin and her face instantly caves in, like a jack-o'-lantern melted by a candle—*

"Oh goody," Lina said. "Here comes the pu-pu platter." She pushed her glass across the table at the waiter. "I need a refill," she said. "Another mai tai."

Mr. T. Tran nodded and took the glass. He pointed at mine—still half-full—and I shook my head.

"Watch, he'll come back with a Coke or something," Lina said.

"Be quiet," I said, and selected a pu-pu, or whatever one of the individual things on the plate was called. Grease dribbled down my chin.

"What about a home nurse?" I asked.

"Too expensive," Lina said.

"What's the other going to cost?"

"Big bucks too," Lina said. "But thank God for Medicare. And Phil's big fat salary. Phil can pay for anything. Mmm, try one of these rolled-up things; they're actually edible. Do you know why Connecticut is called the Nutmeg State? Pammy has to write a report for school."

I shook my head. "Babbo's never even been in the hospital," I said. "I wonder how he'll react when you tell him."

Lina tapped the table with her red plastic swizzle stick. "What do you mean, *me* tell him? You're not getting off easy on this one, pal."

I gave her what I hoped was a frosty look. "Of course I'll be there to tell him," I said. "Just give me the date."

Lina took her calendar out of her purse and turned to her *To Do* list. "I'll start calling around on Monday," she said, writing a note to remind herself. "It's probably just like day care—you have to get on a waiting list for something decent."

I thought about Saint Ronan's, where Mama had lived for three years after her stroke. "All those homes are horrible," I said. "Full of construction paper cutouts and Lawrence Welk on big-screen TV."

"High-school glee clubs in to sing Christmas carols," Lina added.

"Little children marching around in Batman and Barney costumes on Halloween," I said.

"Talk about hell on earth!" Lina finished the last pu-pu and licked the grease off her well-manicured fingers. "Thank God you could come today. I couldn't wait to ditch Pammy and Richie with the baby-sitter. They love the baby-sitter. They hate me." She paused. "Do you think Phil hates me?"

"Of course not," I said.

"Sometimes I wonder," Lina said, smiling, as if the very idea gave her satisfaction.

※

Lina got the Happy Family, which she hardly touched. I got the Perfect Match with white rice, cold sesame noodles, and a spring roll. I tried not to think about Mama and mice and Babbo babbling in Italian as I glumly ate my sour, salty main dish, half-listening as Lina gave me the run-down on the doings at her house.

"Pammy plays 'Frère Jacques'—with two hands—on the piano," she said. "Richie's still padding around in those Big Bird slippers that make his feet stink. Every day when I drop him off at day care I tell the teacher, *Have a good day*. Notice I don't say *nice*. And she says, *Every day is good when you wake up alive*. Like you're gonna wake up dead? I feel like asking her. But I keep my mouth shut because she's still Pollyanna-izing. *Every morning when the alarm clock rings*, she says, *I thank God for another day*. Oh yeah? I feel like saying. Well I think: *Fuck, six-thirty already?* But like I said, I don't breathe a word of this. I keep my mouth shut because I'm afraid if I'm rude they'll molest my kid or cheat him out of his goddamn graham crackers for snack. I mean, once I told Pammy's teacher I didn't have time to sell candy bars. For weeks afterward Pammy complained about how she always got stuck playing with the bald-headed doll during recess." Lina paused. "So what do you think of my exciting life?"

She looked around the restaurant, which was empty except for an older couple sitting in a booth toward the front. Her eyes looked vacant, and the deep plum color on her lips seemed to tremble.

"Bob just wanted me because I looked different," she finally said.

I nodded.

"He wanted me to talk in Italian to him," Lina said. "Like I know more than four or five things to say. I mean, he'd be fucking me and I'd be telling him, *Fish on Fridays*, or *Shut the hell up!* Then he'd come with these great big groans and I'd be saying, *Hey thanks, paesano, you're a real goomba, how goes it?*"

I laughed. Lina shrugged and looked across the table at me. I knew she was evaluating, with dissatisfaction, my green turtleneck and navy sweater.

"Do you ever feel like waltzing into a bar, leading some guy on, and then giving him the wrong phone number?" she asked.

"Nope," I said, using my fork to stab a scallop.

She took another drink. "The minute that mouse looked at me, I knew I needed a face-lift," she said. "I'm getting a face-lift."

"Don't," I warned. "You'll end up looking like Liberace."

Lina sucked on her swizzle stick. "How could we have watched Liberace for all those years and not realized he was the gayest blade on earth? God, wouldn't it be great to be a kid again and not realize anything?" She looked intently at me. "You know, Pammy's got these two black girls in her class. The other day when I pick her up she whispers in my ear, *Daniella and Nicole are different*. So I get all set to roll out the Sesame Street we-are-the-world minilecture when Pammy leans over with a devilish look on her face and says, *They've both got beads in their hair.* Isn't that something? Out of the mouths of babes—"

"Ofttimes come burps," I finished for her. It was a line Phil had coined when Pammy was a colicky infant and screamed herself red in the face until she belched herself out of her indigestion.

The waiter came over and pointed to my empty spring-roll plate. I nodded and he cleared it away. After he was halfway to the kitchen, Lina said, "God, to think I have to pay fifty bucks a month for gloss to get that kind of shine in my hair."

I sighed. I picked a little bit more at my rice, while Lina sat back and opened and closed the tiny umbrella that had been in my drink. She had a dreamy look on her face. All of a sudden I was afraid she might be remembering her days in the high-school drama club. I was scared she might break out into "Shall We Dance?" from *The King and I* or "Happy Talk" from *South Pacific*. To head off trouble, I blurted out, "I'm seeing someone."

Lina dropped the toy umbrella. She leaned forward, her hands pressed flat on the table, and in an exaggerated ladies-lunch voice she said, "Do tell."

I paused, twirling my sesame noodles around my fork. "He's German."

"No way! What's his name?"

I paused. "Dirk Diederhoff."

"Can he change it?"

"I doubt he's ever even considered it."

"Where'd you two hook up?" Lina asked.

"He's from Minnesota," I said, evasively.

"I guess you didn't meet him in a bar, then."

"I don't do bars," I said. "Anymore."

"So where—"

"I answered his ad," I said. "In the newspaper."

"Oh my God!" Lina said. "My little sister answers dirty ads."

"They're not dirty."

"I can't believe it. What did the ad say?"

I pressed my lips together.

"God," Lina said, "I can just imagine the kind you'd answer. *Long walks at Grant's Tomb—*"

"That's full of crack addicts now," I said.

"*Evenings listening to chamber music. Saturday afternoons in the stacks of the New York Public Library.*"

"So what kind would you answer?" I asked.

"I wouldn't answer," Lina said. "I'd *advertise*." She laughed ruefully. *"Bored housewife needs something to keep her out of the mall."* She sucked wistfully on her discarded straw. "I've seen those ads in the paper. I've read them. Do you notice how the men always want a photo?"

"And the women always want a man who can bench-press three hundred but isn't afraid to cry," I said.

"What gets me are the euphemisms for *fat*," Lina said.

"Zaftig."

"Rubenesque," Lina said.

"Statuesque."

"Does he fuck you in German?" Lina asked loudly.

I looked over at the cash register, where Misters V. and T. Tran were conferring. Lina impatiently said, "I'm telling you, they don't get English. One day I ordered the moo shu and they brought the chow mein. Do I look like someone who orders chow mein?"

I shook my head. "Dirk doesn't talk much," I lied.

Lina laughed triumphantly. "Neither does Phil. Bob never did either. It's a male thing. It's like they're afraid their dicks will fall off if they open their mouths." She leaned back in her chair. "The other day Richie pulls down the fly on his jeans—did I tell you how much I hate the way his Big Bird slippers make his feet stink?—and he goes to me, *Mommy, Mommy, I've got a peenie. Great*, says I. *Now you can go out and rob a bank*." She sucked in her cheeks and pursed her lips at me. "Did I tell you I'm going out for Halloween as a dominatrix?"

I looked at her empty mai tai glass. "You're acting like an asshole."

Lina sighed. "I should have been a man," she said. Then she pulled her ear to indicate she was joking. "So this relationship, is it serious?"

I shrugged. "I think so. Yes."

Lina turned and craned her neck. "Where's the waiter? We need our fortune cookies right now. Chop chop."

"Stop it," I told her.

"What's Kirk—I mean Dick's—I mean Dirk's astrological sign?"

"Aries, I think."

"The ram. Great. He'll never be impotent." She took a cup and poured some of the tea that had been sitting in the stainless-steel pot since the beginning of the meal. "I'm going to read your tea leaves."

"That's the Gypsies, Lina."

Lina stared down into the cup. "Ah . . . I see . . . I see . . . life full of great fortune and profound sorrow." She stifled a burp. "Not-so-happy family comes back to haunt you. New family of many blond daughters. One son, strong as ginseng root. But beware the evil tuna fish—"

"Lina, stop it," I hissed as the waiter came over and silently gathered our dishes.

"Do you think I should leave Phil?" Lina asked, watching the waiter stack the plates.

"For who?" I asked, no longer caring about decorum.

"For myself," she said, and then asked the waiter, "Could you wrap this? I want to feed it to my dog."

I got up without excusing myself and disappeared for three or four minutes into the ladies' room. It was a single-stall bathroom, cold and not very clean, and after I had gotten over some of my shame at being related to someone like Lina, I went back into the dining room. Lina was bent over her compact mirror, reapplying her lipstick. She had coated only her bottom lip when Mr. T. Tran came back carrying the check and two fortune cookies wrapped in cellophane on a black lacquer tray.

"You choose," Lina told me, her top lip pale and cracked compared to her coated bottom lip. "You first. You have a future. I only have fate."

I selected the cookie on the left. Lina put down her lipstick and seized her own cookie, as if certain it would contain some secret as to how she should live her life.

We hesitated, then ripped the cellophane and gingerly broke our cookies in half. I thought about how different we were in our approach from Phil and Dirk, both of whom extracted their fortunes by breaking the cookie in half with their teeth.

I looked at Lina expectantly.

"Do not purchase any items from the Home Shopping Channel," she pretended to read from her fortune. "All that glitters is not gold."

I leaned over, took the scrap of white paper out of her hand, and read the real message: *"Good friends stick by your side."*

Lina took mine and read aloud, *"Be confident."* Then she tossed it down to the table. "Have you noticed how shitty these fortunes have been lately? They used to sound like Confucius. Now they sound like your local Girl Scout leader." She looked back toward the kitchen door. "I feel cheated. I demand a refund."

"Lina," I said warningly.

She clenched her fists on the table. "I swear to God, if you marry him—"

"I'm just going out with him," I said.

"You said it was serious, and serious means marriage. Which really means jail."

"You're a sour person, Lina," I said.

"I know," she said. "I'm just like the eggplant Mama used to pickle in vinegar." Lina looked around the restaurant. "Bob used to take me here," she said, as if she hadn't told me that already. Then she told me something I hadn't heard before. "I stole money from Phil to get an abortion."

I sucked in some breath. "How could you?"

"How could I not?" Lina pursed her crooked lips together. She looked all lopsided as she said, "Now when I fall asleep—God, I have so much trouble going to sleep—I dream about tidal waves. I read about them in the *Reader's Digest* in the clinic. They're called nightmare waves. They rush out of nowhere onto the shores of South Sea islands. They're supposed to be sent by a hostile god. Whole families, entire villages, get swept away."

I felt the sharp corners of my fortune cookie melting in my mouth.

"Do you ever have weird dreams?" Lina asked.

"Sometimes I dream in Italian," I told her. "I'm talking, but I don't have the least idea what I mean to say."

I sighed. I reached over for the check, but Lina grabbed it first. "I'll pay," she said. "You know I like to pay."

I AM HAPPY, ARE YOU HAPPY?

AT THE AIRPORT-LIMOUSINE terminal, my sister demanded that Dirk and I bring back the tackiest souvenirs from Italy that we possibly could find. "I want a Pope-on-a-rope key chain from Vatican City," Lina told us. "Plastic statues of Michelangelo's David. Laminated place mats that say *Torna a Sorrento.*"

"They don't want to spend their whole vacation shopping for you," Lina's husband said.

"Who said they did?" Lina countered.

Lina and Phil glared at each other. I looked down at the floor of the terminal, and Dirk looked away.

"Well," Lina finally said. *"Buon viaggio.* Have a ball."

We hugged. I held on to Lina tight. "You'll get to go someday," I whispered.

"Is that an offer to baby-sit?" she asked.

We left them on the sidewalk of the terminal, Phil holding my niece's hand, Lina holding Richie's. With her free hand, Lina blew me kisses that seemed to sting my face. Tears welled up in my eyes, and I turned my face out the window of the limousine so Dirk wouldn't see.

The limousine was empty except for us and the driver. Just outside of Bridgeport, Dirk pushed up his wire-rim glasses—always a signal that he was about to say something important—and told me, "They don't seem to match, your sister and her husband."

"They had to get married," I reluctantly said.

"Oh," Dirk said. I sensed disapproval in his voice. "You should have told me that before."

"And Lina needs a vacation," I said.

"Well, she doesn't need to make you feel bad because you're taking one."

I shrugged.

"Your sister seems to constantly compare herself to other people," Dirk said. "It's mean-spirited. Not to mention unhealthy."

Dirk rarely said anything negative against another person. What lay behind his attack of Lina was his (accurate) judgment that Lina didn't like him. Over the past weekend, which we had spent at Lina and Phil's house, Lina had stared too intently at Dirk, as if challenging him to stare back; she watched him go into the bathroom and wash his hands before dinner and observed how he brushed the crumbs off the table before he stood up to bring in his plate. He was too tidy for her, too precise. Out of his earshot, Lina referred to him as Hans Brinker, the boy with the silver skates.

"Lina's definitely going through one of her bad phases," I told Dirk.

"Good thing it's a phase," he said. "It would be very uncomfortable for you if she always acted like that."

"Look," I said, annoyed, "my sister and I are really close. She's always done a lot for me. I mean, she didn't have to invite us for the weekend. She didn't have to take us to the terminal or volunteer to pay my bills while I'm gone."

Dirk blinked, as if surprised I would stand up for anyone in my family. "I realize that," Dirk said.

"And she's covering my tracks with my father."

"That whole situation is ridiculous," Dirk said. He lowered his voice so the driver couldn't hear. "You're an adult. You should be able to tell your father you're going away with me."

I sighed. How could I explain to Dirk that in our family, a three-week spin of Italy was what two people—if they were lucky enough to afford it—did only on their honeymoon? They certainly didn't do it before they had even announced their engagement. Although my father must have known inside that Dirk and I "were a pair," as he put it, he preferred to ignore the situation. If I had told him we were off to Italy, he would have been forced to acknowledge that Dirk and I were sleeping together. He would have held it against me for a long time, even if Dirk and I eventually got married.

The hint—the threat—that Dirk was going to ask me to marry him hummed between us, in an undercurrent seemingly louder than the jet's engine, all the way across the Atlantic. Dirk held my hand a lot and kept looking at me out of the corner of his eye, as if he were making one last appraisal of an expensive item he was about to purchase. I grew tremendously thirsty and kept on walking back to the stewards' station for more orangeade, which also kept me going back and forth to the bathroom.

At da Vinci Airport, Dirk—who had peed only once on the entire plane ride—left me standing by the baggage claim while he went off to use the bathroom. The hubbub of families and friends reuniting—the loud shouts and greetings, the kisses and hugs—reminded me of a big party from my past. I kept on seeing people—types—that I recognized from my childhood: relatives, people from our neighborhood, church parishioners. When a woman whose hair was darker than mine casually asked me something in Italian, I was pleased that I was able to give a faltering answer back.

But the feeling of belonging disappeared when Dirk came back from the bathroom and joined me. With his hair so pale it sometimes looked white and his scholarly wire-rim glasses, Dirk was clearly a foreigner. As we waited for our luggage, no one said anything to me, and I noticed that a little more space cleared around us, as if people realized that we were different.

That was the way it went for the rest of the trip. Wandering through the ruins of Villa Adriana or down a narrow, winding street in the pale pink light of Siena, people spoke English to us if we were together, and Italian to me and German to Dirk if we were apart. It got to be a joke. At night—lying on the too-soft, grungy mattresses in the only hotels we could afford, our feet swollen from walking and our stomachs gurgling to protest all the wine and the garlic—we would report on how people came up to us and asked for directions to churches, *piazze,* railroad stations. Dirk was tremendously amused at being taken for *un tedesco.* I was slightly annoyed that he could respond more fluently in German (which he had carefully studied from seventh grade through graduate school) than I could in Italian, a language I had grown up hearing—although, admittedly, consciously ignoring—from the time I was born.

My Italian was coarse and unmistakably the language of *contadini.* The further north we traveled, the more my *sh* for *s* and the way I slurred the last syllable became apparent. While in Rome I felt like I was in the midst of a family gathering, in Florence I felt more and more alien among the skinny, chic-looking women climbing out of Fiats onto the crowded streets. The girls jetting around the Duomo on motor scooters—their long, light brown hair flying behind and their faces impassive behind their dark glasses—seemed to have grown up worlds away from me. And yet, with all their bravura, they reminded me of Lina.

By the time we got to Venice, people's faces had sharpened so considerably that they had high cheekbones and hawk noses.

Here Dirk, more often than I, was the one people began speaking to. His precise looks were the rule instead of the exception.

�֎

At a souvenir stall in Saint Mark's Square, I paid ten thousand lire for a black plastic replica of a gondola. When I peered through a little hole in the back of the gondola and clicked the red button on top, I saw colorful, cheesy scenes of the Venice I had longed for years to see: a flock of pigeons scattering in the air in front of Florian's, the Rialto Bridge hung with blazing red flags, the dome of Santa Maria della Salute bathed in a cloud of mist, the lacy facade of the Doge's Palace, the shadowy Bridge of Sighs. When I took the gondola away from my eye, I saw the real St. Mark's Square—the white tables and chairs lined up in front of the cafés, tourists posing for pictures in front of the Campanile, a group of nuns patiently waiting in line in front of the Correr. From the bandstand in front of Quadri's, musicians in white coats played too-slow swing music. Then bells began to ring, and at the top of the tower, the figures of two Moors stiffly swung their hammers, striking the hour.

Dirk came up behind me. The sunlight glinted off his pale blond hair and the rims of his gold wire glasses as he stared at my plastic gondola.

"My Great-Aunt Grazia used to have one of these," I said, slipping it into my canvas backpack.

"So you have to have one too?" he asked.

"It's for Lina."

"Your sister doesn't really want that stuff."

"She told me to bring back the tackiest souvenirs I could find."

"You've done a splendid job of locating them," Dirk said.

Only the thought that the whole afternoon and evening—never mind three more complete days of vacation—loomed in front of us kept me from stalking down the square in silence. I tried to make light of the situation. "You're just jealous of that snow globe of the Vatican that I bought," I told Dirk.

"Don't be ridiculous," he said, slightly smiling to show that he, too, didn't want a fight. "I'd much rather have that hollow replica of the Pietà."

He unsnapped his camera from the case. I waited impatiently while he shot everything in the piazza—the four bronze horses and the mosaics at the top of the basilica, the pigeons on the large white squares on the pavement, the dizzying height of the Campanile. Then we walked down to the Grand Canal. I trailed a little bit behind, watching the leather identification tag swing back and forth from the strap of Dirk's Minolta. Before we left, Dirk had taken his black fountain pen and labeled practically everything he had packed with his name and address. When he quit packing for a few minutes to make a phone call, I borrowed his pen, and like a mother sending her son off to summer camp, I blocked out his name in capital letters on the inside of his underwear. "Very amusing," he said, when he opened the suitcase in Rome and discovered it.

As I walked behind him, I wondered if his name was rubbing off his Fruit of the Looms onto his backside. Then I wondered, with guilt, if Dirk also was thinking something mean-spirited about me. But Dirk didn't hold grudges. He probably had his mind on something dull from another century, some fact from the guidebook he had consulted—and read aloud from—the night before. *In 1756, Casanova escaped from a wooden cell in the Doge's Palace and scaled the walls to his freedom. . . . Black candles were lit on either side of the Byzantine Madonna to comfort criminals about to be executed on the piazza.*

"Where are we going now?" I asked.

"The Frari."

"Does it have any Botticellis?"

"It's a *church*."

Dirk offered me his Blue Guide while we were waiting for the vaporetto. I declined. I held on to one of the posts on the dock and stared down the canal. A crowd had gathered underneath a sign that said SEE MURANO, ISLAND OF GLASS! I wondered if the island was a Venetian version of Cape Cod—the glassblowers fashioning vases and decanters in the shop windows of Murano just as the craftsmen made baskets and candles in the shop windows at Hyannisport. But what did it matter? I'd never see it. In his day planner, Dirk already had worked out an itinerary for the rest of the trip. It was full of churches and museums. Glassmakers, lacemakers, and gondola rides were forbidden.

The night before, our elbows leaning on the windowsill of our hotel room, we had watched the black gondolas glide along the water, their red lights illuminating their hefty cargo: German tourists and vacationers from New York and New Jersey. The gondoliers, in their red-and-white striped shirts and straw hats, sang songs I remembered from my childhood. Sometimes they were accompanied by accordions, whose hum sounded mournful as it faded on the water.

Dirk was scornful of the whole business.

"Lighten up," I said. "It looks like fun."

"It looks like an amusement park."

"I like amusement parks," I said.

"I thought you said you used to throw up on the rides."

"That's because I ate too much cotton candy."

Dirk sighed. "We should have gone to the hill towns," he said. "Assisi. Padua. Ravenna."

"But everyone goes to Venice," I said.

"Yes, every Italian-American."

"I'm Italian-American," I reminded him.

"But you're not on a Perillo bus tour."

"Maybe I wish I was," I said, and walked away from the window.

"Are you premenstrual?" Dirk asked.

"No," I said, carefully watching him. "My period's late."

His face turned ashen, and I laughed. "Don't worry," I said. "I feel it coming."

He blinked, and the anxiety that had just tightened his face disappeared. "Don't do that to me, Angel," he said. "It's not fair."

I shrugged and sat down on the bed. He kept his eyes on me, and I started to feel so uncomfortable that I decided to make him uncomfortable back. "What if I was pregnant?" I asked him.

"*Were* pregnant," he corrected me.

"Whatever!"

"But you aren't," he said. "You just said you probably aren't, so it doesn't bear further discussion."

From below on the canal, I heard shouts of laughter and an accordion begin to play. In the midst of Venice's playfulness, Dirk's pure Midwestern outlook on life annoyed me.

Lina had an affair, I felt like telling him. *With a married man. She got pregnant by him too, and then she had an abortion.*

But I didn't say anything. Dirk kept staring at me, as if trying to see a side of me he never had discerned before. "You know," he said, "sometimes I think you're so jealous of your sister that you even want to make the same mistakes that she did."

"Let's drop the subject," I said.

"My pleasure," Dirk murmured, and sat down beside me on the bed. I felt the tension emanating from his body, and felt my own tension aching to be transformed into something else.

"Do you still have your diaphragm in from this morning?" he asked as he carefully took off his glasses.

The vaporetto sputtered as it pulled up to the dock. Dirk and I climbed aboard. We stood at the back, watching the yellow sign that marked Saint Mark's stop fade away in the distance. We didn't talk anymore until we landed at the Rialto stop.

Once we wandered off the main canal, the paths became

much narrower, and the pastel buildings with their high, tall windows seemed to close us in. Cats climbed on grates and slid in and out of the broken lower windows. Dirk and I went one way, bickered about the best route to take, then turned in the other direction. Dirk stopped at a bridge that arched over a small canal and pulled out a map. "Do you want me to ask someone for directions?" I said.

"There's no one around," Dirk said.

I turned. One door down, there was a linen shop. In the window were cascades of lace, tablecloths, and runners draped over pedestals and hanging from overhead bars. Big wicker baskets were stuffed with napkins and handkerchiefs.

I peered in. Dirk came up behind me.

"It's closed," I said.

When I didn't move away, he asked, "See something you like?"

I pointed. "My mother used to keep a runner like that on the dining-room table." When we dusted the furniture, Lina used to take the runner off the table and drape it over her head like a wedding veil. She picked up some wax flowers, held them like a bouquet, and pretended to solemnly glide up a church aisle.

"Lina took the runner when my mother died," I said. "But Pammy spilled grape Kool-Aid on it."

"Do you want to get her another?" Dirk asked.

I shrugged.

Dirk put his hand around my waist. "I'll get it for her."

I pointed to the handwritten sign on the door. "*È chiuso,*" I reminded him. "Closed."

"On the way back, then."

"We may get lost again."

"I'll remember the way," Dirk said.

As it turned out, we weren't that far from the church. When we rounded the next bend, the curved apse of the Frari jutted out onto the path. An old woman in black sat on the wall, eating a piece of bread. Behind the garden gate, a friar was clipping roses and arranging them in a tin watering can.

After the heat of the sun and the press of the crowds in Saint Mark's, it was a relief to enter the dark church, which we had practically to ourselves. Candles sputtered in the side chapels, throwing shadows on the statues and paintings. The wooden altar rail felt cold beneath my fingers. When I put my backpack down on one of the wooden pews, the knickknacks inside made a loud clatter. Dirk turned around and frowned. He went up to the altar, glancing at his guide book.

I sat down in the pew, watching the greens and purples and blues on the stained-glass windows turn a little less brilliant as the sun shifted. Then, taking up my clattering bag again, I wandered to the back of the church, where a white marble statue by Canova reposed. The sculpture seemed too curvy and suggestive for a church.

Dirk came up behind me.

"This doesn't seem to belong in a church," I said.

Dirk looked around. Seeing the back chapel was empty, he said, "Neither does this." He leaned over, grasped my upper arm, and kissed me. We'd had *panini* for lunch. His tongue was salted with the creamy, smoky flavor of prosciutto and Fontina.

He smiled at me. He couldn't have planned a scenario more exact to my tastes—the empty church, the darkness, the coolness of the marble and the high ceilings, the sun casting blocks of light on the stone floors, the feeling that we had nowhere else to go, but that the whole city lay before us.

"Let's get married," he said.

"Yes," I said. "I mean—I'm not sure. I want to think about it. Talk about it."

"That's fair," he said.

"I don't want to rush into things."

He blinked. "Of course," he said. "I totally agree."

"I mean, there's a lot to figure out," I said. "I'm not sure I know how to have a good relationship. My parents didn't have one—"

"Oh, for people of that generation, that's practically a given," Dirk said.

"Then Lina and Phil don't get along so well."

"Yes, but what does that have to do with us?" Dirk asked.

I shrugged. "Everything. The way other members of your family get married—the way they raise their families—is probably some kind of pattern."

Dirk stared at me. "Why do you always define yourself in terms of your family? They're not you." He took my hand, and his grip felt too insistent. "They're not you," he repeated, as suddenly, from up above, the church bells began to toll the hour.

That night I did everything I could to get to sleep. I breathed long and steady breaths; I said *om* over and over again in my head; I imagined my body filling up with sand and emptying out again; I reconstructed the house I had grown up in room by room; I recited the rosary. As a last resort I imagined myself floating on a gondola past all the lacy arcades of the palaces lining the Grand Canal, counting each gaudy, barbershop-striped pole that marked each landing. But it was useless. At the dock directly below our hotel window, the water taxis came and went, their motors seemingly louder by the hour. Boatloads of people floated by, gondoliers sang "O Sole Mio," and accordions played. The red lights of the gondolas shone through a crack in the shutters and illuminated the walls for a moment before they glided on. Across the canal, the lights of the railroad station shone continuously. Around midnight I heard the melancholy whistle of the last train leaving. Then I lay still for another hour, listening to the click of my travel clock and Dirk's breathing.

At one-thirty I got up, pulled on a pair of shorts and a T-shirt I had left on the chair, and exited the room. The lock snapped when I turned the doorknob. I looked back at Dirk's inert form, relieved that I hadn't woken him.

The stairwell was narrow and had no rail. I trailed my hand along the wall, pulling down a few cobwebs as I groped my way down the steps to the dark lobby. I remembered the lamp was in the corner, and I started to move forward. But before I could reach the corner I heard a click, and the light blazed in my face. For a moment I had the irrational fear that it was Dirk who had thrown the switch. But on the cracked vinyl seat of the couch, his tobacco-stained fingers still on the lamp, sat the night clerk, Nico. He had been dozing on the couch, his feet propped up on the coffee table. He probably was in his mid-thirties, but he looked much older than me because he had two teeth missing on top. Although he was from one of the hill towns, his dental problems caused him to make the same kind of whistling sound when he talked that I associated with southern Italians.

"*Come sta?*" he asked me.

"*Non posso dormire,*" I said.

"*Sta male?*" he asked.

I paused, and he seemed to realize that I suddenly had blocked on all my Italian.

"You know I speak English," he said.

I knew. The previous evening, Dirk had asked him for directions to a restaurant, and Nico had answered in precise but excessively formal English.

I looked into Nico's liquidy dark eyes, then looked around the faded lobby. The stale smells from the faded curtains, the partially emptied ashtrays, and the guest book that no one probably had signed in years, all made the room look uninviting—not to mention I knew it was improper to sit with a man I hardly knew in a dark room in the middle of the night. Yet within seconds I found myself on a too-soft chair sitting kitty-corner to Nico. My throat caught as I admitted, "I'm homesick."

He looked alarmed. "Is a doctor necessary?"

"No, no. Sick for home," I explained. "I miss my home."

He nodded. *"Si, ora capisco."* He paused. "New York?"

"Connecticut. It's next door. Nearby. Close. I grew up there, but now I live in New York."

"Ho un cugino a Baltimore."

"That's pretty far away."

He nodded.

"Have you ever visited the United States?" I asked.

"No, no."

"Maybe someday."

He shook his head and looked intently at me. "When will your husband take you back?"

"Non siamo sposati."

He raised one eyebrow. But if he was shocked, he didn't show it.

"But we're getting married," I said. "We will be married."

"I—" He paused, searching for the right word. "I congratulate you. This will please your parents."

"My mother is dead," I said.

He crossed himself. *"Poverina."*

"And my father's older now. He forgets a lot."

Nico nodded. "That's the way the cookies crumble."

I had to bite my lip to keep from laughing. I wondered what other American idioms he had been forced to memorize: *a bird in the hand is worth two in the bush; don't count your chickens before they hatch?* Then I remembered some of the Italian idioms I had learned, all of which probably seemed equally absurd to natives: *in bocco al lupo!* for good luck; *caspita!* for you don't say; and *ad ogni uccello il suo nido è bello*—every bird likes his own nest, the Italian equivalent for *there's no place like home.*

Nico fell silent. I looked at his hands. They were large and covered with dark hair. He wore no wedding ring.

"Do you have a family?" I asked him. "I mean, besides the cousin in Baltimore."

"I have a mother and a father and the father of my wife. I have four children. Two are sons and two are daughters."

"That's a big family," I said. We sat for a while in silence. "*È contento?*" I blurted out. It was one of the first things I learned in Italian, and I was sure it was a phrase that Dirk had learned in one of his first German lessons: *I am happy. Are you happy?*

Nico shrugged, as if happiness were an irrelevant issue. "*Va bene,*" he said. "My life goes well. It is possible to go better. It is possible to go worse also."

He smiled, and the dark gap in between his teeth glistened with a little saliva. He leaned forward a little, and the springs on the couch creaked. "Hot milk?" he offered, his eyes wet with expectation.

I hesitated, then shook my head. He leaned back again, and the moment was lost. This did not seem to bother him nearly as much as it did me.

❧

In the morning I lay in bed, groggy from lack of sleep, while Dirk went down the hall to take a shower. Then I got up and moved the bag that contained the lace runner Dirk had bought for Lina off the chair. I opened the green shutters, sat down by the window, and looked out onto the Grand Canal. Fog hovered above the dark water. Mossy seaweed clung to the foundations of the buildings. The air was moist and smelled like moldy bread.

At my feet lay the knapsack full of souvenirs for Lina. I sorted through it and pulled out a postcard of the Trevi Fountain. The blue pools of water were full of gold, silver, and copper coins thrown by thousands of tourists who had closed their eyes and made a wish to return to Italy.

I took Dirk's black fountain pen off the table. *Dear Lina,* I wrote. *Rome seems like long ago. It's easy to get lost in Venice, but the natives help you find the way. By the time you get this, I'll be home again. Love, Angel*

In a P.S., I wrote, *Dirk and I are getting married.*

I stared at the P.S. for a moment. It seemed so final now that it was written in black ink. Below, from the canal, I heard a low whistle. On the sidewalk one of the gondoliers in his garish red-and-white striped shirt leaned against a dock post. He looked up and winked at me. I stared at him for a moment before I put the postcard on the table and closed the shutters. Then I went down the hall to use the bathroom. I felt a dull pain in my abdomen—the beginning of cramps—so I took a tampon.

When I got back, Dirk was standing by the window, rubbing one side of his pale hair with one of the rough white towels provided by the hotel. His head was bent down toward the table where the postcard sat.

"What are you looking at?" I asked sharply.

He turned with a puzzled look on his face, and I realized with relief that he couldn't read a damn thing without his glasses.

GOD MOVES THE FURNITURE

AFTER LINA TRIED to kill herself by closing all the windows and turning on the gas oven, Phil went to Sears and bought a new Kenmore electric. I played kickball with the kids in the backyard while the servicemen ripped out the old stove and installed the new. Lina was upstairs, lying in bed. She had assumed the supine position immediately after Phil brought her back from the psychiatric ward, and she had remained in that posture for almost the entire weekend. "We'll have to give Mommy some time to herself," Phil had told Pammy and Richie. "In the meantime, here's Auntie Angel to take her place. Angel's going to stay with us until Mommy's all better, aren't you, Angel?"

I nodded vigorously at the kids, as if I were a stable customer they could rely upon. But inside I felt like a basket case. Insomnia had kept me fitful for weeks, and I actually had been contemplating downing a handful of Xanax when Phil called to tell me that Lina had tried to commit suicide.

"I can't believe it," I said.

"Well, believe it. It's true." He paused. "You sound sick."

"I just broke it off with Dirk," I told Phil.

"Again?"

"This time it's for good," I said.

"Can you come?" Phil asked. "I really need your help. Please come."

Phil's ragged voice—usually so smooth and calm—convinced me that he really wanted me. I called my boss and told her I had a family emergency—I had to be there for my sister. But the truth was I wanted to be there for Phil. For years I had tried to get over the strange feeling I had whenever we were washing dishes and Phil got too close to me at the sink, so close I could smell the detergent on his freshly washed shirt. I had tried to stop waking up in the middle of the night, wet from some dream I had spun about him, even while Dirk slept next to me. I had prayed to God to squelch my obsession with Phil. I had rolled the I Ching and consulted tarot cards and even done high-impact aerobics to sweat him out of my system. But nothing worked. My eyes still were drawn to the slope of his butt, his rumpled collar, his tie askew when he came home from work. Phil was a hospital administrator. He was the kind of dispassionate person who distanced himself from the patients—people like me and Lina, who were either sick in the body or spirit. That distance—plus his unattainability—no doubt attracted me. Or, as the no-nonsense counselor I recently had visited phrased it, *You want him because you can't have him.*

After the servicemen left, the kids stayed outside to play on the swing set and I went back inside. Phil sat at the kitchen table and read the manual for the new oven. Then he took a pen from his pocket—he always carried the silver pen Lina had given him in his shirt pocket—and filled out the warranty card.

To test the new stove, I heated water—coffee for Phil, tea for me. Neither one of us bothered to ask if Lina wanted anything. Like a flu patient or a pregnant woman, she had eaten nothing but soup and saltine crackers since she came home. Whenever I put the tray down on her bed, she pursed her lips and said, "Just the smell of that food makes me want to lose it."

The burner crackled and the coils were a luminous red when I took the whistling copper kettle off the stove. I steeped an Earl Grey tea bag for me and then poured water over the Irish creme beans I had ground for Phil. I stood at the counter listening to the water gurgling through the filter into the cup, then I brought our drinks over to the table. I liked serving Phil. He always looked so delighted when you gave him a cup of coffee or passed him some bread at the dinner table, as if simple courtesy were something extraordinary. Living with Lina had reduced him to that.

Phil smiled and thanked me for the coffee. He finished filling out the warranty card and put it in the pile of mail he had been preparing all morning—hospital bills, insurance forms, thank-you notes. He sighed as he looked at the pile of letters, pushing one of the wayward bills back into the even stack. "She could have died," he said.

He hadn't talked about *the incident*, as he called it, since the first day I had arrived there. I didn't know how to respond, so I nodded.

"If the UPS man hadn't gotten here . . ." he said.

I nodded again.

"If he hadn't come to the side door . . ."

And I thought, *If she hadn't ordered, exactly four days before, two push-up bras from Victoria's Secret* . . . The bras were inside the package the UPS man had delivered—Phil had me open the box. We stared, with embarrassment, at the honey-colored silk lingerie, size 36C. Then Phil took the bras upstairs and told me to throw out the box. "I can't stand looking at it," he said. I wondered where Phil put the bras. Lina and I had the same exact cup size, even though she had given birth to two children and I had never had any babies to stretch my bosom.

I sipped my weak Earl Grey and told Phil, "It's no use thinking about what-ifs."

"That's all I ever think about," Phil said. "Anymore."

"Me too," I said. I kept my eyes focused on the table. It was imitation French country kitchen, pine wood, with inlaid blue-and-white tiles that matched the white brightness of the new stove.

"So what happened with Dirk?" Phil asked me.

"I tried," I said. "I wanted it to work."

"I thought you would have been married by now," Phil said. "I thought you two were going to elope when you went off to Italy."

"Dirk would never elope," I said. "He wouldn't know how many pairs of underwear to bring."

Phil laughed. "You were hard on him, Angel."

"He annoyed me."

Phil blinked. "You looked exactly like Lina when you said that."

I shrugged. I listened to the kids out in the backyard, the creak of the swing, the *whooompft* when Richie threw himself down on the dented slide. The conversation should have drifted on to other things. But then I told Phil, "I just knew it wasn't going to work out with Dirk, that's all. And I knew there would be nothing worse than being in the wrong relationship forever, maybe even having kids in the bargain."

"You made the right choice, then," Phil said.

"So why do I feel so lousy?" I asked.

"I have to admit, I've never considered you a very"—Phil paused, carefully choosing his words—"*buoyant* soul."

"Even when we were kids, Lina and I were never happy," I said.

Phil took a sip of his coffee. "I hope you don't mind my saying it, but your family always has seemed a little warped to me."

"That's the understatement of the year," I said.

"I always got odd vibes when I walked into your house. Like

even the furniture was sad, and the walls were angry." Phil hesitated. "Still, I always felt Lina exaggerated a lot of the things that were wrong in your family. She held grudges. She wanted to blame a lot on your parents. In the hospital, when she was lying there so miserable, the doctor asked her, 'Can you remember a time in your childhood when you were happy?'"

"I'd have to think about it," I said, as if Phil had posed the question to me. Then a memory came to me unbidden: Lina and I sat sprawl-legged on the stained living-room rug, merrily snipping chains of paper dolls, while outside, the hot August sky grew a bloated, bruised purple, then turned pitch as night. Suddenly the wind whipped through, causing the window shades to flap and the paper dolls to scatter. Lina and I turned to each other in wonder. "God's moving the furniture upstairs!" we said in one hushed voice, the moment we heard the first ominous rumble of thunder.

"Why can't Lina remember *that*?" I blurted out.

"Remember what?" Phil asked.

"Nothing."

"That's just what Lina told the doctor: *nothing*. 'There's nothing I remember,' she said, 'and anyway, if memories are all you have, then why stay alive?' So the doctor gave her a legal pad and a pencil and said, 'Make me a list of ten good reasons why you should be alive right now, then.' She sat there with the pencil in her hand and it took her a whole minute to write down *the kids*."

I wondered what number Phil ranked on the list.

"I don't understand it," Phil said. "For the past month, Lina seemed to be more—well, you know, *normal*. She was going to Scout meetings at school and helping Richie learn how to read. She took Pammy shopping for new shoes and then they had lunch at the West Farms Mall. She let Pammy throw a penny in the fountain. She even was playing piano again—just a little, a half hour a day. It drove me nuts, listening to those scales, but I thought, if it makes her happy, why complain? She had the names of some teachers. She was going to call one. Now I can't imagine her taking lessons or putting any kind of strain on herself."

"She's doped up," I reminded him.

"She can't stay that way forever," Phil said. "In the meantime, there's all this lying I have to do, all this covering up for her. People ask me, 'How's your wife, what's wrong with her?' What am I supposed to tell them?"

I shrugged. Dirk had told me that in medieval times they believed that depressed people had too much bile in the blood or the spleen. And I had told Dirk, *I thought they looked at people's auras.* And Dirk said, *If there were auras, yours would be green with envy for your sister, and black with rage around the edges. I'm glad I'll never have to live with it.*

I cupped my Earl Grey in my hands.

"Did you know this man?" Phil asked.

"What man?" I asked, completely thrown off guard.

"Come off it," Phil said. "The guy Lina . . . went around with."

I hesitated before I shook my head.

"But you knew about him?"

"I suspected," I said. "But I don't think she tried to kill herself because of him."

"Well, why?" Phil asked. "What was it?"

It was genital warts, I felt like telling him. *It was an abortion. It was feeling so lonely that your chest aches and feeling so bizarre you wonder if there isn't a sick little man living upstairs, like Rumpelstiltskin, weaving weird dreams in your head.* But I didn't say any of that to Phil. "You heard the doctor," I said. "There doesn't have to be one reason why."

"It doesn't make sense."

"Since when does Lina make sense?"

"Since when does anything?" Phil asked.

We looked at each other, for so long and so hard I heard the fluorescent light over the sink flicker and hum, and I felt a strange energy in the air. Then, out of nowhere, a low sound buzzed, startling me.

"That's the stove alarm," Phil said. "Did you set the timer?"

We got up and went over to the oven. Phil fiddled with the clock, trying to fix it, until I finally leaned over him and turned the dial around to its starting place, and the buzzing stopped. We stood there, looking at each other, and again I smelled the detergent on his shirt, and there was a moment when everything hovered. Then the back door slammed and Pammy marched in, like a little version of Lina with her black hair and eyes.

"What are you doing?" she demanded, and as we stepped back from each other, Phil sharply said, "Nothing. We're not doing anything."

Five minutes later Lina drifted in, looked dispassionately at the new appliance, and told Phil in a monotone voice, "I wanted a double oven."

✳

The next day the kids went back to school and Phil returned to work. I sat downstairs and read, and after a while I heard Lina get up from bed and go into the bathroom. The pipes creaked and then I heard the pounding of the water. I looked at the clock to time her. "You'll check on her every quarter of an hour, won't you?" Phil had asked anxiously that morning, a question I knew was really a command: *Just keep Lina from overdosing on lithium or slitting her wrists in the shower.*

Ten minutes after the water stopped and the blow-dryer went on and off, Lina called me upstairs. To my surprise, she was fully dressed and sitting at the vanity table. She looked at herself in the mirror, a comb in her hand, studying the dullness in her usually shiny black hair. "I need a trim," she said. "Let's go to the beauty salon."

"Sure," I said, sitting down on the unmade bed, on what I knew was Phil's side. "We could do that."

"You'll have to drive."

"That's fine," I said.

"We'll have to go downtown. That's the only place I want to have it done."

"Okay," I said, which for some reason prompted Lina to throw her comb down on the vanity table, turn around, and glare at me.

"Stop acting like everything's normal," she said. "Because it isn't."

I bit my lip. I knew I wasn't supposed to upset her, but I went ahead anyway. "If things aren't normal, who's to blame?"

She turned around again. I watched her comb her long dark hair until I felt like I was going to explode from curiosity and anger. "Why did you try to kill yourself?" I asked her.

She shrugged. "I just felt like it."

"But why did you feel like it?"

"I can't explain. I've tried. Phil asked me. Sixty times. I couldn't answer."

She plugged in her curling iron, and while it was heating up, she put on some cream blush and powdered her nose. I propped some pillows—Phil's pillows—against the headboard of the bed and leaned back, watching her.

"You always seemed so lucky," I said. "I always envied you."

Lina snapped her compact shut. "What in the world for?"

"I don't know," I said. "You had Phil—"

"Oh Phil," Lina said impatiently. "I haven't had sex with Phil in—"

"Don't tell me," I interrupted—convinced she'd say something that would kill me, like *two days.*

Lina tossed her compact back onto the vanity table. "I wish Phil would just throw me on the floor and—and—and—"

"I could stand some *and,*" I said.

"—whatever!"

"I'll take some *whatever* too."

Lina took up her curling iron and wrapped just the bottom of her hair around the hot wand. "What happened with Dick?"

"*Dirk,*" I corrected her, annoyed. "It didn't work out."

"Phil said you two were kaput," Lina said.

"What else did he say?" I asked.

"That you seemed lonely."

"That's a given," I said. "Since I live alone."

"Why don't you—"

"What? Get a cat? I hate cats."

"Get a *dog,* then."

"I don't want an animal," I said. "I want a man I can stand."

"Let me know when you find him," said Lina. "Maybe he has a twin." She finished flipping under the ends of her hair, switched off the curling iron, and took out her mascara. "Do you ever fantasize a man is raping you?" she asked, as she leaned forward and darkened her eyelashes.

"What kind of question is that?" I asked.

She held the mascara wand away from her eyes. "Answer only if it's appropriate," she said.

I hesitated. "Sometimes."

"And does it feel good?"

"Of course," I said. "Otherwise, why fantasize it?"

"What feels good about it?" Lina asked, in a mock-therapist's voice.

I sank my head farther into Phil's pillow. "I guess . . . the loss of control. But knowing you're still in control, because you're the one who's dreaming it."

Lina waited a minute for the first coat of mascara to dry, then began to apply the second. "I've been fantasizing about dying," she said. "For days I've been curled up on the bed, trying to imagine what happens when you lay down your life."

"You're supposed to go through a tunnel of light," I said.

"Mmmm," Lina said. "Now that sounds like some good *and.* Or *whatever.*"

"And be reunited with your loved ones," I added. "Can you imagine being reunited with Mama and Babbo?"

"Sure," Lina said. "In hell." She snorted. "Can you imagine what they'd say?"

I cleared my throat and growled like Babbo, *"This is one devil of a scorcher we're having here."*

Lina shook her mascara wand at me the way Mama used to threaten us with her worn-out wooden spoon. *"I told you to go up, not down—but you don't listen!"* Lina recapped the mascara. "Do you ever imagine Mama and Babbo the way they are now?"

"What do you mean?" I asked.

"You know." She looked down at the carpet. "All worms . . . and bones . . ."

"Of course not," I lied. "I believe in a soul, don't you?"

"I don't know my soul," Lina said. "I only know my ugly face—"

"Lina, your face is anything but ugly."

"And my sagging body." She picked up a lipstick, opened it, rejected the color, and chose another. "When I was thinking about dying," she said, "I kept imagining what would happen to my body. I kept wondering if all those rumors we heard when we were kids were true—like your appendix bubbling up and hissing in the coffin, your fingernails sprouting like claws, and your hair growing to your feet."

"That's morbid," I said.

Lina puckered up and spread gloss over her lips. "Then I thought about the horrible color the morticians would use on my lips—coral or bright pink. And Phil weeping as he said, 'If only she could have seen what a bad makeup job they'd do on her, she never would have killed herself!'" Lina closed her lipstick and turned back to me. Her made-up face looked hard and steely, ready for a fight. "Ready?" she asked.

I got up from the bed. "Sure."

"You have to drive," Lina reminded me again.

"I'll drive you," I said.

"I think I'll stay doped up for a while," Lina said. "I like the thought of being *driven*."

We took Lina's Saab onto the Wilbur Cross Parkway toward downtown New Haven. The sky was a uniform shade of blue, like a plastic picnic dish, and the bare trees stood out in relief as we whizzed through Wallingford into Hamden. After ten minutes the tunnel loomed ahead, like two uniform mouse ears painted onto the side of the mountain. I stripped off my sunglasses and tossed them into Lina's lap; Lina turned to me and smiled.

"Oh Angel, the real tunnel!" she said. *"Ricordi?* Remember?"

As we zoomed into the darkness of the tunnel, we shouted in gleeful unison just as we did when we were two giddy girls: "Who turned off the lights?"

ABOUT THE AUTHOR

RITA CIRESI is the author of the novels *Blue Italian* and *Pink Slip* and the story collection *Mother Rocket*, which won the Flannery O'Connor Award for Short Fiction. She lives with her husband and daughter in Wesley Chapel, Florida.